Always With Me

Whisper Lake #1

BARBARA FREETHY

BARBARA
FREETHY
—BOOKS—

Fog City Publishing

PRAISE FOR BARBARA FREETHY

"I love the Callaways! Heartwarming romance, intriguing suspense and sexy alpha heroes. What more could you want?" — *NYT Bestselling Author Bella Andre*

"I adore the Callaways, a family we'd all love to have. Each new book is a deft combination of emotion, suspense and family dynamics." — *Bestselling Author Barbara O'Neal*

"Once I start reading a Callaway novel, I can't put it down. Fast-paced action, a poignant love story and a tantalizing mystery in every book!" — *USA Today Bestselling Author Christie Ridgway*

"A fabulous, page-turning combination of romance and intrigue. Fans of Nora Roberts and Elizabeth Lowell will love this book." — *NYT Bestselling Author Kristin Hannah on Golden Lies*

"Powerful and absorbing...sheer hold-your-breath suspense." — *NYT Bestselling Author Karen Robards on Don't Say A Word*

"Freethy is at the top of her form. Fans of Nora Roberts will find a similar tone here, framed in Freethy's own spare, elegant style." — *Contra Costa Times on Summer Secrets*

"Freethy hits the ground running as she kicks off another winning romantic suspense series...Freethy is at her prime with a superb combo of engaging characters and gripping plot." — *Publishers' Weekly on Silent Run*

PRAISE FOR BARBARA FREETHY

"PERILOUS TRUST is a non-stop thriller that seamlessly melds jaw-dropping suspense with sizzling romance, and I was riveted from the first page to the last…Readers will be breathless in antici-pation as this fast-paced and enthralling love story evolves and goes in unforeseeable directions." — *USA Today HEA Blog*

"Barbara Freethy is a master storyteller with a gift for spinning tales about ordinary people in extraordinary situations and drawing readers into their lives." — *Romance Reviews Today*

"Freethy (Silent Fall) has a gift for creating complex, appealing characters and emotionally involving, often suspenseful, some-times magical stories." — *Library Journal on Suddenly One Summer*

Freethy hits the ground running as she kicks off another winning romantic suspense series…Freethy is at her prime with a superb combo of engaging characters and gripping plot." — *Publishers' Weekly on Silent Run*

"If you love nail-biting suspense and heartbreaking emotion, Silent Run belongs on the top of your to-be-bought list. I could not turn the pages fast enough." — *NYT Bestselling Author Mariah Stewart*

"Hooked me from the start and kept me turning pages throughout all the twists and turns. Silent Run is powerful romantic intrigue at its best." — *NYT Bestselling Author JoAnn Ross*

ALSO BY BARBARA FREETHY

Whisper Lake Series

Always With Me (#1)

My Wildest Dream (#2) - Coming Soon

Don't miss the Callaway Series that inspired Whisper Lake!

The Callaways

On A Night Like This (#1)

So This Is Love (#2)

Falling For A Stranger (#3)

Between Now and Forever (#4)

Nobody But You (A Callaway Wedding Novella)

All A Heart Needs (#5)

That Summer Night (#6)

When Shadows Fall (#7)

Somewhere Only We Know (#8)

For a complete list of books, visit Barbara's Website!

ALWAYS WITH ME

CHAPTER ONE

"WELL, if it isn't the runaway fiancée. You can put a ring on her finger, but you can't get her down the aisle."

Gianna Campbell turned away from the cash register at the Big Sky Café to look into the mocking smile of a man she'd once allowed to put a ring on her finger, her college boyfriend, Jeremy Hutchins. Jeremy had put on a few pounds and his brown hair had thinned on the top. He'd also lost the cheerful smile he used to give her. Now there was only anger simmering in his dark eyes.

She and Jeremy had grown up on the same street in Whisper Lake, then gone to college together in Denver, and had impulsively gotten engaged the night of their graduation. But six months later, she'd broken things off. That had been eight years ago. Jeremy should have moved on by now, but clearly her most recent failed engagement had only reinforced his theory that something was wrong with her, and he had never been to blame for their breakup.

"Leave her alone," Chloe Morgan chided, as she set down Gianna's coffee. Chloe was a pretty brunette with warm hazel eyes. She was not only one of the most popular women in town, she was also one of Gianna's best friends, although that was a relationship Gianna had neglected the past couple of years, something she hoped to correct in the next several months.

"It's just a joke," Jeremy defended. "Gianna used to be able to take a joke."

"And I still can." She fought the urge to toss her hot coffee into his smug face. Why she'd ever wanted to marry him she couldn't even fathom now, but at twenty-one she just hadn't seen him clearly. In fact, that was true of most of her life. She would like to say she was a good judge of character, but, clearly, she wasn't. She tended to see people as she wanted them to be and not as they were. "How have you been, Jeremy?"

He looked taken aback by her casual question. "Uh, well, fine. I'm great. I took over my dad's auto shop."

"Good for you." She handed Chloe a ten-dollar bill and asked her to add a turkey wrap to her order.

"How's your aunt doing?" Chloe asked, as she took a wrap out of the refrigerated case.

"Her leg is broken in three places. She's out of commission for at least six weeks. My parents are busy with their own business, so I told Aunt Lois I'd come back and run the antiques shop until she can return to work."

"It's nice that you had the time."

"I'm making time. It has been awhile since I spent a summer in Whisper Lake. I'm looking forward to it."

"It's probably easier to make time since you're not getting married—again," Jeremy put in. "Third time, right? Guess three wasn't the charm for you."

"I see news still travels fast in this town." She turned back to Chloe, who was running a hand over her large baby bump. "It's getting close to your due date now, isn't it?"

"I'm three and a half weeks out," Chloe said with a smile. "I'm almost to the finish line. But I need Kevin to come home before the baby arrives."

"Is there a chance he won't?" she asked with concern. "Where is he deployed?"

"I'm not sure. He's in some special unit now. Everything is very secret. But he told me he wasn't going to miss the baby's birth."

"I'm sure he won't."

"We need to catch up, Gianna. Let's have a girls' night this weekend. What are you doing Saturday night?"

"I haven't gotten that far. I just arrived yesterday. But I would love a girls' night."

"We'll figure it out."

"Sounds good."

She moved away from the register as Chloe tended to her next customer. The café was crowded for a Thursday, especially since it was in between breakfast and lunch. On the other hand, it was late June, and with the Fourth of July holiday less than two weeks away, there were already plenty of tourists in town.

Jeremy followed her out the door. "Hey, you weren't upset by what I said, were you?"

"You were just trying to be funny."

He cleared his throat. "Sorry things didn't work out."

"No, you're not," she said candidly. You're happy that you weren't the only man I walked away from."

"Well, you obviously have a problem with commitment. How many women get engaged three times and call off the wedding three times?"

"I don't know, but I have to go."

"Back to the shop?" he asked, dogging her heels as she walked down the street. "I was sorry to hear about Lois."

"I'm not going to the store. I'm picking up inventory at the old summer camp." She paused by her aunt's black pickup truck. "Apparently, there's a new owner, and it's going to be completely rebuilt."

"I heard that. You know, Gianna—you look good. Not happy, but still good."

She didn't know what to make of his awkward words or the odd look in his eyes. "Thanks." She got into the truck and slammed the door on whatever Jeremy was planning to say next. She didn't know what he was after, nor did she want to find out. She quickly backed out and headed down the street.

A mix of emotions coursed through her as she drove through town. Jeremy's words had stung. She suspected he'd told his joke more than a few times to more than a few people. She should be used to teasing. She'd spent her childhood and teenage years being the gawky art girl, who had paint on her fingers, braces on her teeth, and wild blonde hair that could never quite be contained in a ponytail.

She had grown out of most of that awkwardness. Her blonde hair now swung about her shoulders in styled waves. Her teeth were perfect, and she did most of her art on her computer, although she could occasionally be found with paint on her fingers on the weekends. But despite the outward changes, she was still the same girl on the inside, and that girl couldn't seem to get her life right.

She didn't know why she kept saying yes to the wrong men. She supposed she should feel lucky that three men had wanted to marry her, but none of those guys had really known her. There was always a disconnect. She'd felt like they were marrying their vision of her—not the woman she really was, which begged the question…*who was she?*

Maybe it was time she figured that out before accepting any more rings.

While this trip home hadn't started on the best note, she had hopes it would be a good break for her. She'd been back to Whisper Lake for holidays, of course, but her visits had been very brief the last eight years. She was looking forward to reconnecting with her parents, her friends, letting the majestic Colorado mountains and the beautiful waters of Whisper Lake heal her battered heart and bring her clarity.

She needed to start over—both personally and professionally. She hadn't just blown up her engagement, she'd blown up her job. Her boss had also been her fiancé. Thankfully, she had enough freelance graphic gigs plus a small salary from her aunt's business to get her through the next few months.

She grabbed the turkey wrap out of the bag and bit into it, needing some fuel for the drive. She actually appreciated the opportunity to drive up to the camp. It would help clear her mind. After finishing her snack, she rolled down the windows, welcoming the warm, dry air that blew through the truck.

It was after noon, and the temperature was climbing into the mid-seventies. The tall conifers, pines, and aspens that towered on the hills were thick with leaves after a snowy winter, and the creek that ran next to the road was full and rushing toward the lake where it would swell the water level to even greater heights.

It would be a good summer for boating, skiing, tubing, fishing —all the things that kept her parents' action sports business thriving. And when summer ended, they would be renting skis, boards and snowshoes for cross-country treks.

Thinking about her parents brought a smile to her face. They were both superior athletes. At sixty-five, her still-agile dad, Dave, led rock climbing tours and hikes into the wilderness. Her mom, Jeannie, a former professional skier, continued to light up the slopes with her speed and style. She, on the other hand, had no athletic skill whatsoever.

To go along with her lack of physicality, she had very strong fears of heights and deep water, which was why she'd spent most of her childhood engrossed in art and books, and why she'd spent her twenties in Los Angeles, where yoga wear was as much for running errands as it was for actual yoga.

While she loved the city life, she had to admit to feeling waves of nostalgia now that she was back in the mountains that had sheltered her and inspired her. That feeling intensified as the two-lane highway turned into one long and winding road, and the traffic thinned out as she headed around the eastern side of the lake.

The south shore of Whisper Lake was the most populated, with eight thousand or so full-time residents and an even greater number of tourists coming in and out of town depending on the season. The north shore was more wild and rugged and catered to the serious winter sports enthusiasts, boasting a population of about two thousand full-time locals. The eastern and western portions of the lake were dotted with remote cabins and a few mom-and-pop grocery stores and gas stations.

Seeing the sign for Echo Falls Camp, she made a turn onto an even more narrow road that was filled with potholes and pebbles. The two-mile drive into the campgrounds had once been pristine and well-kept. The camp, named after a nearby waterfall, had been a mecca for kids all over Colorado, offering everything from horseback riding, to canoeing, arts and crafts, wildlife exploration, and water sports. She'd spent a few summer weeks there, the last and most notable when she was fifteen.

Her smile faded at that thought. She wanted the carefree memories back, but all she could see in her head now was Zach's face—his sparkling green eyes, wavy brown hair, and slightly crooked smile that had charmed all the girls, especially her. He had been great...until he hadn't.

She shook his image out of her mind and focused on what was happening now.

The camp had closed six years earlier when the owner, a widower by the name of Tom Rowland, had become ill. Over those years, the property had fallen into complete disrepair as Tom battled cancer, and his heirs debated what to do with the vast property.

Tom had passed away five months ago, and his estate had apparently found a buyer, someone who wanted to bring the camp back to life. His heirs had been in touch with her aunt and asked her to take the few pieces of antique furniture that were on the property, which was what had brought her to the camp today. She hoped nothing was too heavy, and that it would all fit into her truck, but she'd get what she could, and if she had to make a second trip, she would.

She had to admit it would be nice to see the camp working again, to hear kids' laughter. Right now, it just looked depressing.

As she drove closer to the lake, the long pier came into view. There had once been rowboats and canoes tied to the dock. Now, it was empty. As she slowed down, more memories flooded her brain.

Impulsively, she pulled over to the side of the road and got out. Maybe she'd just take a quick minute to look around...

She walked past the three camper cabins closest to the pier, noting that most were still boarded up, and all showed signs of age and weather. When she got to the pier, she strolled out to the end, which was about fifty yards from the shore. It was dead quiet out on this part of the lake. During summer camps, this cove had been filled with action: canoes, Jet Skis, a floating dock with a slide and basketball net, and kids everywhere. Today it was so still she could hear nothing but the breeze through the trees, whispers of long-ago voices. She smiled to herself, thinking that that was exactly how the lake had gotten its name. The early settlers had felt like the wind was whispering to them that this was home.

It still felt like home to her, even though she'd been gone a long time. She had so many memories in this small part of the world. Fourteen years ago, she'd stood on this pier and wondered what her future held: what would come next, where she would go to college, who she would marry...

She still didn't know the answer to the last question. Her life was a work in progress. She was twenty-nine and thirty was looming. It was a big birthday. It made her feel like she was a little behind. Deep in her heart, she knew she had accepted the last engagement ring because she'd been feeling the pressure to settle down, move on to the next stage of her life. Eventually, she'd realized she wasn't being fair to herself or to Jeff. Ending the engagement had been a better decision than starting it—at least, she hoped so. She was beginning to doubt if she was making any good decisions at all.

With a sigh, she turned around. It was time to stop thinking and get back to what she'd come here to do.

The sudden sound of a motor drew her glance toward the trees. A pickup truck was coming down the road. *Did it belong to Tom's son? Or someone else?* She suddenly felt very alone, very vulnerable.

That was crazy. This was Whisper Lake. She wasn't in danger. But she did need to get back on solid ground.

As she took a few steps forward, she heard a loud splintering sound, and she froze, not sure what was going on. Then her foot went through a broken board. She tried to scramble backward, but another board broke apart, and another. The pier was crumbling beneath her, and all she could see was the deep, dark water.

She flailed her arms, searching for some way to get her balance back, but there was nothing to hang on to. She crashed into the water, hitting her head on the way down. The stunning blow, along with the cold water, made her heart stop and her brain went numb. She went under, deeper and deeper. It felt like there was no bottom, but there had to be.

Panic ran through her. She'd never been a great swimmer. *Why the hell had she come out onto the pier?*

She kicked and kicked, weighed down by her clothes and her shoes, but finally she reached the surface. The shore felt like a mile away, even though it was probably only about thirty feet. She tried to swim, but she couldn't seem to get anywhere. And then she saw someone running toward her.

He wouldn't be able to get to her because the pier was completely gone.

That didn't stop him. He kicked off his shoes and jumped into the water, and in that moment, she had a sense of déjà vu—this had happened before. Not exactly like this, but close.

Or was she losing her mind?

Was the bump on her head turning her rescuer into the guy she'd just been thinking about—into Zach Barrington?

As he drew closer, she saw dark hair and startling green eyes.

Her stomach turned over.

No way! It couldn't be!

"I've got you," he said, grabbing her arm.

She stared back at him in shock and saw an echo of surprise in his expression.

"Gianna?" he muttered.

"Zach?"

"You're bleeding."

"What?"

"Your head. Come on, we need to get you out of the water."

"What are you doing here?" she asked in a daze.

He didn't answer, just put his arm around her waist and started dragging her toward the shore. She kicked along with him, relieved when she could feel the ground under her feet.

They staggered out of the water, onto the shore, and then stopped and stared at each other. It was a long look filled with so much emotion—shock, curiosity, sadness, anger...

"I can't believe it's you," he muttered.

"Are you sorry?" she asked, the words spilling out before she could stop them. "That you pulled me out of the water?"

His gaze narrowed. "Am I going to be?"

CHAPTER TWO

ZACH COULDN'T BELIEVE Gianna Campbell was standing in front of him. She was taller now, not as skinny as she'd been as a teenager, no braces on her now straight white teeth, and her light-brown eyes still sparked with gold when she was angry or upset, and she was clearly feeling both of those emotions, just as he was.

He'd volunteered to redesign the camp, because he'd needed to come back to Whisper Lake for a few different reasons. Gianna hadn't been one of them. He'd heard she'd left the area years ago. Apparently, she was back.

"What are you doing here?" he asked.

She folded her arms in front of her chest, perhaps aware for the first time that her sleeveless blouse was clinging to her breasts, and beautiful breasts they were. She'd filled out since he'd last seen her. At fifteen, she'd been skinny—all gangly arms and legs, not a single curve. That had definitely changed.

"What are you doing here?" she countered, a puzzled frown drawing her brows together.

"I'm an architect. I'm handling the camp remodel."

Wonder widened her eyes. "Seriously? I thought you were going to be a pro baseball player."

"In my dreams maybe. I grew up and realized my fastball

wasn't all that fast." He tipped his head. "Now, it's your turn. What are you doing here? I didn't think you were living in Whisper Lake anymore."

"I'm visiting for the summer. I've been living in Los Angeles, but my aunt broke her leg, and she needed help with her antiques shop. I had some time, so here I am."

"You work in antiques? I thought you'd be doing something in art."

"I'm actually a graphic artist. I'm just helping my aunt out."

He nodded with understanding. "That makes more sense. You couldn't sit in front of anything without trying to draw it. What are you doing here at the camp? Just taking a journey down memory lane?"

"No. Tom Rowland's son put some furniture aside for my aunt when they cleaned out Tom's apartment. Do you remember Tom?"

"Of course. Tom was the one who sent me home after you accused me of stealing your necklace."

Gianna cleared her throat at the reminder. "Right." She stared back at him, as if she had no clue what to say next, and to be honest, he didn't, either. "Thanks for pulling me out of the water," she said finally. "The water was so cold, I felt like I couldn't breathe. I'd forgotten how icy the water is in early summer."

"No problem. I think I did it once before."

She flushed at his words. "It wasn't quite the same."

"Close enough. You were in trouble, and I saved you."

"I could have made it to shore—both times," she said defensively.

He shrugged. "I guess we'll never know."

"Would you have rescued me if you'd known it was me when you jumped in? I know you don't like me, Zach."

"And you don't like me, but my feelings about you didn't factor in."

She stared back at him, as if she wanted to say something but couldn't find the words. Finally, she said, "I need to get down to the lodge and pick up the furniture."

"What you need are some dry clothes. I have an extra sweat-shirt in my truck if you're interested."

He thought she would immediately reject the idea, but appar-ently her soaking top was enough to get her to consider borrowing his shirt.

"I wouldn't say no to that," she said slowly.

"Follow me." He walked over to his truck and opened the door to the cab, pulling out his suitcase. Setting it on the ground, he unzipped his bag and took out a gray sweatshirt. "Here you go."

"What about you? You don't need this?"

"I have another shirt." As he pulled his wet T-shirt over his head, he tried not to like the appreciative reaction in her eyes. All too quickly, her appreciation turned to concern, and he realized his mistake. His scars were six months old now and sometimes he forgot they were there.

"What happened?" she asked, her gaze fixed on his chest, on the white lines, the blistered skin.

"It doesn't matter." He picked up a dry T-shirt and pulled it over his head. He'd change his pants later.

While he was doing that, Gianna managed to shimmy out of her wet shirt while under cover from his sweatshirt that hung down to her thighs.

"Thanks," she said. "I feel better now. I can deal with wet jeans."

He reached back into the truck and pulled out a paper towel. "You have blood on your forehead. You might need a stitch."

She took the towel and dabbed at her head. He would have offered to do it for her, but there was a stiffness to her posture that told him that would not be a welcome suggestion.

"There's not a lot of blood," she murmured, glancing at the paper towel.

"The cut doesn't appear to be deep, but you have a nice bump. Does it hurt?"

"It's not too bad. I'm sure it's fine." She paused, giving him a speculative look. "Are you staying here at the camp?"

"No, I'm at the Firefly Inn, although I haven't checked in yet. I just arrived and wanted to take some measurements before I lost the light. I don't know if Hunter has had the electricity turned on in the lodge yet."

"Hunter?"

"Hunter Callaway. He's one of the new owners. He should be arriving soon."

"Arriving from where?" she asked curiously. "What's his story? Why is he buying this old camp?"

"Hunter is from San Francisco. He's a firefighter, but he has been looking for a career change. His cousin Lizzie Cole runs the Firefly Inn. Do you know Lizzie?"

"Yes. I've known Lizzie and her siblings since we were kids. The Coles came to the lake almost every summer to visit their grandparents, who lived down the street from me. I heard Lizzie had purchased the inn and is completely redoing it."

"It's mostly done now, from what I understand. Anyway, Lizzie told Hunter that the camp was for sale. He got a family group of investors together to purchase the property. He and his fiancée Cassidy Ellison will be managing it once it's ready to reopen."

"How did you get involved in the project?"

"Hunter and I are friends. I've been living in San Francisco the last ten years. He mentioned the camp to me, and I told him I spent one eventful summer here. He asked me if I'd like to design the remodel."

"And you said yes after the way you left? Why? I would think you'd hate this place, that it would be the last project you'd want to work on."

"I have more good memories than bad. And a job is a job."

She gave him a doubtful look. "That's it?"

He wasn't going to get into his other reasons for wanting to come back to the lake. "Isn't that enough?"

"Not really. I don't understand why you would care about this camp. You got kicked out."

"But the six weeks before that brought me back to life after my dad's death. It was a great place to heal, and even though I don't like that I was blamed for something I didn't do," he said pointedly, "I still have a soft spot in my heart for this place."

"I can't believe you're still denying that you took my necklace."

"Because I didn't take it, and that will be the truth forever, Gianna."

Her lips tightened. "Fine. We don't need to get into all that. It was a long time ago. I have to get down to the lodge." She headed toward the truck that bore the logo and name of her aunt's antiques shop.

He tossed his suitcase into the back of his vehicle as anger ran through him. He was pissed off that she still didn't believe him. But she was right about one thing. It was a long time ago, and there was clearly no point in getting into it, especially when her mind was as closed as ever. Once she picked up her antiques, hopefully they would never have to speak again.

―――――――

Zach Barrington—how could he possibly be here?

As Gianna slid behind the wheel and sucked in a deep breath, she could smell his musky cologne. She could feel his warmth, as if it were his arms around her, and not the sleeves of his sweatshirt.

It was crazy to have such an intense physical and emotional reaction to him. It had been fourteen years since they'd spent six weeks together. They'd been teenagers then, flirting with all the feelings of attraction and connection. He'd been her first real kiss, her first slow dance, her first make-out session—and her first heartbreak.

She drew in a shaky breath. Zach was even more handsome now. His body had filled out. She'd seen that when he'd ripped off his wet shirt to reveal a very fit male physique. He had the muscled arms and rippling abs of an athlete, not an architect. *But what about those scars?*

It looked like he'd been in a fire or something...

Clearly, he hadn't wanted to talk about it. *And why would he?*

They weren't friends. They hadn't been in a long time.

Zach was a man now. He'd had a day's growth of beard on his jaw. The planes of his face were hard. There were lines around his eyes. He'd lived a lot of life between now and when they'd last seen each other, and so had she.

But some things were the same. His wavy brown hair was still just long enough to imagine running her fingers through it. And his eyes—his deep-green eyes were as expressive as ever, although he seemed more secretive now. Back in the day, every emotion had played out in his gaze, including desire.

She hadn't really understood it then. She'd been so young, so naïve. Boys had been a mystery to her, especially popular, handsome boys, who didn't usually pay her much attention. But Zach had liked her drawing. He'd always wanted to see what she was doing. He hadn't made fun of her for choosing art when everyone else was boating or swimming or horseback riding.

He'd turned out to be an artist himself. Maybe that's why he'd appreciated her skills. As an architect, he'd obviously done some drawing over the years.

But why he'd come back to this camp still confused her. Sure, it was a job, and it was for a friend, but she had a feeling there was some other reason he'd decided to take on the assignment.

Did that reason have something to do with his scars?

Dragging her mind back to the present, she swerved to avoid a large pothole near the old barn and stables that had been abandoned for years. When the grand lodge came into view, the knot in her throat thickened. The three-story building had once housed a large kitchen, dining hall, living room and library on the first floor, and then a half-dozen bedrooms on the second floor that had housed camp staff.

Tom's apartment had taken up the entire top floor. As a kid, she'd felt like the lodge was a luxurious mansion. The long, wide porch had always been set with Adirondack chairs, and she'd spent many an afternoon reading in one of those chairs. Now, everything just looked sad and unhappy.

She parked in front of the lodge as Zach did the same. Before getting out of the truck, she checked her reflection in the mirror.

She had a big bump, but the cut didn't look too bad, and the bleeding had stopped. At least she hadn't knocked herself out—one good thing in a fairly troubling day.

She met up with Zach on the large porch. He unlocked the door and waved her inside.

The grand foyer was as depressing as the outside of the lodge. It needed everything: a new floor, new paint, new stairs. And it smelled awful.

She wrinkled her nose. "Do I want to ask what that smell is?"

"Probably better not to know. What did you say you're here to pick up?"

"All this stuff." She walked over to the grouping of random furniture pieces. There was more than she expected: three arm chairs, two dressers, a bookcase, two side tables, a coffee table, nightstand, several lamps, a half-dozen paintings, and three large boxes.

"You think that's all going to fit in the truck?" Zach asked, doubt in his voice.

"It looks like it will take two trips. My aunt didn't know what Tom's son was sending to the store. But she didn't want to say no to anything without seeing it for herself. She has found a lot of trea-sure in what looks like junk."

"None of this looks like treasure."

She didn't think so, either. "You never know. It might be worth something with a little attention."

"Or not."

"Well, I'll leave it to my aunt to determine that. Were you expecting the lodge to look like this?"

"I have to admit, I didn't think it would be this run-down."

"Tom was sick for a long time. He didn't want to leave. He lived upstairs until the very end. This place was his life. Now he's gone. It feels strange."

"Did you return to camp after that summer we were here?"

"No. I never came back."

He stared back at her, a hard gleam in his eyes.

She took a quick breath. She didn't want to talk about the past, because she was terribly afraid of how emotional she felt right now. It wasn't just seeing Zach again after so many years; it was everything else that had happened in the last year. She'd come home to get away from her problems, from heartbreak. Having to deal with Zach was not what she wanted to do.

The sound of a car horn broke through the tension between them.

Zach moved toward the front door, and she followed more slowly, hovering in the doorway as he jogged down the steps to greet an attractive man in his early thirties, who had just arrived in a white SUV.

"Hunter. You made it," Zach said, giving his friend a hearty handshake.

"Sorry I'm a little late."

"No problem. I just got here."

"Are you...wet?" Hunter asked, his gaze narrowing.

"I took an unexpected dip in the lake."

"In your clothes?"

"I had to rescue someone." As Zach turned in her direction, she wished she'd stayed inside the lodge. "Gianna, come down and meet the new owner." He turned back to Hunter. "Gianna took a walk on the pier and it broke. She ended up in the water, and I jumped in after her."

"Hi," she said, as she moved toward the men, giving Hunter a sheepish smile. "I didn't realize the pier was in such a bad state."

"I'm sorry," Hunter said, worry in his eyes. "I guess we should put warning signs up. I'm Hunter Callaway—the new owner."

"Gianna Campbell."

"Do you need to see a doctor?" he asked with concern. "You have a good bump on your forehead."

"I'm fine. Don't worry about it. And I'm very happy that you're bringing the camp back to life. It was a great place for a long time. It would be nice to see it that way again."

"That's the plan."

She cleared her throat. "You're probably wondering why I'm here. My aunt runs an antiques shop, and the Rowland family left some furniture and boxes in the lodge for her to pick up. She sent me in her place."

"That's fine," Hunter said. "Can I help you?"

"Actually, that would be great." More helping hands would enable her to leave that much sooner. "I'm not sure it will all fit in my truck, but I can make a second trip."

"Zach should be able to take the rest of it in his truck," Hunter said, as they moved toward the lodge.

"I could do that," Zach agreed, giving her a speculative look.

"That's an imposition."

"I'll be going back to town in a few hours anyway—if you can wait that long. It's up to you, but I'm happy to do it. Why don't you give me your number, and I'll text you when I'm headed that way?"

She hesitated, but pragmatism won out. It would be faster and more convenient if she allowed Zach to help her. "All right. Whenever you come by is fine. The shop is on Fourth Street—Antiques Galore. I'll either be there or in the apartment upstairs."

"Sounds good." He gave her a cool smile that told her he knew she wasn't thrilled about accepting his help.

He'd always been able to read her a little too well. It looked like she was going to have to see him again—at least one more time.

CHAPTER THREE

AFTER LOADING UP BOTH TRUCKS, and sending Gianna on her way, Zach and Hunter headed back into the lodge.

"Do I need to worry about a lawsuit from Gianna?" Hunter asked. "She probably has a case considering the pier wasn't closed down, and there weren't any signs."

"I wouldn't think so, but who knows? Gianna can be surprising and not in a good way."

Hunter gave him a thoughtful look. "Is there something going on that I'm not aware of?"

"Why would you ask that?"

"Because there was tension between you and Gianna, which seems weird, since you pulled her out of the lake. But I'm guessing today isn't the first time you've met, is it?"

"No. We knew each other when we were teenagers. She was here the summer I came to camp. We were friends and then we were enemies."

"Does she have something to do with the fact that you got kicked out of camp?"

"Yes." He'd never told Hunter exactly what had happened, only that he'd gotten into trouble and had been asked to leave.

"Care to elaborate?"

"There's not much to say. She accused me of stealing her necklace. I had foolishly taken it once before as a joke, so when it disappeared again, I got blamed. But I didn't do it. By then, I knew how much it meant to her. It was the only thing she had from her biological mother. Anyway, once I knew the story, I felt horrible that I'd ever used it to tease her. But she didn't believe me. No one did. And, in case you were wondering, she still thinks I'm a thief. She has not changed her mind in the last fourteen years."

"Sounds like kid stuff."

"It was, and it wasn't…"

Hunter's eyebrow lifted in question. "You two were having a summer romance?"

"We were. Then we weren't."

"And this is the first time you've seen her since then?"

"Yes. I couldn't believe it was her when I pulled her out of the water. It felt like a dream."

"Or a nightmare?" Hunter suggested with a sly grin.

"Maybe. By the way, thanks for volunteering me to take the rest of the stuff to her store. Now I have to see her again."

Hunter laughed and gave him a knowing look. "You want to see her again, if for no other reason than to prove she was wrong about you."

"I don't think there's a way to prove that. I'm not going to waste time trying. Anyway, shall we go through the lodge and talk about the plans? We have to submit the preliminary drawings to the planning commission by next week if we want to get on the July review schedule."

"Which we do." Hunter walked over to the mantel and waved his hand toward the engraving of a train and the inscription—*All who are lost are now found*. "I wanted to talk to you about how we can preserve this wall or use the engraving and the slogan in another way. I read a lot about the camp's history, about the Orphan Train used in the 1920's to transport orphans to Western towns. The train broke down just north of Whisper Lake, and the kids ended up spending the winter here, doubling the town's population in one big snowstorm."

"And when the spring came, the kids stayed with their new families," he continued, knowing the story well. "Tom Rowland made a point of saying that the camp would always be welcome to anyone who was lost, whether it be physically or emotionally. Those who needed a home, a family, would always find it here. That was true for me. I felt lost when I came to this camp after my dad died. And it changed me. It was a time of healing. I think we need to keep this wall intact and perhaps build even further off the theme."

"I agree. I like the idea a lot. Is that why you took this job, Zach? Do you need to heal again after Rebecca? After the fire?"

"Yes." He sucked in a breath at the reminder, but his reasons for coming to the lake were more complicated than Hunter knew. He needed to fill him in; he just wasn't quite ready. "Let's get to work."

After returning to the antiques shop, Gianna got help unloading the truck from Kellan Ferguson, a nineteen-year-old, red-haired, college kid who worked in the store part-time, mostly handling pickups and deliveries. But a college final had prevented Kellan from making the run up to the camp.

Hopefully, Zach would help unload the items on his truck when he brought them by later. She wasn't looking forward to that, but first things first. She needed a shower and some dry clothes. While the drive back from the camp had settled her nerves, there were still too many questions rocketing through her mind, all of them having to do with Zach's unexpected return.

She couldn't stop thinking about him, about those troubling scars on his chest... He'd been through something terrible and painful, and her heart hurt for him, which was strange since she'd spent so much time hating him.

Pushing him out of her mind, she headed up to her apartment. After a long shower, she put on black leggings and a T-shirt and then went back downstairs to see how she wanted to organize what she'd picked up from the camp.

The sound of a car turning in to the back lot made her heart jump, but when she opened the door, she saw the silver SUV belonging to her mother, Jeannie Campbell. As her mom got out, her heart filled with love for the tall, willowy brunette whose smile had always made her feel better, and today was no exception.

"Mom." She hurried forward to give her mother a hug. "I said I was going to come by tomorrow night to see you and Dad."

"Well, I couldn't wait, and I was afraid you might not actually make it. Yesterday you were too tired, and you wanted to work in the store tonight. I couldn't help wondering if you were avoiding us."

She looked into her mom's warm brown eyes and felt a wave of guilt. "Sorry. I guess I'm a little embarrassed."

"Oh, honey. You have nothing to be embarrassed about."

"Three failed engagements would say otherwise. Dad is disappointed in me. I could hear it in his voice when I told you both the wedding was off, and I haven't spoken to him since. He's been busy every time I've called."

"That's a coincidence."

"Is it? It's been three months. How busy can he be?"

"Your dad wants you to be happy, as do I. You haven't found the right person yet, and that's okay. Better a failed engagement than a failed marriage."

"I know that's what you think, but it's not what Dad thinks, is it?"

"Your dad needs a little more time," her mom said lightly. "He'll get to the same realization when he thinks about it long enough. He's just worried about you, Gianna."

"Maybe he has reason to be. I ran into Jeremy in town. He was practically gleeful at the fact that I'd called off yet another wedding. He told me I clearly have a problem with commitment."

"Well, Jeremy is an ass," her mother said bluntly. "Don't let him get to you."

"He wasn't wrong, but he is also an ass," she said, exchanging a smile with her mom. "Do you want to come into the store?"

"Actually, since you said you weren't free to see us until tomorrow night, your dad and I are going to a birthday party for Linda Glenn. You can come if you want."

"I'm not really up for a party," she said, especially not one with a bunch of gossipy women like Linda Glenn. "I'm going to ease my way into town life."

"I figured you'd say that, so I brought you something." She moved back to her car.

"That wasn't necessary."

"It was necessary. I wanted you to feel like you're at home, even if you have decided not to stay with us." Her mom pulled out a casserole dish and put it in her arms. "I made you a lasagna."

"My favorite. You're the best."

"I really am," her mom said with a laugh.

"You are. And I decided to stay here because it's more convenient, and the apartment is empty."

"You're also dreading talking to your dad. I know Dave can have strong opinions, especially when it comes to your choices, but he loves you no matter what. You two need to have a long conversation."

"We will."

Her mom grabbed another bag from the car. "I also have garlic bread and the fixings for salad."

"It smells wonderful. But you didn't have to go to the trouble to cook for me. You're so busy right now."

"I ended up getting off a little earlier today, and I made a second lasagna for Linda's party." Her mother paused. "Have you spoken to Jeff?"

"Not since I gave him back his ring several months ago, and I don't expect that I will. Now that I'm no longer working for his company, we'll never run into each other. I also realized after the breakup how few friends we had together. So, it's not like I lost much there. But it's still sad, and I feel guilty for stringing him along."

"I don't think that's what you did. You just changed your mind."

"You're being very supportive."

"I will always have your back, Gianna. And this painful period will pass."

"Not soon enough," she said with a sigh.

"Shall I carry this in for you?"

"I can take it." She put the grocery bag on top of the casserole. "Have fun at the party."

As her mom hopped into the car, she went back inside. Not wanting to go all the way upstairs, she stashed the lasagna in the storeroom refrigerator and decided to dig into the boxes she'd picked up at the camp. While her aunt would be the final arbiter on the furniture, if there was nothing worth selling in the boxes, she could get rid of the trash in tomorrow's pickup.

She opened the first box and discovered it was filled with photos. She spent a good thirty minutes picking out her friends in old camp pictures and looking for shots of herself. Eventually, she found one of herself standing in front of an easel on the porch in front of the lodge during art class. Zach was looking over her shoulder at her painting, and his hand was on her back.

That moment in time flashed into her head. She could feel the heat of his fingers through her thin top. And she remembered thinking if she turned her head, their lips would touch, he was that close. She drew in a breath and let it out. *What the hell was going on? Why was she still so affected by his memory?* She'd dated other men. She'd told three of those men she loved them, and she would marry them.

So why the sudden obsession with Zach again? Was it just because she was feeling so lost right now? Was she looking for some answer to the problems in her life in a very old crush?

But Zach was not the answer to any problem—in fact, he'd always *been* the problem. She tossed the pictures into the box and set it aside, then moved on to the next one, only to find more photos.

Before she could look through them, her phone buzzed with a text from Zach that he was almost at the store. Her pulse leapt with excitement at the thought of seeing him again, while her brain cautioned her not to forget how much he'd hurt her.

She told him to park in the back and then returned her attention to the box at hand, happy to have a distraction.

These pictures were much older, probably going back thirty-five to forty years. She wondered if her parents were in any of the photos. Her dad had gone to the camp when he was a kid.

As she picked up a close-up shot of a teenage girl standing by the pier, her gaze caught on the chain at her neck, on the glittering gold locket, and her heart stopped.

The locket looked exactly like the one she'd lost.

It probably didn't mean anything, she told herself. It wasn't like she had a one-of-a-kind locket. But it was still so strange to see it around the neck of someone else. The girl had blonde hair. She looked to be about sixteen. There was something about her expression that felt vaguely familiar.

"Gianna."

She jumped at the sound of her name. She'd been so engrossed in the photo she hadn't heard Zach park in the lot or open the door.

He gave her a funny look. "Everything okay?"

"I—I don't know."

"What are you looking at?" He walked over to her. "Where's that photo from?"

"It's from the boxes I picked up at the camp. This girl—look at her neck." She pointed to the locket. "That necklace looks like the one I had."

He frowned at the picture. "You think this girl took your locket?"

"No. The picture is old. All the photos in this box are from thirty or forty years ago. There are dates on some of them, but you can also tell by the clothes and the faded images."

"So, she had a locket just like yours. What's the big deal? Was the locket that unique?"

"Not really. I don't know," she muttered, as a wild thought ran through her head.

His speculative gaze returned to her face. "What are you thinking?"

"It's crazy."

"Say it."

"I told you that the locket was the only thing I had from my biological mother. This girl, she kind of looks like me..."

Awareness dawned in his eyes as he met her gaze. "You think this girl is your mother?"

"I told you it was a crazy idea." She drew in a breath. "But what if she is?"

CHAPTER FOUR

ZACH STARED BACK AT HER, an unreadable expression on his face. Gianna didn't know if he thought she was insane or on to something. She didn't know, either. "Now it's your turn to talk," she suggested. "Do you think she looks like me?"

He glanced at the photo once more. "I don't know. The picture is old and grainy. Was your biological mother a local girl?"

"I was told she was not, but the camp has never been just for locals. She could have gone there from anywhere."

"Do you know anything else about her?"

"She was a teenager when she had me. That's it. And there's no information on my father. It was a closed adoption."

"I thought that even closed adoptions could be opened after a certain age. Have you ever tried to find her?"

"I haven't."

Surprise flashed in his eyes as he met her gaze. "Why not? You told me back at camp that you wanted to find her one day. What stopped you?"

"I was going to look for her when I turned eighteen, but the summer after I graduated from high school, my mom was diagnosed with breast cancer. The next year was all about chemo and desperately praying that she wouldn't die. I put all thoughts of my biological mother out of my head. I couldn't abandon the woman who had raised me, and it felt like a betrayal to even want to know the person who didn't want me. I decided to leave her in the past."

"That makes sense. How is your mom now?"

"She's good. She's in remission. And hopefully she stays that way."

"I'm glad."

"Me, too. I really thought I had put all those questions out of my head. But now…" She glanced back at the photo. "I'd like to know who this girl is."

"Maybe you can find out. But if you start asking questions, you won't be leaving your past in the past."

"I know. But my past seems to be coming back in different ways—not just with this picture but also with you. I never expected to see you again, Zach."

"I'm sure that would have been your preference."

"I always thought so. But…" She shook her head, not sure what she wanted to say.

"But," he pressed, a question in his gaze.

"It was a long time ago. We were kids. And maybe you didn't take my locket." She couldn't believe she was saying that after so many years of thinking he was guilty.

"What? You're saying you believe me now?"

"Well, I can't see why you'd continue to lie after all these years."

"I'm not lying now, and I wasn't lying then. I never understood why you were so quick to call me a liar, Gianna. You knew me. We were more than friends. We were…"

As his voice drifted away, she said, "We were what? That's the thing. You didn't want to acknowledge what we were. That last day of camp, I heard you tell Tony that you didn't really like me, that you were just messing around. That what we were doing together was no big deal."

Guilt flittered through his eyes, but he didn't deny it.

"I thought you took my locket," she continued, "so that you could prove to the other kids that you didn't care about me. It all made sense at the time. I heard what you said to Tony, then my locket was gone. I connected the two events, and I felt betrayed. I had been stupid to think that someone like you could want someone like me. You were way out of my league. Every girl wanted you, and every guy wanted to be you. What you said to Tony confirmed what I'd always wondered—whether you were using me, or if I was just some challenge, some dare."

"You weren't a challenge or a dare," he said forcefully. "And I did like you. When Tony and some of the other guys started giving me a hard time about you, I admit that I played it down. I was an idiot teenager, and I didn't handle the situation well. To be honest, the way I felt about you was so different that I didn't know what to make of it. I didn't want everyone teasing us. I thought if I played it cool, Tony and the others would drop it. I'm sorry for hurting you."

She nodded, drawing in a quick breath at the apology she'd waited a long time to hear. "Thanks for saying that."

"I didn't know you'd overheard my conversation with Tony. All I knew was that you believed I took your necklace after you'd told me what it meant to you. I was pissed that you could think that, and I felt betrayed. I thought you knew me better than that."

"I thought I did, too. But if you didn't take it, who did? That's the question I could never answer."

"I honestly have no idea. It could have been anyone—even one of the girls."

"Well, it doesn't matter anymore. We can move on."

"I hope so. It looks like we'll be in the same place for a while, and I'd rather not be enemies, Gianna."

"I don't want to be enemies, either." She sighed. "I have enough people in town who don't like me."

His brow shot up. "You have people who don't like you? I have trouble believing that."

"Really? Up until five minutes ago, you didn't like me," she said dryly. "Where is the difficulty coming from?"

He smiled. "That's true, but now we've made our peace. What problem do you have with all the other people who don't like you?"

"You don't know?"

"Know what?"

"I'm a joke around town these days. I've had a couple of broken engagements—actually three, one a few months ago. My first fiancé, Jeremy, still lives here in Whisper Lake. He has dubbed me the runaway fiancée. He finds it very amusing that I can't make it down the aisle. It makes him feel better to not be the only man I disappointed. He told me earlier today that I have a problem with commitment. I can't say he's wrong."

"Three engagements, huh? That's a lot. But it's better than three divorces."

"That's what I think. But I know it's not great. I've hurt people with my poor decisions, and I need to do better."

He gave her a thoughtful gaze. "I have to say it seems a bit out of character, Gianna, but then I guess I don't really know you."

"You don't know me, Zach. We spent six weeks together when we were teenagers."

"We had a lot of fun that summer—up until the end."

She met his gaze and saw the shared memories running through his eyes. "We did have fun. You were my first boyfriend, my first everything—kiss, slow dance, broken heart. We packed a lot into the short time we had together."

"We didn't do everything," he pointed out, a wicked spark in his gaze. "Even though I thought about it a lot, especially when we were making out."

"I was fifteen. I was not going to have sex with you. I was not ready for that."

"I was sixteen, and I was definitely ready. But we ran out of time."

"We ran out of our relationship, which wasn't much of one, if it could be broken so easily."

His expression changed, a thoughtful gleam entering his eyes. "Maybe you blamed me for taking the locket, because you were afraid things were going too fast. Maybe I was the first guy you wanted to get rid of."

Anger ran through her. She didn't like his suggestion at all—not one little bit—mostly because it had an odd ring of truth to it.

Had she used the locket to push Zach away? Had her pattern started well before she'd gotten involved with Jeremy?

"Nothing to say?" Zach pressed.

"I don't think that's what happened," she said slowly.

"I never would have thought you were a girl who couldn't commit. I saw the way you committed to your art. You were obsessed with painting. You put it before everything else. You were so sure that you were going to grow up and do something with it, and you did."

"Apparently, I can commit to a paintbrush, but not to a man."

He grinned. "Paintbrushes don't talk back, and you can control them."

"Yes, I can, most of the time. Sometimes the brush seems to have a mind of its own." She cleared her throat as another long look passed between them, and a rush of emotions made her hot and uneasy. "Should we unpack the truck?"

"Why don't we get dinner first? I'm starving." He sniffed. "Unless you just ate. It smells good in here."

"My mom dropped off a lasagna. It's in the fridge."

"Is it big enough to share?"

"It is," she said slowly.

"Are you going to invite me to share it?" he asked, with the same sparkle in his eye that had once made butterflies dance through her stomach.

"I feel like that's a bad idea, Zach."

"Why? We've cleared the air. Apologies were made. We agreed not to be enemies. What's the problem?"

"My life is complicated, and I need a break from men."

"It's dinner, Gianna. I promise not to propose." He cleared his throat with a guilty gleam in his eyes. "Too soon?"

For some reason, his bad joke eased the tension between them. "Definitely too soon. But if you want to share my lasagna, I guess I'm okay with it. There's way too much for one person." She couldn't believe she was offering to have dinner with him, but there was a part of her that wasn't ready to say good-bye.

"That's all I'm asking—a little pasta, a little conversation."

"Good. Because that's all I have to give." She might have made a habit of falling in love too fast and too recklessly, but she was not going to make that mistake again—and definitely not with Zach. "We can eat upstairs." She walked over to the refrigerator and pulled out the casserole dish, handing it off to Zach. Then she grabbed the salad and bread and headed up to her apartment.

The one-bedroom unit was very basic, with a couch and an armchair in the small living room, a table for two by the galley-style kitchen, with a small bedroom and bath. Her aunt had often rented the apartment, but the last tenant had moved out several months ago, and she hadn't gotten around to repainting or putting it back up for rent.

"This doesn't fit you," Zach muttered, his gaze sweeping the room. "It's too gray. You like color."

"I do," she admitted, surprised that Zach had had the same reaction she'd had when she'd first seen the place. She set the lasagna on the counter as she turned on the oven to heat. "But it's convenient to the store. I can access the stairs from the street or the storeroom. Plus, it's free."

"If you're going to be here longer than a few days, you'll have to do some decorating. At least put some of your art up." He paused in front of the blank canvas resting on an easel by the window. Her paints were ready to go, but her creative brain was not. "What are you going to do with this?"

"I'm not sure yet."

"You were rarely sure when you started sketching. You told me that was part of the fun, being able to see what your brain would come up with if you didn't think too hard."

His words resonated with her, reminding her once more of the girl she used to be. *Where had that girl gone?*

"What other pieces do you have here?" he asked. "I'm curious as to how your art has progressed."

"I didn't bring anything with me."

He raised an eyebrow. "Why not? You didn't anticipate these empty walls?"

"They weren't a priority. I moved out of my apartment in LA and put everything in storage."

"You moved out? You're not going back?"

"I will return to LA, but I'll start over, somewhere new and fresh."

"You said you're a graphic artist. What does that mean exactly?"

"It can mean a lot of things. For me, it has involved designing ads, logos, websites, and collateral materials for small businesses. For the past two years, I've been working at an advertising agency."

"Do you like it?"

"I always like the creative part, but with clients, it can be constraining at times. It pays the bills, though." She put the lasagna in the oven. "This needs to heat up for a few minutes. Do you want some water or coffee? I'm afraid I haven't shopped yet. I just arrived yesterday."

"Water is fine."

She tossed him a bottled water as he sat down at the table. He caught it with a deft hand. Zach had always been good at sports. He'd won every contest they'd had at camp. And it looked like he'd kept in shape over the years. He'd changed out of the clothes he'd been wearing earlier, now in jeans and a dark-green knit shirt that matched his very compelling eyes.

Her gut clenched as he met her gaze. Forcing herself to turn away, she moved into the kitchen and pulled a bowl out of the cupboard for the salad. It felt good to keep busy, so she didn't have to look at Zach.

"Can I help?" he asked.

"My mom dropped everything off. I'm just tossing it together."

"I'm surprised you're not having dinner with your parents."

"They had a birthday party to go to, and to be honest, I'm not looking forward to speaking to my dad."

"Why not? I thought you had a great relationship with your parents."

"It used to be great, but I've hurt them with the failed engagements. They lost deposit money on the first two weddings, and while I wasn't going to ask them to pay for anything on the last one, I still feel like I let them down, my dad especially."

"I'm sure he wouldn't want you to marry someone you didn't love."

"He doesn't think I have a realistic expectation of what love entails. That's what he said after engagement number two. I've tried to avoid talking to him since this last one blew up." She finished mixing the salad and then brought it over to the table. "Do you want to start on this or wait for the lasagna?"

"I'll wait. Why don't you sit down?"

"Okay. I'll pop in the garlic bread at the last minute." She let out a breath as she sat down. "This still feels awkward."

"I know," he agreed, his easy smile belying his words.

"You don't seem uncomfortable at all."

"I hide it better than you."

"I do tend to wear my emotions on my sleeve."

"We'll be running into each other around town. It's best if we get this awkwardness out of the way."

"Do you think we can do that?"

"Now that we've cleared the air, yes." He sipped his water. "Tell me about your ex-fiancés."

She sighed. "Really?"

"I'm curious as to what kind of men they are."

"They're all different. As I said, Jeremy was the first. We grew up on the same street and ended up at the University of Colorado in Denver. We gravitated toward each other, because we were scared of being alone at a big school. We started out as friends and senior year, it evolved into something more. He asked me to marry him the day of our graduation. We were wearing our caps and gowns and drinking champagne, and I thought it was romantic and exciting. But our year-long engagement turned into one endless fight. We argued about everything—what jobs to take, where we should live, what kind of ceremony we wanted. I called off the wedding three weeks before the date. Jeremy was furious and embarrassed. So were his parents and his siblings—my parents, too. It was awful."

"You were young—twenty-one, twenty-two…"

"Twenty-two and way too young. After that debacle, I wanted to leave Colorado, so I found a job in LA, and I moved to California. It felt good to be in a place where no one knew me, even though it was lonely at times." She paused. "This is pretty boring, isn't it?"

"I've never thought you were boring, Gianna, not ever."

She flushed at his words. "That's an exaggeration, I'm sure."

"No, it's not. Keep going. When and where did you meet bachelor number two?"

"It was about three years post-Jeremy. I met him through my roommate at the time. Her boyfriend worked at a tech company, and he brought his buddy, Victor, to a party one night. Victor was completely different than Jeremy, who had waffled over what he wanted to do with his life. Victor had a two-year plan and a five-year plan and a ten-year plan."

"Sounds like a lot of plans."

"He was a finance guy. Everything had to add up for him. I liked his confidence, his ability to make a good life for himself. He liked to direct things and I was okay with it, because his choices were usually well thought out. We were opposites, but I thought we'd complement each other."

"But you didn't?"

"In the beginning, his decision-making usually took me into consideration, but it became more and more about him. He wanted children by a certain date. He wanted to live in a specific kind of house in a particular neighborhood. He insisted I be his supportive partner at every business event, whether or not it fit into my schedule. I broke up with him two months before the wedding, so I got out a little earlier than I did with Jeremy, but Victor was still really angry at me for messing up his plan."

"It sounds to me like you escaped at the right time. You can't live your life according to someone else's plan."

"He even had our kids' names picked out. The boy was going to be Edward after his grandfather. I hated the name. Who names their kid Edward in this day and age? But Victor was really pushy about it, and I gave in, like I always did. I realized I was losing myself in him. I had to get out."

Zach nodded. "Good decision. Although, I have no problem with the name Edward."

She smiled. "Fair enough."

"And fiancé number three?"

"This conversation is making me feel really bad about myself."

"So far, I haven't heard anything that should make you feel that way."

"But you're only hearing my side."

"True. Are you lying?" he challenged.

"No," she said firmly. "I can completely acknowledge I had blame in both those relationships, and in the last one, too. I met Jeff a year and a half ago. Where Victor and I had nothing in common, Jeff and I had too much in common. He's an art collector. He loves museums. That's where we met. And he ran the ad agency where I was employed as a graphic designer. Art was a big draw between us."

"He sounds better. What was his fatal flaw?"

"Our work and personal life blurred together. He'd take credit for my ideas. We were partners in private, but in public, it was more about him. When it came to the client, he acted like I was his assistant. It was insulting. When I talked to him about it, he kept telling me we were a team, but my skill was in the art, and his was in the pitch. I couldn't say he was wrong, but I felt a little used. I noticed that he did it with other people, too, with both men and women. He took what they had to give, and then he moved on."

"So, you moved on first."

"I did. I don't know why it takes me so long to see people for who they really are. Although, I'm sure each of the guys would give you a different story." She cleared her throat, unsure why she was telling him so much. "What about you, Zach? Do you have a woman in your life? I don't see a ring on your finger, but not all men wear one."

"I've never been married, but I was engaged once."

"Only once? Amateur," she said lightly.

His lips curved into a small smile that didn't quite reach his eyes. "Once was enough."

"How long were you together?"

"Four years."

"That's a considerable length of time. Why didn't you get married?"

"We couldn't seem to find the right time. There was enough uncertainty in our relationship that we never got around to setting a date."

"When did the relationship end?"

"About six months ago."

There was a hint of pain in his voice, and she couldn't help wondering who had broken up with who. "Are you okay?"

"I'm getting there."

She licked her lips. They'd gotten very personal very fast, and she wanted to take it even further. "Can I ask you a question?"

"That depends on the question."

"What happened to you, Zach? How did you get those scars on your chest and your back?"

He stared at her for a long minute, his gaze filling with shadows. Finally, he said, "I was in a fire."

Her pulse leapt. "A fire? I'm sorry. That must have been a terrible experience."

"The worst of my life." His expression was grim. "But I was lucky. I survived."

She took a quick breath. "Was there someone who didn't survive?"

"My fiancée."

"Oh, God, Zach. I thought it was just a breakup." She felt terrible for pushing him into the confession. "I shouldn't have urged you to talk about it."

"You asked me earlier why I came to the lake. It healed me once before. I was hoping it might do so again."

She had a lot more questions she wanted to ask him, but the oven timer went off, making her jump. She'd been so caught up in Zach, she'd lost all track of time. "Our pasta is ready. I'll put the bread in."

"Sure."

She pushed back her chair and stood up, feeling like they'd both said too much, and at the same time wondering if there wasn't more that needed to be spoken.

Zach met her gaze, and she now understood better the hard lines around his eyes and mouth. What he'd been through made her broken relationships pale in comparison.

"It's okay, Gianna," he murmured. "You didn't know."

"I wish I could find the right words, but I'm not sure what they are."

"I don't need words, but lasagna would be good. I'm starving."

She gave him a faint smile as he deliberately eased the tension between them. "Well, that's one problem I can solve, and I can't tell you how happy it makes me to actually be able to fix something."

"I know that feeling."

Zach's phone buzzed. He pulled it out and frowned, then slipped it back into his pocket.

"If you need to get that…"

"I don't. Let's eat."

She wondered who was trying to reach him, but she'd already asked him far too many questions. Maybe it was better if she didn't know anything else.

CHAPTER FIVE

Zach let out a breath as Gianna moved into the kitchen. He hadn't planned on telling her about the fire or Rebecca. But the words had just come out. Not all the words, though...there was a lot he hadn't said. He probably shouldn't go any further now, not while everything was so up in the air.

She returned to the table, setting the casserole dish between them, and handed him a spatula. "Help yourself. I'll grab the garlic bread."

He took a healthy serving of the meat and cheese pasta, his stomach rumbling at the delicious garlic aroma wafting through the air. He added salad to his plate while Gianna set a platter of garlic bread on the table, then took her seat across from him.

"Do you need anything else?" she asked.

"I don't think so," he said, scooping up his first forkful. It was every bit as good as he'd imagined. "Wonderful. Your mother is an excellent cook."

"She is, and her lasagna is one of my favorite meals. I've tried to replicate it, but it never comes out the same. My mom always makes it when I come home, although I didn't expect her to deliver it to me. I'm very spoiled."

"I'm sure they're happy to have you back in Whisper Lake, even for a short time."

"My mom is, but, as I mentioned, things are still awkward with my dad, and it bothers me a lot. My parents and I have always been close, a circle of three. I don't know if I told you, but they tried to have a baby for over five years before they turned to adoption. It took another two years before they were able to adopt me. They've always told me how I completed their family, how loved and wanted I was, which is why I've always felt conflicted about looking for my biological mother. It feels traitorous. I should be grateful with who I ended up with and not who gave birth to me."

"But you can't quite get there." He could see the glimmer of uncertainty in her eyes.

"I would like to know my family history, my medical history. And as much as I try to convince myself that who I am is who I am and has nothing to do with my birth parents, I still have questions. Do I look like my biological parents? Were they artists? Did I inherit their creativity? Or am I nothing like them?" She took a sip of water. "My mom and dad are super athletes, and I am as clumsy as they come. I wonder what it would feel like to have a skill like my parents. It's crazy, because I don't think I could be any closer to anyone than I am to my parents, but I still wonder."

He considered her words. "Biology doesn't always mean parents and children will share anything. You could find out you have even less in common with your birth mother than you might think."

"That's true."

"But you're going to try to track down the girl in the photo, aren't you?" He didn't really need her to give him a verbal answer, because he could see the truth in her eyes.

"I shouldn't."

"That's not what I asked, Gianna."

"I just found the photo. I haven't had time to process."

"You don't need time. A big clue dropped in your lap, and you won't be able to look away from it. Why don't you talk to your mom? See how she feels. Have you ever actually asked her?"

"Not in a long time. Like I said, I put it all away."

"Until you found the picture tonight. You can't un-see it, Gianna."

"I was thinking I might ask around, see what I can find out. It doesn't mean I have to do anything."

"But you would do something. You can't lie to yourself and say you'll just get to a name and that's it. Because it won't be it. You won't be able to go that far and stop. So, before you take the first step, you need to think it all the way through."

"That's probably good advice."

"All my advice is good, no probably about it."

"You always were confident, Zach."

"Tell me something… If you found your biological mother, what would you say?"

She drew in a breath and let it out, indecision in her brown eyes. "I don't honestly know. I guess it depends on who she is— what her story is. She could be married to someone other than my birth father, which is likely. She might not want him to know about her past. And she could have other kids—children she'd want to protect."

"There's a lot to consider."

"There is. And what if I didn't like her at all? What if she is a horrible person? Would I be better off never knowing than knowing that kind of truth?"

"She could be wonderful."

"You're not helping, Zach."

"I'm just pointing out the different possibilities."

"I need to think about it. It's not like anything has to happen immediately. I've gone this long without knowing, I can wait a little longer."

He wondered if that was true. He had a feeling that picture was going to haunt her dreams until she took some kind of action. But it was her business, her truth to pursue, and he had his own problems to worry about.

They finished the rest of their meal in silence.

"Do you want more?" Gianna asked, as she put her fork down.

He sat back in his seat. "I'm stuffed. Thank your mom for me."

"I'm not going to do that," she said with a smile.

"Why not?"

"Because then she'd ask me a million questions about you."

"Does she know anything about our camp romance?"

"She knows that a horrible boy named Zach stole my necklace and made me cry for a few weeks."

"Great. Maybe don't mention I'm in town then," he said dryly.

"I wasn't planning on it."

"We did have a great summer, Gianna."

"I was really happy until the end," she admitted.

"Me, too." Feeling like he was in danger of getting too deep into the past, he pushed back his chair and stood up, grabbing both their plates and taking them over to the sink.

"You don't have to clean up," Gianna protested.

"It's the least I can do." He rinsed the plates and put them in the dishwasher while Gianna covered the lasagna dish and placed it in the fridge.

"Sorry I don't have dessert," she said.

"I definitely don't need more food. We should probably head downstairs and get the truck unloaded."

"That's right. We still have to do that."

"It shouldn't take long. You had most of the pieces in your truck. Did you unload those yourself?" he asked, as they moved down the stairs.

"No. My aunt has a college kid who works part-time and provides the occasional muscle. Tonight, that muscle will have to be you."

"I think we can manage. You don't have a lot of room in here," he added, noting the crowded storeroom. "Your aunt has a lot of stuff."

"Yes, she does. She had just picked up quite a few items from an estate sale when she broke her leg. She didn't have time to tag the pieces or get them into the showroom. That will be one of my jobs. But my main goal is to get the store opened tomorrow in time for the weekend."

"Does your aunt have any other help besides the muscle?"

"She has two other part-time employees, but my aunt has always considered this store her baby, and she spends all her time tending to it. She doesn't give up control easily. She didn't feel comfortable with one of her employees taking over in her absence, and apparently none of them wanted to work full-time, so she was thrilled when I offered to come and help out. I used to work here when I was in high school. It has been awhile, but I think I can handle the business."

"What about other family members?"

"Lois's husband died almost ten years ago now, and they didn't have any children. She has a lot of friends in Whisper Lake, but no significant other that I know about. Although, my mom did recently mention that Marty, a local handyman, seems to be doing a lot of projects around my aunt's house, so who knows…"

They walked into the parking lot. He unlatched the back of the truck and hopped on. He grabbed a nightstand and pulled it toward the edge. "This one isn't too heavy." He set it on the ground.

She tested the weight. "You're right. I can carry this myself."

While she did that, he got the bookcase off the truck and onto the ground, as well as a small dresser and a chair. When Gianna came back, they moved the bookcase into the store, and then went back for the remaining pieces.

"Thanks for bringing these," she said, as they finished. "You saved me another trip to the camp."

"No big deal. We got a chance to catch up."

"It was weirdly nice to talk to you again."

He smiled at her choice of words. "I feel the same way. If you decide to look for that girl in the photo, maybe I can help."

"Why would you want to do that?"

"You talked about your desire to find your birth parents a lot the summer we were together. It weighed on your mind. I'd like to see you get the answers you've spent your entire life looking for."

She stared back at him, measuring the sincerity of his words with a cool, speculative glance. "I'm sure you'll be busy at the camp."

"I can make time."

"How long are you staying in town?"

"Several weeks. I'm not completely sure of my plans."

"That's a long time. I thought you were going to say a few days, maybe a week. Don't you have other jobs to get back to?"

"This is my priority at the moment, and I'm still working my way back into my career. The fire put a lot of things on hold."

"It took you awhile to recover, didn't it?"

"Too long," he said tersely.

Her gaze narrowed. "I feel like you have another reason for coming back here, Zach. Am I wrong?"

He shrugged. "Maybe not wrong, but I'm not ready to talk about it." He extended his hand. "Friends again?"

She hesitated, then slid her hand into his. The warmth of her fingers sent an old, familiar wave of desire through him. Touching her had definitely been a mistake. There was an odd glitter in her eyes as well. The attraction that had burned so bright as teenagers was still there. That was both exciting and disturbing.

He couldn't afford to be distracted by Gianna. He had too much on the line.

They exchanged a look that went on far too long, and then she abruptly pulled her hand away from his.

Before he could say good night, his phone buzzed. It was Mitch again. "I need to take this."

"Of course. We were done anyway."

He wasn't so sure of that, but he didn't have time to argue the point. "I'll see you later."

"See you," she muttered, as he headed out the door.

"Mitch—what's up?" he asked, as he got into the truck. "Did you talk to your parents?"

"I did," Mitch replied, a heavy note in his voice. "They're not interested in working anything out with you. As far as they're concerned, you have no legal standing, and they blame you for what happened to Rebecca. I've tried to tell them the truth, but they've always had a blind spot where my sister is concerned.

They've never been able to see her as anything but their perfect angel. It's always everyone else's fault."

"Do they know I'm in Whisper Lake? That I'm working on the camp remodel?"

"I didn't tell them, because I thought you might change your mind, knowing how they feel about you."

"I'm not changing my mind, and I'm not leaving town anytime soon."

"You should reconsider, Zach. My father is very powerful. He's on the city council. He can muck things up for you—for the camp. He has friends in the building department. Even if it wouldn't bother you to go up against him, what about your friend?"

Mitch made some good points. He could go toe-to-toe with Ron Carver, but it wasn't just him; Hunter was also involved. "I'll think about what you said, but I want to see Hailey. Can you help me out?"

Mitch didn't answer right away. Finally, he said, "I'm supposed to take Hailey to ballet class on Saturday morning at ten. We're going to hit the park at Grove Square after that. Anyone could wander by and say hello, but that's all I'd let anyone do."

His pulse jumped. "I'll see you then." He ended the call and drew in a breath. At least he'd get to see Hailey. That was a start. But a start to what? As much as he wanted to refute the Carvers' claim to Hailey, he didn't have any legal rights. What he needed was communication, understanding, compromise. *Was he going to get any of that from Rebecca's parents?* It was doubtful, but he had to try.

He needed to see the little girl he considered a daughter. And she needed to see him. He didn't know why the Carvers couldn't understand that, but he was done being patient. He'd given them time to come to terms with their grief. Now, they were going to have to come to terms with him.

Gianna opened the store at ten a.m. on Friday morning. She'd spent way too much time thinking about Zach the night before. There was something going on with him that he hadn't shared with her, and she was very curious as to what that was. But she was taking a hiatus from men, and she didn't need to get any further involved with Zach.

Picking up a dust cloth, she wiped down the furniture in the showroom, moved items around so that they could be seen better, and tried to familiarize herself with the inventory, but there were a lot of items in both the showroom and the storeroom, and it would take time to know where everything was and how valuable, unique or historical it was.

Two ladies came in a little after eleven, spending a good hour browsing, one eventually buying a set of silver candlesticks, the other a small end table. The items were inexpensive, but at least they hadn't left empty-handed. After that, the doorbell pealed every few minutes as more shoppers came to browse. The locals expressed their sympathy for her aunt's injuries, one leaving cookies and a few others dropping off cards. It reminded her how small and close the community was. However, there were also shoppers from out of town, some vacationing at the lake, others making a day trip to her aunt's well-known antiques store.

As the clock ticked past one, the door chime rang once more, but this time it was Chloe who entered the shop.

"How's it going?" Chloe asked, as she set a paper bag from the Big Sky Café on the counter.

"It has been busy since I opened the doors, not a tremendous number of sales, but quite a few shoppers."

"Your aunt has built a good business. People come from all over."

"There are definitely more out-of-towners than I remember when I used to work here as a teenager."

"I figured you'd be busy, so I brought you some lunch. Have you eaten yet?"

"I haven't. And this is very sweet. I'm surprised you could get away from the café."

"I have a doctor's appointment in a half hour, so I was on my way out."

"Everything okay?"

"It's just the usual checkup," Chloe replied, one hand gently pressing against her belly. "I thought you might be avoiding the café and other restaurants in town after your encounter with Jeremy yesterday."

"I have to admit I'm not eager to see all the gossips and hear what they have to say about me."

"There's no avoiding that, but there are plenty of people in this town who love you and care about you. They will have your back —myself included."

"Thanks. It's really nice to hear that." She paused. "There's a sparkle in your eyes I didn't see yesterday."

Chloe gave her a happy smile. "I heard from Kevin this morning. We actually got to video chat. It was good to see his handsome face. He's been gone so long."

"How long has it been?"

"Eight months. We didn't even know I was pregnant when he left." Chloe's eyes grew moist. "I had to tell him over the phone. This whole time he kept thinking he'd be able to get back, but every time something came up. There was a mission, the team needed him, he didn't have a choice—all the usual explanations." Chloe's sparkle faded with her words.

"Are you all right?" she asked, as a tear ran down Chloe's cheek.

"Don't mind me; I'm hormonal. I go up and down." Chloe wiped her eyes with her fingers. "I feel like Kevin has missed the whole pregnancy, and I'm terribly afraid he'll miss the birth."

"I'm sure he won't. Aren't first babies often late?"

"Yes, and I hope this one is, too."

"Kevin will make it in time," she said confidently. "He'll move heaven and earth to be with you. He adores you. He has loved you since you were sixteen years old." She'd been there through their early years together, and there had never been a doubt in Kevin's mind, even when they were in high school, that Chloe was the one for him.

"We've been together for twelve years, but the last five years Kevin has been gone a lot. I have to admit this isn't what I thought I signed up for. I just hope it will change after the baby comes, because I don't know if I can take care of our son by myself."

"You're having a boy?" she asked with delight.

"Yes. I'm going to be outnumbered by males."

"I'm so happy for you. You will be an amazing mother. When we were kids, and we used to play house, you were always the mom, remember?"

Chloe laughed. "I do remember. You were the artist visiting from Paris, Keira was the model or the fashion designer, and Hannah was the nurse. Funny, how we pretty much became our childhood dreams. Except for Keira, of course. I never thought she'd go into real estate, but after her mom had that horrible accident, she needed someone to run the business, and Keira jumped in. She's doing well, but I wonder if she's happy, if she's doing what she really wants to do. Anyway, we need a girls' night, which is another reason I came by. I spoke to Lizzie Cole, and she and her sister Chelsea are in for tomorrow night, as is Hannah. I'm still working on Keira."

"That would be fun. I'd love it."

"I'll text you the details when I have them. I've missed you, Gianna. I haven't heard much from you the past year."

"I know. I've been feeling so embarrassed by my bad choices that I didn't feel like I should get in touch."

"That's ridiculous. We all love you."

"But there is something tragically flawed within me; I just haven't figured out what it is yet."

Chloe gave her a sympathetic smile. "I don't think you are tragically flawed. Frankly, I was happy when you and Jeremy split, because he was wrong for you. I didn't know Victor too well, and I never got to meet Jeff, but if they weren't right for you, then the right guy is still out there. You simply have to find him."

"I am not looking. I'm done."

"Maybe that's a good thing. Maybe he needs to look for you."

"I'm taking a break from men."

"We'll see," Chloe said, skepticism in her eyes. "I better get to my appointment."

"Thanks again for lunch."

As Chloe left, another woman walked in. While she was pleased to see a customer, she was not as happy to see Helen Carver. She'd spent most of her teenage years at odds with Helen's daughter, Rebecca, including the six weeks she'd spent at camp with Zach, where Rebecca had been determined to get Zach for herself.

Helen frowned when she saw her. "Where's Lois?" she asked shortly.

"My aunt broke her leg. I don't know if you remember me; I'm Gianna Campbell."

"I know who you are. When will your aunt be back?"

"Not for a few weeks."

"Well, that's disturbing."

"Can I help you?"

"My husband put some furniture on consignment last week and I need to know where it is." Helen glanced around the room. "I don't see anything in here."

"There are a lot of pieces in the back room. If this was last week, it's possible that it's waiting to be priced and put on the floor. I'm still playing catch-up. Is there something in particular you wanted to know about the pieces?"

"I need to know if anything has sold yet."

"Why don't I check with my aunt, and I can give you a call?"

Helen frowned. "Can I look in the storeroom?"

"I'm sorry. I'm not allowed to let anyone but employees back there. Is your number in the computer?" She opened the screen in front of her. "I know my aunt takes contact information for anyone who puts items on consignment."

"That was my husband. I'll give you my number," Helen said. "Don't bother Ron with this."

She picked up a pen. "All right. Go ahead." She jotted down the number.

"Please call me as soon as you can," Helen said. "It's important."

She didn't really understand the urgency in Helen's voice, but she wasn't going to question it. "I will."

The door opened again, and, to her surprise, Zach came through the door. She hadn't expected to see him so soon, and she couldn't deny the spike in her heart rate. He really was an incredibly attractive man.

"You," Helen said, fury blazing in her eyes as she looked at Zach.

He stopped in his tracks, an odd expression crossing his face.

"What the hell are you doing here?" Helen demanded. "How dare you come here? How dare you? After what you did? You're a murderer."

"Mrs. Carver," he began.

"Don't talk to me. And don't come near the house, or I'll get the police involved." Helen stormed out of the shop.

"What was that about?" Gianna asked in shock, noting the pallor of Zach's skin, the furious look in his eyes. "Why did Mrs. Carver call you a murderer?"

CHAPTER SIX

ZACH DIDN'T ANSWER RIGHT AWAY. FINALLY, he drew in a breath and said, "I told you my fiancée died in a fire. That was Rebecca."

"What?" She hadn't thought she could be more surprised, but she was. "You were engaged to Rebecca Carver? How did you not tell me that yesterday?"

"It's complicated."

"And she died? I can't believe I never heard that." Usually her mom kept her in the loop with town news, but she couldn't remember hearing that piece of information. Although, she'd been quite wrapped up in Jeff and wedding plans the last six months. Maybe her mom had said something, and it just hadn't sunk in.

"Well, it's true. Rebecca is dead," he said grimly.

She shook her head. "I'm sorry. I still don't understand. You said you hadn't been back to Whisper Lake since you were sixteen and at the camp. How did you and Rebecca even get together?"

"We ran into each other in San Francisco four and a half years ago and we started hanging out."

"Why?" she asked, confounded by the fact that Zach and Rebecca had been in a relationship. "I didn't think you liked her at all when we were teenagers. You said she was shallow and a mean girl."

"When we met as adults, she was different. She had changed."

"In what way?"

"She was nicer, not as stuck-up, less cocky. I realized her teenage attitude had been her way of covering up her insecurities."

"What did she have to be insecure about? She was tall and skinny with big boobs and legs for days. Her hair was shiny and smooth. She didn't have a zit to mar her perfect face, and she never even had to have braces. She was born perfect."

"She wasn't perfect. She had a lot of problems, more than I realized until we got involved."

She wasn't quite sure what to make of his words. "So, what happened? Why does Mrs. Carver think you're responsible for Rebecca's death? Did you set the fire?"

"No. I wasn't there when it started. I'd been out of town on business. I actually came home early, because I hadn't been able to get Rebecca on the phone for a few days, and I had a bad feeling. When I arrived, the apartment was fully engulfed in flames. I tried to get to Rebecca, but the ceiling fell down on me. By the time the firefighters pulled her out, it was too late."

She felt a rush of guilt at her negative thoughts. Rebecca was dead and that was a terrible, terrible tragedy. "I am sorry she died. I know I just went off on a rant, but I wouldn't wish what happened to her on anyone."

"I know." He stared back at her. "There's more, Gianna. Do you want to hear it?"

Her stomach tightened. "Yes. Tell me."

"There were two other people in the apartment when the fire started—a man who was hooking up with Rebecca, bringing her drugs, encouraging her addiction, and Rebecca's seven-year-old daughter Hailey."

She drew in a breath and let it out. "What happened to her little girl?"

"I got Hailey out of the apartment first, but when I went back inside, that's when the ceiling came down. Rebecca and her male friend died."

"He wasn't just a friend. She was cheating on you with him."

"Yes."

"Why? Were you not happy together?"

He let out a breath. "It wasn't really about me. Rebecca had a drug problem. I didn't know how bad it was for a long time. She hid it really well. But it got worse and worse. The last year and a half were a nightmare. She went to rehab twice, and the last time, I thought she'd finally kicked it, but then she met this guy, and he got her back into it. Actually, I can't even blame him, because I'm sure the reason she was with him was to get drugs."

"That's terrible. What about her daughter? Was Rebecca even trying to be a mother?"

"She loved Hailey. But she was weak and when she was in a spiral, she couldn't see past her own needs. Luckily, I was there to pick up the slack. Hailey and I became very close."

"What happened to Hailey's father?"

"He was apparently a one-night stand when Rebecca was in college. He wasn't interested in being a father, so Rebecca was doing it on her own."

"Where is Hailey now?"

"She's with the Carvers. While I was recuperating from my burns, they came and got her. I haven't been able to see her since the night I pulled her out of the apartment. The Carvers believe that I'm responsible for everything that went wrong for Rebecca. They don't want Hailey to have anything to do with me, even though I was a father to her for four years."

"I don't understand. Why are they blaming you? You were a victim of their daughter's drug problem as well."

"They don't acknowledge there was a problem. They said Rebecca was unhappy with me and I wouldn't let her out of the relationship. I had to be crazy to suggest she was addicted to anything."

"Was the fire related to her drug use?"

"It was; I'm sure of it. But the apartment was destroyed, so any evidence of drug use vanished, and the fire department wasn't able to pinpoint exactly how the fire began. The Carvers have convinced themselves it was faulty wiring."

She shook her head as she tried to make sense of it all. "Can you go to court to get visitation?"

"I'm talking to a lawyer, but I don't have the law on my side. Rebecca and I were not married, and she didn't have a will. Her parents have legal custody of Hailey. I just want to be a part of her life. I *need* to be a part of her life."

Hearing the fierce passion in his voice, everything suddenly made a lot more sense. "That's why you came back. It wasn't just because of the camp."

"No. The camp gave me a good reason to be here for a while. I'm hoping I can change the Carvers' mind about me."

"You didn't tell them you were coming, did you?"

"They wouldn't talk to me. I did speak to Rebecca's brother, Mitch. He has been trying to act as a middleman."

"I remember Mitch. He was several years younger than us."

"He's a good guy. He knows who his sister was. But his parents won't let him say a negative word about Rebecca. There is a lot of dysfunction in that family, which is another reason why I want to be here for Hailey. I can't even imagine what she thinks about me now. She must feel that I abandoned her." His last statement was filled with intense emotion.

"Wow," she murmured, her heart going out to him. It was a good thing there was a counter between them, because right now all she wanted to do was put her arms around him. "You've had a rough time. I'm sorry."

"I thought about telling you last night, but I didn't know where to start. And since you'd just decided I wasn't as horrible as you thought, I didn't want to change your mind quite so soon."

"I don't think you're to blame for Rebecca's death. Obviously, I don't know the whole story, but you didn't create her addiction, unless you were feeding her drugs?"

"I wasn't. But maybe she was unhappy, and I did try to hang on to her for too long. I wanted to make our relationship work. I had fallen in love with her kid, and I had this vision of us being a family. I'd missed being part of a family." He drew in a hard breath. "I wanted something in my life to last. I kept thinking I could fix her. Maybe if I'd let her go…"

"You don't know what would have happened. She could have ended up in exactly the same situation and her daughter might have died with her."

"Maybe." He met her gaze. "It is good to talk to you again, Gianna. I always felt like we could be honest with each other. You were the first person I ever spoke to about my dad's death."

"I remember," she said softly. "And because of that, I understand why you might have felt compelled to try to hang on to Rebecca. You always believed your dad should have fought harder for his family and not as much for his career."

"Yes, I did. Anyway…now that Mrs. Carver knows I'm in town, I need to figure out a way to convince her and her husband to let me see Hailey."

"After the way she reacted to you, I think you only have one choice."

"What's that?"

"Make them see Rebecca for who she really was."

He immediately shook his head. "If I go negative, they'll continue to shut me out."

"What's the alternative, Zach? She called you a murderer. She won't change her mind without evidence."

"Whatever I say about Rebecca could hurt Hailey."

"Whatever the Carvers say about you could also hurt her. She has to think of you as her dad. She has to wonder where you are. Why haven't you seen her before this?"

"I was recovering from my injuries, and I was trying to work things out with them by phone. But when that stopped working, I drove up here two months ago. The Carvers wouldn't let me through the front door, and then they sent me letters from their lawyer telling me they'd take out a restraining order if I tried to come back."

"That's crazy. Why the tough stance?"

"Anger, grief, I don't know… That's when I got my own legal advice, which basically told me I had no rights. I continued to call, to send letters, but there was no response. I realized I wasn't going to change anything unless I was here in town. When Hunter offered me the job, I jumped on it. I thought it would be a good way to show the Carvers what kind of man I am and to prove that I can be trusted. But I have to be cautious and not give them any ammunition to keep me out of Hailey's life permanently."

"Sounds tricky. If you're not going to convince the Carvers their daughter was a drug addict, what are you going to do?"

"I was thinking of a charm offensive," he said with a half-hearted smile.

"You are pretty charming."

"I was also hoping Mitch could smooth the way, that enough time had passed that maybe they were seeing things more clearly now. But obviously they still have very negative feelings toward me."

"Clearly."

"Do you know them, Gianna? Would you be able to put in a good word for me?"

"Sorry. Rebecca never liked me, nor did her mother."

"Okay."

She saw the pain in his eyes and suspected that it probably ran deeper than anyone knew. While Zach had always come across as the happy-go-lucky, funny, charming guy, he'd also had a quieter side that he tended to keep hidden from most people. But he hadn't kept it hidden from her. She'd heard a lot about his dad that summer, about his heartache, about his mom and brother.

"What about your family?" she asked. "Did they ever meet the Carvers? Would your mom have any input?"

"No, she didn't meet Rebecca or her parents. I'm not close to my mother."

"Why not?"

"She remarried years ago and has a completely separate life."

"What about your younger brother?"

"He fits into her new life better than I do."

Zach's words were cold and unemotional, but she had a feeling that was a cover for another deep hurt.

"Anyway…let's change the subject," he said. "How are things going here?"

"Fine. There have been quite a few customers up until now." She paused. "Why did you come here, Zach?"

"I've been walking around town, reacquainting myself with Whisper Lake. I saw the sign and decided to say hello."

She wanted to say she was glad to see him, but she feared she was walking a dangerous line. She was a little too interested in Zach for someone who was supposed to be off men.

"I was also curious as to what you decided to do about the photo," Zach added.

She let out a small sigh. "I'm still indecisive. I'm seeing my parents tonight for dinner. I'm thinking I should maybe mention it before I start asking questions that might get around town. But I'm on thin ice with my dad as it is. I have a feeling going on this quest will make that worse."

"You could always take me to dinner at your mom's house. I could be a buffer."

"I don't think my dad would react well to seeing me hanging out with another man quite so soon, even though we're just friends," she added hastily. "I need to simplify my life, not complicate it."

"I understand. We both have a lot going on. But it's nice to know you're around."

It was nice for her, too.

As three women entered the shop, Zach tipped his head. "I'll let you get back to work. I'll see you soon."

His promising words sent a shiver down her spine, and she found herself watching the door long after he'd left. Zach was going to be trouble. She knew that with utter certainty. She also knew she wasn't going to stay away from him, even though she should.

———————

After leaving the antiques shop, Zach walked downtown. He felt unsettled and uneasy after his encounter with Helen Carver. That hadn't been the way he wanted to see her, but he should have figured it might go down like that.

He glanced down at his phone as it buzzed—*Mitch.*

"Hello?"

"I just got off the phone with my mother," Mitch said. "She was freaked out. She told me she's going to call the police on you."

"For doing what? Walking into an antiques store?"

"I tried to calm her down. I told her you were in town to work on the camp, but that set her off even more, because then she realized I knew you were coming and didn't warn her."

"I'm sorry about that. I would have told her myself, but after calling me a murderer, she stormed out. What else did she say?"

"That you were never going to see Hailey, that I needed to tell you to leave, that they want nothing to do with the person who killed Rebecca. I tried to tell her again that Rebecca's drug problems were not your fault, but she wouldn't hear me. She was completely panicked."

He frowned, wondering why the Carvers were so shaken by his presence. "Why are they so upset? Your parents have legal custody. They have all the power."

"They're afraid of losing it."

"I just want to see Hailey. I want to spend time with her. She was my daughter for four years. I don't want her to think I abandoned her, even though I'm sure that's exactly what your parents have told her. But I need her to know the truth. I need her to understand that I will always be there for her."

"I get it, Zach. I do. But my parents think you're the person responsible for Rebecca's death and they can't see you any other way. Look, I can't meet you tomorrow. It's too soon. Give me some time to talk to my dad. Maybe he can help get my mom off the ledge."

"I won't push for tomorrow, but I've already waited a long time, Mitch."

"I'm on my way over to my dad's office now. Let me see if I can get him to speak to you."

"All right. I do appreciate your help. Thanks." He blew out a frustrated breath as he hung up the phone. He was in Whisper Lake, only a few blocks from his daughter, but he still felt a million miles away. But he wasn't giving up. And the Carvers would eventually realize that.

He continued on down the street, walking more briskly as he headed toward the Firefly Inn. Work had been the only thing getting him through the past few months, and he needed to get back to it.

The Firefly Inn was a two-story mansion at the far end of downtown. It had a sweeping front porch that wound around the front and side of the building, with buckets of flowers hanging from the eaves. The inside was charming and inviting with dark paneled walls, sleek hardwood floors, colorful rugs, and furniture that invited lounging and relaxation.

When he entered the lobby, Lizzie stood behind the front desk, chatting with a dark-blonde woman. She motioned him over when she saw him.

"Zach, I want you to meet my sister, Chelsea."

Chelsea turned, smiling at him with light-blue eyes that reminded him of both Lizzie and Hunter. The Coles and their cousins, the Callaways, had apparently all inherited that particular shade of blue. "Nice to meet you, Chelsea."

"You, too," she replied. "Lizzie filled me in on the camp remodel. I'm looking forward to the reopening. The kids in my classroom are very excited about it."

"You're a teacher?"

"Yes—at Powell Elementary. I have a few boys who would really benefit from some organized outdoor adventures. They come up with way too many bad ideas when left to their own devices."

"Sounds like what my teachers used to say about me."

"Do you want some coffee?" Lizzie asked. "I just made a fresh pot." She waved her hand toward the nearby credenza. "There are cookies, too."

"No thanks, although they smell delicious. From what I've

seen, you're at the top of your game when it comes to hospitality and good food."

Lizzie beamed at his words. "Thanks. The inn is still a work in progress. At some point, I'd like to add dinner, but we need a few more guests to make that happen."

"This summer should do the trick," Chelsea put in. "Once people stay here, they'll become repeat guests."

"I hope so."

As Lizzie finished speaking, the front door opened. The man stepping into the inn had dark hair and blue eyes and wore a police uniform.

"Well, look who's here," Lizzie exclaimed. "Another one of my siblings."

"Lizzie, Chelsea," the man said with a nod. "How's it going?"

"Good. Did you come by for afternoon cookies?" Lizzie asked with a sparkling smile.

"No. I'm looking for one of your guests, and I think I may have found him."

Zach started as the officer's gaze turned on him. "Are you looking for me?"

"Are you Zach Barrington?"

"I am."

"I'm Adam Cole. Can I have a word with you—alone?"

His gut tightened. "What's this about?"

"Probably best if we speak in private."

"I'm fine with you saying whatever you have to say right now."

"Adam, what's going on?" Lizzie asked in concern. "Why are you glaring at Zach like he's some sort of criminal?"

Adam frowned. "All right. If you want to do this here, we will. I got a call from one of our city councilmen, Ron Carver. He said that you're harassing his family."

"What?" Lizzie exclaimed.

Adam ignored his sister, his hard gaze focused on him. "Care to explain, Mr. Barrington?"

"I'm not harassing the Carvers," he said evenly, determined to keep the anger out of his voice. After Mitch's call, he should have expected this visit from the police. "I came to town to see their granddaughter, Hailey. I've basically been her stepfather the last four years."

"You were involved with Rebecca?" Adam asked.

"Yes, I was."

"Do you have a legal claim to the child?"

"I'm working on that, but at the moment, no. I'm not trying to take Hailey away from her grandparents; I just want to see her. I'm talking to Mitch Carver as well as to a lawyer in an attempt to make that happen."

"It sounds complicated," Adam said, crossing his arms in front of him.

"It is complicated, not only by facts, but by misunderstandings and grief."

"So, you weren't married to Rebecca? Nor did you adopt her daughter?"

"No. But I lived with both of them for four years."

"According to Mr. Carver, you were responsible for getting their daughter into drugs, which led to her death."

"That isn't true," he said tersely.

"All right, putting that aside, if the Carvers have legal custody of Hailey, and they don't want you to see her, you don't see her," Adam said flatly. "Not until you get a lawyer to tell me otherwise. Do I make myself clear?"

"Perfectly."

"Don't be such a hard-ass, Adam," Lizzie said. "Hunter knows Zach. He's a good guy."

"I'm just doing my job."

Zach didn't want to be the source of tension between the Cole siblings, but he was happy that Lizzie had spoken up for him, even though she didn't know him very well.

"So how are things coming at the camp?" Adam asked, switching into a friendlier tone. "Has Hunter bitten off more than he can chew?"

"It's a big project," he conceded. "We'll have initial drawings into the city next week."

Adam nodded. "I hope that goes well. You might consider having Hunter be the point person with the building department. Ron Carver has a lot of friends in local government. Anyway, I need to take off. Please remember what I said."

"I'll walk out with you, Adam," Chelsea said. "I want to talk to you about one of the kids in my class. I'm concerned about his welfare."

As Adam and Chelsea left, Zach turned to Lizzie. "Thanks for the vote of confidence."

"I wish I could do more," she said, a worried gleam in her eyes. "I know Mr. Carver has a lot of influence in this town. I would hate to see him use it against the camp."

"If that looks to be the case, I'll bow out. Hunter can hire another architect."

"But you've already done a lot of work."

"It doesn't matter. The camp needs to be reopened. But even if I step away from the project, I won't leave Whisper Lake. I need to talk to Hailey."

"I didn't know Rebecca well. I met her a few times over the years, but I remember hearing about the fire and her death. It was sad. I didn't realize there was a child left behind."

"It is sad," he agreed. "But I'm not the Carvers' enemy, and they need to realize that."

"If I can help in any way…"

"I'll ask. Thanks for the offer."

"No problem. And just so you know, Adam is a good guy. He can sometimes see things very black and white, but when it comes down to it, he usually does the right thing."

"I'm sorry the Carvers put him in the middle of a private situation." He paused, thinking he needed a jolt of caffeine to clear his head. "Maybe I will have a coffee."

"Of course," she said, moving over to the credenza. "Do you take anything in it?"

"Black is fine. You're a good hostess."

"It's all I ever wanted to be," she confessed, as she filled a mug. "Even as a child, I was the one hosting the tea parties. I started out as a party planner, but when my partner and I had a chance to buy this inn, I knew this was what I really wanted to do. I've always loved the lake. My grandparents used to live here, and my parents brought us here all the time when we were kids. Now with Chelsea and Adam working here, it's feeling even more like home. If I could get my parents and my two other brothers here, it would be perfect."

"Where is the rest of your family?"

"My parents and my oldest brother Grayson are in Denver. My other brother Nathan is currently in New York. We'll see if he hears the call back to the mountains." She paused. "I'm also very excited to have Hunter and Cassidy settling here. Hopefully, more of the Callaways will come for a visit."

"I've heard a few stories about Hunter's very large family."

"There are a lot of us," she said with a smile. "I've missed some of the family drama, not being in San Francisco, but my mom keeps in touch with her siblings, so she's almost always in the know. Is your family in Denver?"

"Not anymore. My family is very small compared to yours. And while you'd think that would make us closer, it has actually had the opposite effect."

Sympathy filled her gaze. "You've had a rough year, haven't you?"

"Unfortunately, yes."

"I'm really sorry about what happened with you and Rebecca and Hailey. I hope you can find a way to work it out."

"I'm going to give it my best shot."

CHAPTER SEVEN

"HI, MOM," Gianna said, as she stepped into her parents' house that evening and gave her mother a hug.

"Hello, honey. I'm glad you made it. How was your day?"

She set her purse down on the table in the entry. "Busy. I got a lot of questions, not all of which I could answer. I'm going to run them by Aunt Lois tomorrow morning and see if she can give me some tips. I know art, but I don't know furniture that well."

"No one knows the antiques as well as your aunt does. Come into the kitchen. Your dad is watching the Rockies take on the Giants."

She wasn't surprised to hear that since her dad had always been an avid baseball fan. She followed her mother down the hall into the great room at the back of the house, which combined the kitchen, dining room, and family room in one large space. Her dad was sitting in a brown leather recliner, a newspaper on his lap, the remote control in his hand.

"Hi, Dad." She walked over and gave him a kiss on the cheek.

"Gianna," he said, a cool note in his voice.

"Why don't you turn that off, Dave?" her mother suggested. "So we can talk."

"It's the ninth inning," he protested. "I'll let you two catch up."

"We're all going to catch up," her mom said firmly. "And the Rockies are up by five, so you can mute the sound at least."

"Fine," her dad grumbled.

She sat down on the couch next to her mom. "How was the party at Linda's house last night?"

"It was all right," her mom said rather carefully.

"Why don't you tell her the truth?" her dad put in.

"Dave."

"You wanted me to talk. Now you want me to be quiet?" her dad asked, an irritated note in his voice.

Her heart sank. This visit was not starting out well. "What happened at the party?"

"Jeremy was there." Her dad gave her a pointed look. "He mentioned that he saw you yesterday, that you seemed unapologetic about calling off another engagement."

"I don't think that's exactly what happened. He was making fun of me at the café. I didn't appreciate his humor. I also don't like that he's talking crap about me all over town."

"Well, you've given him plenty to talk about." Her dad moved his recliner into the upright position, his brown eyes hard. "He didn't say anything that wasn't true."

"Dave," her mom interjected. "Gianna hasn't done anything wrong."

"She led on three different men. How is that not wrong?"

"I didn't lead on anyone," she defended. "I just changed my mind, and each situation was different. They also didn't happen in one year. Jeremy and I ended our relationship seven years ago. I'm sorry that I've embarrassed you and Mom, that I've put you in a bad position, but I'm not sorry I called off the weddings, because they weren't right."

"Are you sorry you said yes in the first place?" he challenged. "One broken engagement is understandable, maybe even two, but three? Why do you keep saying yes?"

"That's a good question. I really thought I loved each of them. But as time went on, as the wedding date got closer, I realized it wasn't right."

"Which is a good reason for calling the wedding off," her mom said.

She gave her mother a smile, grateful for her support. "I'm sorry I've disappointed you both," she said, turning her gaze back to her father. "Clearly, I need to do some serious thinking about what I want in my life."

"Yes," her dad agreed. "I never expected you to be so flaky, Gianna."

She winced at his words. "I'm going to do better. I know I've made mistakes. I can't blame everything on the guys. I think the problem is I don't know who I am." As the words came out, she realized she was moving into dangerous territory.

A shadow ran through her mother's gaze, and her dad's lips tightened. She hadn't intended to bring up the photo she'd found or the fact that she might want to look for her biological parents, but she'd inadvertently gotten there anyway.

"You're going to blame your actions on the fact that you're adopted?" her father challenged.

"That's not what I meant. It's that I've come to realize I tend to be whoever these guys want me to be—at least in the beginning—and then I see what I'm doing, and I realize I'm not really the woman they want, and they're not the man I want. I don't know if that makes sense."

"Why would you try to be someone else?" her dad asked.

"I need to figure that out."

"Hopefully, you do that before you accept another ring."

"You don't have to worry about that. I'm taking a break from romance."

"Good," her father said, his gaze moving back toward the television.

"I'll get dinner ready," her mom said, getting to her feet. "Gianna, why don't you help me?"

She followed her mother to the kitchen. "What can I do?"

"I actually have everything under control, but I thought the two of us could chat."

"Good call. What did you make?"

"Roast chicken with mashed potatoes and glazed carrots."

"Another one of my favorites. You're bringing out all the hits."

"I try," her mom replied, a strained look in her eyes. She checked the oven, then added, "It will be a few minutes. Do you want something to drink?"

"Not yet." She paused. "Maybe I shouldn't have come. I could leave."

"Don't you dare. You and your father needed to talk."

"I'm not sure it did any good."

"It's a start. You do need to figure out what you want in your life and who you want to share that life with, but it's what you said about not knowing who you are that makes me a little sad."

"I wasn't just talking about being adopted; it's that I can't seem to really be myself."

"Maybe it is about you being adopted. I know you've been curious for most of your life. But I thought you'd made your peace with it."

"I have. Or I thought I had," she mumbled. "I love you and Dad. You're my parents. You're wonderful. I couldn't have asked for a better family."

"But you still want to know who your real mother is."

"Not my *real* mother—that's you. My biological mother."

"Perhaps you should try looking for her. I'm not sure you'll get far, but maybe just taking that step will make a difference."

She licked her lips. "I did find a rather interesting photo last night. I had to pick up boxes and furniture from the camp for Aunt Lois, and in one of those boxes was a picture of a teenage girl. She was wearing a locket, exactly like the one I had."

Her mom's eyes widened. "Really? Who was she?"

"I have no idea. There was no name on the picture. And it was at least thirty years old, maybe more. I know the locket wasn't that special. It could be a coincidence."

"Do you have the picture?"

"It's at the apartment. Do you want to see it? I could bring it by tomorrow."

Her mother's gaze filled with uncertainty. "I don't know. Maybe this is something you need to do on your own."

Guilt ran through her. "I don't want to hurt you, Mom."

"I know that. But you have questions. You should try to get them answered. You have my blessing."

"Well, she doesn't have mine," her dad suddenly barked out, as he got up from his chair and came toward the kitchen. "You're now going to go off on some search for a woman who gave you away? Why don't you look for answers inside yourself instead of everywhere else?"

"Dave, it's okay that she has questions," her mom said.

"No, it's not, Jeannie. I think this picture you found is just another distraction, another reason for you not to examine your own actions too closely, Gianna."

She couldn't say her father was completely wrong. Searching for her mom did feel like a good break from feeling bad about ending her relationship with Jeff. But she couldn't make herself feel better by hurting her parents. "You're right. I don't need to do anything with the photo."

"He's not right," her mom said, shooting her dad a dark look. "We've danced around this subject before—when you lost the locket at camp, when you graduated from high school, when I got sick...it's time. I want you to figure out who you are and if you need to find the woman who gave birth to you to do that, then you have my support."

Her father rolled his eyes and stomped out of the kitchen.

"Don't worry about him," her mother said. "He's being protective of me. But I understand your desire to know your personal history. I might feel the same way."

"Really?"

"Really," her mom said, meeting her gaze.

"Maybe I am just looking for a distraction from my problems. I want you to know I didn't come home with the intention to look for anyone. It was the camp; it was seeing Zach again, and then the photo."

"Wait! Zach?" her mom interrupted. "Isn't that the boy who

took your locket? The one you cried over for weeks after you came home that summer?"

"That's the one. I ran into him at the camp on Thursday."

"What on earth was he doing up there?"

"He's the architect on the remodel. He's friends with the new owner."

"Well, that's quite an interesting turn of events."

"Yes. He's definitely the last person I expected to see there. He brought back a lot of memories, some of which had to do with the locket, which he again denied taking. I think I believe him now. Maybe I did just lose it. Or someone else took it. Anyway, I saw him, and then I found the photo, and everything started to snowball."

Her mother nodded. "That's completely understandable. You know, Gianna, I've always felt a little insecure because we didn't share blood, but that's my problem, not yours."

"I love you so much, Mom. I don't want you to ever doubt that."

"I love you, too. But you should try to find your biological mother, because if you don't, you'll always wonder."

"She could be horrible."

"I wouldn't wish that for you. I wouldn't want her to disappoint you."

Her mother's generosity only added to her emotional conflict. But there was a part of her that knew she did need to at least try to find an answer to the question that had plagued her entire existence.

"Why don't you show the picture around town?" her mom suggested. "Put it up in the store. A lot of people come through there. Someone might recognize her."

"That's an interesting idea. But once I do that, I won't be able to take it back. Are you ready for that? Will Dad be ready for what might come?"

"We can handle whatever happens. The real question is —can you?"

Gianna was still thinking about her mother's question on Saturday morning as she drove to her aunt's house. And she still didn't have an answer.

While it was nice to have her mom's blessing, her dad would not be happy if she pushed forward. They hadn't discussed it over dinner, a meal that had been so forced with trivial conversation, she'd been relieved when it was over. It was the first time in her life that she'd felt out of place within her own family. She needed to think hard about how a search would affect their relationship.

She parked in front of her aunt's one-story ranch house, located several miles from the downtown area, on a woodsy lot, with a view of the lake. While her parents preferred to live close to the harbor and their business, her aunt had always liked quiet when she was done with work.

Grabbing a tote bag filled with treats, she walked up to the front door and used the key she'd gotten from her mom to open the door. Her aunt was on crutches, but it was still painful for her to move around.

"Hello? Aunt Lois?"

"I'm in the sunroom," her aunt called back.

She walked down the hall and into the sunny sitting room with floor-to-ceiling windows that looked out over the water. Her aunt was in a big armchair, her casted leg up on the ottoman, a pile of books on the table next to her, and her laptop computer on the ottoman.

"How are you?" she asked, leaning down to give her aunt a hug.

Lois was her father's younger sister, and like her dad she had dark-brown hair and eyes, but whereas her father was always more guarded, her aunt had an open, welcoming expression.

"I'm doing all right," Lois replied. "My friend Pam comes by every morning to help me bathe and dress. Then she makes me breakfast and puts lunch and dinner in the fridge. I'm going to gain weight while I'm healing."

Since her aunt was genetically blessed with a lean frame, Gianna didn't think she had to worry about that. "I'm glad you're eating and that you're being well cared for," she said, perching on the chair across from her aunt.

"I'm blessed with good friends and a very caring niece. How is the store?"

"I opened yesterday, as I told you, and we had a busy afternoon. I sold a few pieces. Nothing particularly big, but hopefully that will change, and I can get some of the furniture out of the back room and into the store."

"I know it's crowded. I had just gotten new inventory when I broke this damn leg."

"And you now have more inventory from the camp."

"Well, don't worry too much about what isn't in the showroom already. I can catch up when I get back."

"I will keep putting items on display as we get space. I need to confer with you on the pricing of various pieces, though. I took some photos and wanted to run through them with you."

"That was very smart of you," her aunt said approvingly.

"By the way, I saw two very cool guitars in the back room, one signed by Halston Cooper, who is a huge country-western singer. Should I get those on display? I think they'll sell right away for a lot of money. In fact, I was looking at your website and thinking they should be on the front page."

"No, you need to leave the guitars where they are. I'm not putting them up for sale."

"Why not?"

"Because I don't think the woman who gave them to me really wants me to sell them. And one day, I believe she'll want them back, so I'm keeping them safe for her."

"Who is the woman?"

"Chelsea Cole."

"Lizzie's sister?"

"Yes. Chelsea is a fantastic singer-songwriter. She was on her way to the top of country music when she suddenly quit and came to Whisper Lake. She asked me to sell her guitars, and then she got a job as a music teacher at the elementary school."

"What do you think happened to her music career?" she asked curiously. "Why did she quit?"

"There are rumors that she had a nervous breakdown or a possibly a romantic breakup with another singer. Someone else said that she had a stalker, and she wanted to live a more private life. I don't know the truth."

"That all sounds terrible. I saw her and Lizzie the other night, and Chelsea definitely seemed withdrawn, a little haunted, but she didn't say anything, and Lizzie told me later that she doesn't even know the whole story."

"Well, I hope Chelsea can come to terms with whatever happened. In the meantime, keep the guitars off sale."

"You're very thoughtful, Aunt Lois."

"I just know that some decisions should be thought over for a longer time."

"Well, I'm glad I asked you. Are there any other pieces in the storeroom that you don't want to sell?"

"No, just the guitars."

"Okay. By the way, I also had a visit from Helen Carver yesterday, and she wanted to know what was happening with the items her husband had put on consignment. But I don't know which pieces belong to them."

"Oh, right," Lois said, a frown on her lips. "Ron sent those over the day before I broke my leg, and I wasn't able to get them into the showroom. We can price them while you're here, and Kellan can help you put them out. Is Nora working today?"

"Yes. She said she'd be in around noon." Nora was a retired librarian, who worked part-time in the store, mostly to keep herself busy.

"Good. I don't want you to have to work every shift."

"I'll be fine. Getting back to the Carvers. I heard Rebecca died. That's very sad."

"It is sad. But I guess they're blessed to have their grandchild now." Lois paused, tilting her head as she gave her a thoughtful look. "You seem rather curious about the Carvers, Gianna."

"I am. When Helen was in the store, a man came in that I used to know when I was a kid—Zach Barrington. Helen looked at him and turned as white as a sheet. She started screaming at him, asking him why he was there. She called him a murderer."

Her aunt's eyes widened. "That's crazy. He's someone you know?"

"I knew him one summer a long time ago, but he was Rebecca's fiancé. He told me that Rebecca died in a fire, that she had a drug problem. He saved her daughter, Hailey, but he wasn't able to save Rebecca. While he was recovering from his injuries, the Carvers came and got Hailey and brought her here. They don't want him to see Hailey, and he's very upset about it."

"Ron told me that Rebecca had gotten involved with the wrong people and that's why she died, but he didn't elaborate. How did this Zach Barrington react to Helen's accusation?"

"He didn't say anything; Helen didn't give him a chance. She took off. But she was shaken. So was Zach. It seems like a bad situation."

"It does. I'm a little surprised Helen screamed at him. She's usually very reserved and difficult to read."

"I don't know about that. I've always been able to read her dislike of me."

Lois gave her a disbelieving look. "Why would she dislike you?"

"Because Rebecca didn't care for me, and her mother thought she hung the moon, so she didn't like me, either. I think the dislike even extended to Mom."

"I'm glad I never had children—all the politics that go along with kids and their mothers…"

"Speaking of Mom, there's something else I wanted to talk to you about."

Lois smiled. "Well, this visit is getting more and more interesting. I thought we were just going to discuss furniture."

"We'll get to that, I promise." She dug into her bag and pulled out the photo. "I found this picture in one of the boxes I picked up at the camp. The teenage girl is wearing a necklace that looks exactly like the one that came with me when I was adopted."

Lois's eyes widened. "Oh, this conversation is about your adoption. I thought you'd decided against looking for your biological parents."

"I had put it aside. But going to the camp was like a trip down memory lane and finding the photo...well, it brought everything back up. I spoke to Mom last night, and she gave me her blessing to try to find this girl."

"Well, that's good. What about your father?"

"He's angry with me, not only for bringing up my biological mother, but for ditching three men on my way to the altar."

"Your father has high expectations, not only for himself, but for everyone around him, and that includes his beloved daughter. But you know he loves you."

"I know. I just hate disappointing him."

"Show me the photo."

She handed the picture to her aunt. "I realize it's a leap to think this girl might be my mother. It sounds ridiculous when I say it out loud."

"The locket looks like the one you had," Lois murmured.

"I don't suppose you recognize the girl."

"I wish I did. She does have features similar to yours."

"I thought so, too, but maybe it's wishful thinking. My biological mother was probably sixteen or seventeen when she had me. I'm twenty-nine, so she'd be around forty-five or forty-six now."

"Which makes her about eight years younger than me and about thirteen years younger than your mom and dad. I doubt we ran in the same circles, if she even lived here."

"True. I'd like to put the picture out in the store, see if anyone recognizes her. What's your opinion on that? If you don't like it, I won't do it."

"I don't have a problem with you asking customers about the photo. But it's a long shot."

"I feel like I need to try. Do you hate me?"

"Why would I?"

"Because it feels like I'm making a statement about Mom and Dad, that they weren't enough for me."

"You just want to know your history; I can't blame you for that, Gianna. Your mom and dad will always be your parents, no matter what you find out."

She was relieved to have her aunt's support. "Thanks. Shall we get to work? Let's go through the furniture, starting with the pieces you got from the Carvers. She's waiting for me to call her with an update."

CHAPTER EIGHT

ZACH SPENT Saturday morning exploring the camp. He'd gone through every cabin and every room in the lodge as well as the old barn. He'd made sketches by hand, then got on his laptop computer at a table in the dining room and used architectural software to bring his ideas to life. He was feeling good about his progress when Hunter arrived.

"How's it going?" Hunter asked as he set a bag on the table.

"Very well. I have some new drawings to show you."

"Perfect. We can talk about them over lunch." Hunter sat down across from him and opened the bag. "Lizzie stocked me up with sandwiches, salads and her famous chocolate chip cookies."

"Great. I'm starving."

As Hunter unpacked the lunch, Zach stretched his arms high over his head, feeling the knots in his neck loosen and unravel. When he was deep in concentration, he tended to hunch his shoulders, and all of his stress ended up there.

"You can take breaks," Hunter said, noting his long stretch.

"I was caught up in some new ideas. I was thinking about the Orphan Train and incorporating the theme of trains into the camp, and then it hit me—we should have an actual train. The younger kids would love it. There is a ton of space available."

"Good idea."

"Being out here has gotten my creative juices flowing. It's the first time in months I've felt excited about something."

"Sounds like the lake is working its magic."

"It is. Have you heard from Cassidy? Is she coming up today?"

"No. She had to change her flight. One of her landscaping jobs has to be finished by the Fourth of July, and she's running behind. I told her there was no hurry to getting up here. We have plenty of time to get settled."

"Do you think you'll be happy running a camp instead of running into a burning building?" he asked curiously.

"Absolutely. I have loved being a firefighter, but I've been ready for a big change for a long time. Once I reunited with Cassidy and we started talking about the dreams we had as kids, I knew it was time to stop putting off what I really wanted to do. I've always wanted to run a camp and Cassidy loves being in nature. We thought we could do something special for kids who might need it. I know you've heard a little about Cassidy's past, but there was a lot of darkness in her early life, a lot of pain. She suffered as a kid, and she wants to help other kids now. We're both very excited about making Echo Falls Camp a place of healing and a place of fun."

"As it was for me. It's a good thing you're doing."

"I'm grateful for my family. If they weren't supporting this endeavor both financially and emotionally, it wouldn't be happening. But with my grandfather, my parents, my brothers Dylan and Ian, my uncle Jack, and my cousins Burke, Emma, and Aiden, I was able to get enough funding to make this a reality. There may be other family members coming on board as well, including some of the Coles, although they're already invested in Lizzie's inn."

"The Callaways and Coles are taking over Whisper Lake."

"I wouldn't go that far, but we do try to support each other."

"Do you think your family investors will be silent or want to share their opinions during the remodel?"

"Callaways always have opinions," Hunter said with a grin.

"I'll make sure they all have a chance to give their input, but for the most part, the decisions will be made by Cassidy and myself."

"It's best not to have too many people in charge."

"Totally agree."

"Speaking of you and Cassidy running things, the former owner lived on the top floor. What are you two thinking?"

"That we will not be living in the lodge—at least not permanently. We should keep the top floor of the lodge as an apartment, and we will start out there, but down the road, it might be used by a camp director or other staff member. I want to build a cabin behind the lodge, some place that's just ours. But that can happen in phase two."

"Good plan. You'll want your own private space."

"Exactly. We don't need to show the cabin on the current drawings. I want to keep everything focused on the camp. I don't want to run into any problems with local officials if this project gets too broad."

"Agreed. On that note, we need to talk."

"That sounds ominous. You're not breaking up with me, are you?" he joked.

"I probably should be."

Hunter frowned. "What are you talking about?"

"I told you Rebecca's parents live in Whisper Lake."

"Yes, and that you're hoping to open up communication with them, so you can see Rebecca's daughter."

"Right. Well, what I didn't tell you is that Rebecca's parents blame me for their daughter's death, and they've rejected every attempt I've made to see Hailey, Rebecca's daughter."

"Why would they blame you for her addiction?"

"Because they're in denial. I thought their attitudes might change once enough time had passed, but they're still bitterly angry with me."

"Have you seen them since you got here?"

"I ran into Mrs. Carver yesterday at the antiques store. She flipped out when she saw me. She called me a murderer and ran out of the store. She said she'd contact the police if I didn't stay away."

"I'm sure that was an empty threat."

"It wasn't. I got a visit from your cousin, Adam Cole, last night. The Carvers had already been in touch with him."

"That's crazy. They called the cops on you?"

"They did."

"Well, you haven't done anything wrong."

"Adam suggested I keep it that way by staying away from them, but that's not going to happen, because I need to see Hailey. She was basically my daughter for four years."

"Hailey is a sweet kid. I remember when you used to bring her to our basketball games."

"I can't imagine what she thinks about me not being with her."

"I didn't realize that there was so much animosity between you and the Carvers. I thought you'd agreed that Hailey's grandparents should raise her."

"I didn't have a choice. They have legal custody and when they first took over, I was in the hospital. But I want you to know that this job is still my priority. I will give you my absolute best, Hunter. However, I also want to use the time to try to bridge the gap between me and the Carvers."

"Completely understood."

"But there's a problem. Ron Carver is on the city council. He has extensive connections in the building department. The last thing I want to do is make my problems yours or be responsible for anything getting hung up."

"I can't see how a councilman could do that."

"I do," he said bluntly. "And you should not underestimate this problem. I'm willing to step back if you want."

"Are you kidding? You just came up with a train!"

He smiled. "I can pass my ideas along."

"And then what? Go home?"

"No, I'm not leaving the lake until I see Hailey. I've cleared my schedule for the next few months, so I can either stay here and work on the camp or stay here and work on seeing Hailey."

"Well, I think you should do both. Let's keep going. I'm not going to worry about Mr. Carver until I absolutely have to."

"I just wanted to be up front with you." He paused at the sound of an engine. "Are you expecting someone?"

"No." Hunter got up and looked through the window. "It's an older man. Maybe it's someone from the Rowland family."

He rose and walked over to the window, his heart sinking. "Remember when you said you weren't going to worry about the Carvers until you had to? Well, you're going to have to, because that is Rebecca's father."

As Hunter opened the door for Ron, Zach hung back in the entry, noting Ron's thinning gray hair, and the stomach paunch that seemed to get bigger every year. Ron was wearing black slacks and a light-blue button-down shirt that showed patches of sweat from the heat.

When Ron saw him, he pushed past Hunter and stomped over to him. Ron was a good four or five inches shorter than he was, but what he lacked in stature, he made up for in his always aggressive posture.

"What the hell are you doing here?" Ron demanded.

"I'm redesigning the camp," he said, keeping his voice as calm as possible.

"That's not why you're in Whisper Lake."

"It's not the *only* reason," he agreed. "You know I want to see Hailey. My phone calls, texts, and emails have gone unanswered, so I decided to come here and let her know that I haven't abandoned her."

"I told you months ago that you will not be a part of her life. That little girl has been through too much pain. I won't allow her to suffer anymore. And I have the law on my side."

"I won't cause her pain. I simply want to reassure her that she hasn't lost the person she considered to be her father the last four years of her life. You might want to think about her feelings."

"You are not Hailey's father. You were not Rebecca's husband. You are nothing," Ron said, practically spitting out the last few words.

As Ron stepped forward in a menacing fashion, Hunter moved in. "You need to back off," Hunter told him.

Zach appreciated his friend's defense, but he wasn't afraid of Ron. "It's fine," he told Hunter. "Ron and I have needed to have this conversation for a while."

Hunter gave him a speculative look, then nodded. "All right. I'll leave you to it, but I won't be far."

As Hunter left the room, he said, "I did not kill Rebecca, Ron. You know that. You have no reason to keep Hailey away from me. I am not a danger to her."

"You got Becca into drugs. And then you threatened to leave her. That's why she got so depressed, confused. She was terribly unhappy. You're the reason she's dead," Ron argued.

It was difficult to hear the spin Ron was putting on his past, but he knew the truth. "I'm not the reason Rebecca is dead. She was a drug addict. I got her into rehab twice, and both times I took care of Hailey while she was gone. I hoped when she came home clean and sober that it would last. It didn't. Her problems were always simmering right beneath the surface. She was haunted by things I couldn't understand. And through it all, I tried to stick with her. But she didn't make it easy. You know she was with another man the night of the fire. I'm sure you know he had a long rap sheet when it came to dealing drugs."

"You should have saved her," Ron said, a broken note in his voice now. "You were right there. Why couldn't you get her out?"

"I tried. I went back for Becca after I got Hailey to safety, but there was a wall of fire…" A knot entered his throat, choking off the words. He could feel the terrible heat, smell the intense smoke. "I couldn't get to her…"

"You didn't want to get to her. She was cheating on you. You were angry."

"That's not true. I did not want her to die. I did everything I could to save her, and I'm not just talking about the night of the fire."

"It wasn't enough. I lost my little girl." Ron turned away from him, obviously struggling for control.

While he had no love for the Carvers, he respected their grief, and he had to find a way to work with them, not for himself or for them, but for Hailey, who was caught in the middle.

Finally, Ron turned around, having gotten his emotions under control, but his face was still flushed red, his eyes filled with anger and pain. "Hailey is happy now. She has a stable home. Let her be."

"I need to see that for myself."

Ron gave an adamant shake of his head. "I can't allow that. She was traumatized after the fire. She cried for weeks. She had terrible nightmares. It's only been the last few weeks that she's starting to act normal. Helen and I can't allow you to mess that up. She's finally getting to a better place. You'll remind her of what she's lost."

"I love her, Ron. And she loves me. I'm sure she asks about me."

"No, she doesn't," Ron said flatly.

His words cut deep, but Zach didn't believe them for a second.

"If you loved Hailey," Ron continued, "you could have adopted her, but you didn't. You could have married Rebecca, but you didn't. You just lived with her, used her. The last time I saw Rebecca, she told me she wanted to be your wife, but you weren't ready to set a date or plan a wedding."

He didn't know if Rebecca had said that or if Ron was embellishing, but he was going to set the record straight. "Rebecca had a lot of problems she needed to work through. Getting married wasn't the answer. I realized that when she made her first trip to rehab a year ago."

"That's what you say now, but you never told us about her problems. You didn't let us know she was in rehab, that she was having issues. We were kept in the dark."

"That was Rebecca's choice. She asked me not to speak to you.

She was embarrassed and ashamed. She was always worried about what people would think, so she kept her secrets very close."

"We're not people; we're her parents."

"But not parents she was close to. I saw you maybe five times in the four years we lived together, and she didn't see you any more than that. She had a lot of problems with Helen. She didn't want Hailey to spend much time with her. She never allowed her daughter to come to Whisper Lake for an overnight with you and Helen, no matter how many times you asked. I don't think she'd be happy that you're keeping me out of Hailey's life."

"We're doing what's best for Hailey. Rebecca was perfect until she met you. She didn't have any problems before that."

"Are you lying to me or just to yourself? Or maybe you really believe that. But having seen Rebecca try to work through her problems, I know they started a very long time ago, when she was a kid, when she was living with you."

"I don't believe you," Ron said flatly.

"It's the truth."

"You want to smear Becca's name."

"I don't want to do that; I just want to see Hailey."

"So you can fight us for custody? Because that will never happen. Hailey is our blood. You have no legal rights."

"Why are you so afraid of me?" he asked wearily. "I'm not a monster. I took care of your daughter and your granddaughter for years."

"And I'm taking care of my granddaughter now, and my wife. Helen and Hailey are fragile, and I need to protect them."

"Because you couldn't protect Rebecca?"

"How dare you—"

"You're not to blame," he said, cutting the older man off. "It's not your fault that Becca was an addict."

His words put shock and wariness in Ron's eyes. "Well, I know that. I just said it was on you."

"It's not on me, either. Although, I have blamed myself. This disease belonged to Rebecca. She struggled with it. And, ultimately, she died because of it. We can't change the past. We can only control what happens now. Let me speak to Hailey. I'll come to your house. You can be in the room. It's a conversation."

Ron hesitated, then shook his head. "No."

"I'm going to keep asking, Ron, and I'm not leaving town."

"You'll have to do that if this project doesn't get approved."

He heard the threat in Ron's voice. "I'll walk away from the project if I need to. But I won't walk away from Hailey."

"We'll see about that," Ron said, full of bluster once more. He strode to the door, slamming it so hard on the way out that a piece of trim broke off.

He blew out a breath, not sure what to think. He'd had a chance to say more than he'd ever expected to say, but Ron hadn't agreed to let him see Hailey, and he'd threatened to hurt Hunter's project. He couldn't let that happen.

When he returned to the dining room, Hunter was sitting at the table, finishing up a sandwich.

Sitting down across from him, he said, "Ron Carver threatened to keep this project from getting approved in order to drive me out of town. I told him I'd walk away from it, and I'm thinking I should do that sooner rather than later."

"I'm not afraid of Ron Carver."

"Maybe you should be. Even if he can't sink the project, he can force you to jump through expensive hoops, he can cause you delays, who knows what else—"

"I won't let him bully me into accepting your resignation. You're my architect. And we move forward together—unless you're having second thoughts about staying in town?"

"I'm even more determined now."

"Then have a sandwich and show me the rest of your ideas."

"Are you sure?"

"Positive."

"All right. I have to warn you that some of my ideas are going to be expensive."

"I figured," Hunter said with a grin.

"And thanks," he added, meeting his friend's gaze. "I know this is not an obstacle you were anticipating."

"Maybe not. But I've spent the last ten years of my life running into burning buildings, where surprise was a given. I know how to work a problem."

"Then you better get ready to work."

"Always ready. On another note, tell me why you were in the antiques store yesterday. I thought you were going to deliver the furniture to the beautiful Gianna after you left on Thursday night."

"I did. But I just happened to be walking by on Friday…"

Hunter laughed. "Is that your story?"

"It is," he said with a smile. "And I'm sticking to it."

CHAPTER NINE

GIANNA CLOSED up the store at six o'clock on Saturday night, then spent another hour organizing the storeroom. She had finally located all the pieces that the Carvers had put on consignment and had priced them and put them in the showroom. She left a message to that effect on Helen's phone, relieved that she hadn't had to speak to her in person.

At a little before seven thirty, she locked up and headed downtown to Micky's Bar and Grill, a local brewery. Chloe had set up a girls' night for dinner and drinks, and she couldn't wait to relax and kick back with her friends.

When she walked into the restaurant, Chloe was standing next to a dark-blonde with pretty blue eyes—Chelsea Cole.

"Chelsea, Chloe," she said happily, as they exchanged hugs.

"It's been a long time," Chelsea said.

"Too long," she agreed. "I heard you're teaching in Whisper Lake now."

"Elementary school. It's fun."

"That's great."

"Lizzie is on her way. She just texted me," Chelsea added. "And she's bringing Hannah."

"Hannah is coming, too?" she asked with delight. "That's wonderful. What about Keira?"

"Unfortunately, no," Chloe interjected. "She has been out of town, and she's getting in later tonight. But she's having her annual pre-Fourth of July barbecue tomorrow, so you can see her then. Did you get the invite?"

"Yes. I'm planning to go."

"Great. I'll check on our table," Chloe said, heading to the hostess.

"I was sorry to hear about your broken engagement, Gianna," Chelsea said, giving her a sympathetic smile.

"Thanks. How have you been? You're not singing anymore?"

"I needed a change."

Shadows filled Chelsea's eyes, and Gianna flashed back on the beautiful guitars in her aunt's storeroom. As long as she'd known Chelsea, she'd been attached to her guitar. The fact that she would give up her instrument was mind-boggling. Something had happened, something beyond just Chelsea needing a change.

"Oh, look, here's Lizzie," Chelsea said with relief, as her sister entered the restaurant, followed by a beautiful redhead with pale skin and brown eyes—Hannah Stark.

As she hugged them both, she felt like she'd really come home. This was the friendship, the warmth, the love that she'd missed— people who had known her for a very long time, especially Chloe and Hannah, who she'd grown up with.

A moment later, the hostess escorted them to a round table in the restaurant.

"This place has changed," she commented, as she took her seat. "I remember it being dark and smelling of spilled beer. Now it's bright and airy, with an open kitchen, and good music."

"Micky's son Josh redid the inside after his father retired," Lizzie put in. "I've been sending a lot of our guests here. They all love it. Especially Josh's homemade brew, which we should definitely order."

"I'm in," she said. "It feels like the generations are all transitioning. New camp, new brewery, new inn…"

"It does feel that way," Chloe agreed, meeting her gaze. "I'm running the café for Kevin's parents. The world keeps spinning at its own pace, no matter how much we want it to go slower or faster."

There was a darkness to Chloe's words that sent an odd quiet around the table.

"Well, I killed the mood, didn't I?" Chloe asked more lightly. "Sorry about that. I'm super aware of time at the moment. I'm ready for this baby to be born, but I'm not ready to do it without Kevin. I want the days to go faster and slower at the same time."

"I can understand that," she said, giving her a sympathetic smile. "Did you speak to Kevin today?"

Chloe shook her head. "No, we didn't get a chance to connect." She squared her shoulders. "And that is enough about me. Tonight is for catching up."

"Not only for catching up," Hannah said with a laugh. "We're going to do karaoke later—like we used to."

Gianna groaned. "I am the worst singer. I'll pass."

"You're not passing, and after a few beers, you'll be fine," Hannah said decisively. She'd always been a forceful personality in the group, but she combined that force with so much love and genuine caring that everyone usually followed her lead. "I'm sorry Keira couldn't make it. But we'll see her tomorrow. Everyone is going to her barbecue, right?"

"I can make it," Chloe said. "Unless this baby has other plans."

"I'm in," Lizzie said, glancing at her sister. "Chelsea?"

"I'll see," Chelsea replied vaguely. "I have some projects to work on for school."

"It's Sunday—they can wait," Lizzie said.

"Like I said, we'll see." Chelsea gave her sister a pointed look.

"What about you, Gianna?" Hannah asked.

"It sounds like fun. I'd love to see Keira."

"There will probably be other people there who you know. Keira loves to throw parties," Hannah said. "And she tries to make sure there are some single men."

"That doesn't interest me at all," she said.

"I'm sorry about Jeff," Hannah said. "I don't know if you want to talk about it..."

"I really don't. I'd much rather hear what you all are doing."

"Well, aside from Chloe here, we're all single," Hannah said. "Unless Lizzie or Chelsea have some news to report."

"I don't," Lizzie said. "I have been so busy opening the inn, I haven't had a second to think about dating."

"Me, either," Chelsea said. "I've been busy with school."

"It's summer now," Hannah pointed out.

"And there's summer school," Chelsea said.

"What about you, Hannah?" she asked.

"I was dating a paramedic, but that ended about two weeks ago, which is when he started to ghost me. What an idiot—like he's not going to run into me at the medical center," Hannah added, rolling her eyes. "And it's not like Whisper Lake is a huge city. Men are stupid."

"Sorry," she said, giving Hannah a sympathetic smile.

"It's fine. We didn't have much more in common than medicine, and better to end it now than waste any more time. What's everyone having to eat?" Hannah asked, picking up the menu. "I think we should order appetizers plus dinner."

"I'm game."

After perusing the menu, they ordered drinks and dinner and then Hannah started an hour-long conversation that began with, *do you remember* and then went off into multiple directions.

Gianna loved not only talking about the past but also hearing what the other women were up to. Hannah's tales from the ER were both gory and funny. Chloe provided more information than she needed to hear on pregnancy woes, and Lizzie had plenty of tales on unusual guests coming through the inn.

Chelsea spoke the least. No one seemed to want to press her, and Gianna didn't know if that was because they all knew what Chelsea had gone through, or because it was clear Chelsea did not want to talk about herself. There was definitely a shadow hanging over Chelsea's head.

After dinner, they moved into the bar and ordered another round of drinks as the karaoke began.

"I'm going to take off," Chelsea said, not bothering to grab a seat.

"Don't leave," Lizzie protested, giving her sister a pleading look. "It's early. And we never hang out anymore. You don't have to sing."

"I'm tired. It was a long week. You all have fun."

"Is everything okay with her?" Gianna asked Lizzie, as Chelsea took off.

Lizzie shrugged, an unhappy look in her eyes. "Not really, but she's very private, and I don't even know all of it. I just know it's been a rough year for her."

"I'm sorry to hear that. I guess that rough year has something to do with her not singing anymore?"

"I'm sure it does, but she doesn't want to discuss her decision to quit. I don't get it. But I am happy that she's living here now. I missed her the last few years when she was on the road."

"I'm sure she'll open up at some point," Chloe interjected. "She just needs whatever time she needs."

"I hope so. But my sister has always kept things deep inside. Anyway, let's talk about who's singing."

"Not me," Chloe said, patting her abdomen. "The baby does not want me to sing—burp maybe—but sing, no."

Gianna laughed. "That's too bad. Because, as I recall, you have the best voice of all of us."

"I don't know about that. Hannah is good."

"I'm just loud," Hannah said with a grin. "I can't help myself. It feels good to belt out a song. You're excused, Chloe, but not you two." She wagged her finger at Gianna and Lizzie. "You're both going on stage with me. It will be fun."

"I don't think she's taking no for an answer," Lizzie said, glancing at Gianna. "Shall we be a girl trio?"

"I guess we could," she said, not wanting to let them down.

Before they could get up, a man came over to the table. He was tall and handsome, with dark hair and striking blue eyes. He wore dark jeans and a gray knit shirt.

"Adam," Lizzie said. "It's nice to see you out of uniform."

"I heard you and Chels were hitting up this place. Where is Chelsea?"

"She took off," Lizzie said, exchanging a concerned look with Adam.

"Too bad." His gaze swept the group. "Hello, ladies—Hannah, Chloe. And you must be Gianna."

"I don't know if I must be, but I am," she said.

"I'm Adam Cole, Lizzie's brother."

"Right. I don't know if we ever officially met when we were kids. Although, I have a vague recollection of three Cole brothers jumping off the dock and splashing us when we were trying to sunbathe on the pier at Pelican Point."

Adam grinned. "That was probably me. The good old days. It's nice to see you again."

"You, too. You Coles are taking over Whisper Lake."

"Lizzie is determined to get us all here. She's also working on the Callaway side of the family, too."

"Yes, I met Hunter at the camp. I'm thrilled he's going to open it up again."

"The whole family is getting involved," Adam agreed. "Anyway, I don't want to interrupt ladies' night, so I'll leave you all to it."

"Actually, we're going to do some karaoke. Care to join us?" Lizzie asked.

"No way. I don't sing."

"I'm not singing, either," Chloe said. "You can keep me company."

He gave her a warm smile. "Now, that's an invitation I like."

"You can have my chair," Lizzie said, as she got to her feet. "Let's go, girls."

While she would have rather hung out at the table with Chloe and Adam, Gianna followed Lizzie and Hannah to the stage.

While the guy before them was singing, they looked over their song choices.

"This is perfect," Hannah said with a grin, pointing to a title. "'Girls Just Want To Have Fun'. What could be better? It describes us perfectly."

"I don't think we've been girls who just want to have fun for a long time," she said with a laugh. "We've all been really busy with work the last decade or so."

"True, but we can be fun tonight, can't we?"

"I'm in," Lizzie said. "I have been working a lot. I could release a little tension."

"I could, too," she admitted, although it was her personal life that had been adding to her stress levels, not her profession.

As they moved onto the stage, her gaze swept the room, and her stomach tightened. Jeremy had joined Chloe and Adam, which was not awesome. She now had her own personal heckler in the crowd.

Thankfully, as the stage was lit up, she couldn't see Jeremy anymore, only a blur of lights and shadows.

As the song began, she concentrated on reading the music and trying to keep up with Hannah and Lizzie. Hannah, as predicted, was the loudest. Lizzie was actually pretty good, and she just tried to blend in.

Although, it struck her that one of her biggest faults was always trying too hard to blend in, to be whoever people wanted her to be.

A surprising amount of applause followed their act, probably because Hannah had sold their performance with her big smile. As they stepped off the stage, she was surprised to see Hunter and Zach heading in their direction, and her heart skipped a beat. *When had they arrived?*

"Good job," Hunter said with a grin. "Are you girls having fun?"

"Ha-ha," Lizzie said, giving her cousin a hug.

"Aren't you going to introduce me?" Hannah asked, giving both men a curious look.

"Sorry," Lizzie said. "This is my cousin, Hunter Callaway, the new owner of the camp, and his friend and architect, Zach Barrington."

"Nice to meet you both. I'm Hannah Stark." She paused, giving Zach a thoughtful look. "Your name sounds familiar."

"Does it? Maybe you met me at camp? I went to Echo Falls when I was sixteen."

Gianna's stomach tightened as Hannah's questioning gaze swung to hers.

"Is this *the* Zach?" Hannah asked.

"Zach and I knew each other at camp," she admitted. She couldn't remember exactly how much she'd told Hannah about Zach, but she had a feeling she'd moaned about him for at least a few weeks after they'd split up.

"Right. Camp Zach," Hannah said, her tone losing its warmth, as she now gave Zach a suspicious look. "How long are you staying in town?"

"Not sure of my plans yet."

"We should get back to Chloe," Gianna suggested. While she appreciated Hannah's protectiveness toward her, it wasn't necessary. She walked over to the table, not sure who would follow, but everyone came over, with Hunter and Zach pulling up extra chairs. Frowning, she realized in her haste to get back to Chloe that now Zach and Jeremy were sitting next to each other.

"Great job, girls," Chloe said with an approving smile. "An excellent song choice. I was singing it along with you."

"After that baby comes out, you'll be singing it with us," Hannah said.

"Are you sure you were really singing, Gianna?" Jeremy cut in. "As I recall, you couldn't carry a tune, not even in the shower."

"I never claimed to be a singer," she said lightly, seeing the aggressive look in his eyes. He was determined to make trouble for her.

Jeremy looked over at Zach. "Gianna and I were once engaged. Did you know that?"

"Really?" Zach murmured, giving her a thoughtful look.

"I was her first fiancé. The first of many," Jeremy added. "She loves to get engaged but getting married...not so much."

"That's enough, Jeremy," Chloe said firmly. "You don't need to keep digging at Gianna."

"Just making conversation," he replied, with a careless shrug. "It's not like everyone in this town doesn't know she's the runaway fiancée."

"Let's talk about something else," Hannah put in. "When do you think the camp will reopen, Hunter?"

"Our goal is next April. We'd like to do a soft opening over spring break," Hunter replied. "But there's a lot to do before then, so we'll see."

"Shall we get another round of drinks?" Jeremy asked, apparently needing to bring the attention back to him.

"I'm done," she said. "I'm going to head out. It was great to see all of you."

"I'll walk out with you," Zach said, getting to his feet.

"Uh, all right."

"We'll see you tomorrow—at the barbecue," Hannah reminded her.

"Great." As she turned to leave, Jeremy gave her and Zach an odd look. She really wished Zach hadn't decided to walk out with her, but she didn't want to make a bigger deal of it than it was.

And it was definitely not a big deal.

CHAPTER TEN

As THEY LEFT MICKY'S, Gianna was struck by how warm it still was. It was almost midnight, but it had to be in the seventies. She didn't even need the light sweater she'd thrown over her sleeveless dress.

"Nice night," Zach commented. "Did you park near here?"

"I walked. It's only about six blocks to the store."

"But it's late."

"And this is Whisper Lake. I'll be fine."

"Why don't I make sure of that? I'll walk you home."

"You don't have to do that, Zach."

"I don't have to, but I want to. Are you okay with that?"

She hesitated, but his dark-green gaze on hers made her nerves tingle, and she couldn't say no. "I guess I can live with it."

The night got quieter as the music from the bar drifted away. The rest of the buildings on this particular block were all closed. "I forgot how quiet it can be here," she murmured. "LA is not like this. There is always the sound of traffic, sirens, airplanes, people…"

"Cities have a different energy."

"They do. I went to San Francisco once. I really liked it. The steep hills, the water views, the magnificent bridges."

"It's a great city."

"What part do you live in?"

"Rebecca and I lived near Golden Gate Park, but I moved into an apartment in the Marina after the fire. I have barely any furniture there. It doesn't feel like home, more like a pit stop."

"On your way to where? Here?"

"Maybe here. I want to be with Hailey. And this is where she is."

"Would you really consider moving to Whisper Lake on a permanent basis? Can you do that with your job?"

"I could make it work. I was at a big firm until a year ago. I actually quit because I thought I needed more flexibility for Hailey. With Rebecca going in and out of rehab, I was a single dad for weeks at a time."

"That must have been difficult."

"It was hard, but Hailey and I really bonded during those times. I decided to go solo and started taking smaller jobs I could handle on my own. I found I liked the freedom of being my own boss."

"I can see that, but I'm sure there's not nearly as much business in this small town."

"I can do my job from anywhere. I can fly out to job sites. I can make it work here if that's what needs to happen."

She could hear the sense of purpose in his voice. "You really love Hailey, don't you?"

"Very much. It happened so fast. She was this sweet, funny, adorable little girl, and she needed a dad. She actually needed both a mom and a dad, although I didn't realize that at first. But soon it became clear that while Rebecca loved Hailey, she had too many internal struggles to really give Hailey the attention she needed. So, I was there, wiping Hailey's hot forehead with a cold washcloth when she had a fever, reading to her at night, comforting her when she had a bad dream, laughing at her silly jokes. Just because I'm not her legal anything didn't mean we don't have a relationship."

"Why didn't you make it legal?" she asked curiously. "Why didn't you marry Rebecca? You said you were engaged..."

"I didn't realize until after we'd gotten engaged and moved in together that Rebecca had significant substance abuse problems. So, we put the brakes on. I wanted her to get clean first." He paused as they came to an intersection. "Do you want to walk and talk a little longer? There's a path to the lake through the park."

"It's late," she said, making a weak protest because she thought she should.

"But such a nice night. And I like talking to you."

His words sent a rush of warmth through her, and she wanted that feeling to last a little longer. "I guess we could keep walking and talking."

"Good." He put a hand on the small of her back as they changed directions.

It was a brief touch, but one she liked way too much.

Zach let go of her as they crossed the street and moved through the beachfront park toward a running path that wound along the lake. There was an empty bench past the swings that looked out over the water about ten feet away.

She sat down on the bench as a slightly cooler breeze lifted her hair, but it was welcome in the warmth of the night and the heat of Zach's presence.

"You're not cold, are you?" he asked.

"No, it feels good." She drew in a breath. "I love the air up here, the sound of the lake rippling against the shore. It's peaceful and at times like this, I feel like it's just the two of us."

"I used to feel that way a lot when we were hanging out—that it was just the two of us, and everyone else faded away."

"That's because we were always sneaking away from camp, trying to find a private spot. The counselors really should have done a better job of keeping track of us. We could have gotten into even more trouble."

"Very true."

"You were a bad influence on me. I never broke rules until I met you." She glanced over at him as a smile curved his lips. "But I have to admit you made breaking the rules very fun."

"We didn't get into too much trouble together. I did most of that on my own time." Zach leaned back against the bench, so close his shoulder was almost touching hers.

She looked up at the sky, at the bright full moon, and the multitude of stars. "It's so bright out here."

"You look good in the moonlight."

"That's a good line. But you don't need to waste time flirting with me. I'm off men."

"For how long?"

"As long as it takes me to figure out what the hell I'm doing with my life."

"So, a couple of days?"

She made a face at him. "Probably a little longer than that."

"The guy at the bar—Jeremy…he was fiancé number one, right?"

"Yes," she said with a little sigh. "I seem to be running into him every time I turn around."

"He's a little bitter."

"You think? I don't know why. It was a long time ago."

"Maybe having you in town has brought some feelings back."

"Feelings of hatred, perhaps. It's sad. We were friends at one time, even before we got romantically involved. But to be honest, now he feels like a stranger—an angry stranger."

"I assume he's still single."

"That's what I hear. He dated someone for a couple of years after me, but I don't know what happened. Anyway, let's not talk about him. Did you make progress on your camp drawings? Is there going to be anything new and exciting at the camp?"

"How about a real train to ride?" he asked with a cocky smile. "How cool would that be?"

"Very cool. The kids will love it."

"Hunter wants to incorporate the history of Whisper Lake and the role the Orphan Train played into its creation."

"The train has always been an important part of camp and town lore. It embodies the spirit of welcome and family, even if the family isn't tied by blood." She paused, thinking that Zach's attempt to get Hailey back into his life was very much in keeping with that theme. "It's like you, trying to forge a family with a little girl you love but isn't legally yours."

He tipped his head. "I wish I could get the Carvers to think that way. Ron Carver came by the camp today. He tried every threat he could think of, including sabotaging the plans for the camp build."

"Can he really do that?"

"He seems to feel he has power. I'm sure he can make Hunter's life fairly miserable. I offered to bow out, but Hunter wants to keep me on. He doesn't like bullies."

"Neither do you. You always stood up against them at camp. Remember Joe Spagnoli? How he used to torture little Evan Kinsey? But you took Joe down one day. You stepped right in front of Evan, just in time to take Joe's fist to your face."

"He felt the force of my fist, too."

"But you had to clean the lodge floors for a solid week after that. I never thought it was fair you got into trouble for fighting when you were standing up for Evan."

"It was worth it to shut Joe down." He smiled. "And I think I scored a few points with you at the time."

"I did think you were amazing," she admitted. "My own personal hero."

"And then I failed you."

She didn't want to talk about that anymore. "Let's get back to the present. Besides threatening you, did Ron have anything else to say? Did he tell you how Hailey was doing?"

"He said she's good now, and he doesn't want her to slide backward because I show up. He swears he's protecting her. Maybe he genuinely believes that. But this isn't the end. I'm not going to quit. I will find a way to see her."

"I'm surprised you haven't shown up at their house."

"I did two months ago, but they wouldn't let me in. And then I got legal counsel who suggested I find a way to make my peace with them. I'm trying to be patient, work through Mitch, but nothing is happening, and Ron and Helen are digging in deeper."

She could hear the frustration in his voice. It was killing him to have things so unsettled with Hailey. "They're probably afraid that one visit will lead you to want custody. They don't want to give you an inch for fear you'll take a mile."

"I don't think I have the ability to get custody. If Hailey was older, maybe she could say what she wanted, but she's seven. I'm also not married. And the fire has suspicions attached to it. If we go to court, they'll do everything they can to portray me as the man who got Rebecca into drugs and the reason she lost her life. While we could possibly shield Hailey from that now, what about the future? What about when she's old enough to ask what happened, maybe even to read court transcripts? I don't want her to hate her mother. I don't want her to realize that she could have died because of what her mom did that night."

"I don't know if you'll be able to protect her from that truth forever. Secrets have a way of coming out and kids grow up to be adults who want answers."

"You're right. Speaking of which…"

"I wasn't trying to change the subject to me," she said quickly.

"I'd be happy to talk about you. Anyone recognize the girl in the photo?"

"Not yet. I only asked a couple of people. It felt awkward. I probably need to keep thinking about whether I'm taking the best course. But that is a decision for another day." She let out a sigh. "Tonight was fun. I've missed seeing my girlfriends, just relaxing and having a good time. I forgot what it was like to be with people who've known you your whole life."

"Your friends seemed very nice, and I liked your singing. I didn't think you were off-key at all."

"Oh, I'm sure I was, but it wasn't about that; it was about doing something fun with Hannah and Lizzie."

"Hannah seems like a firecracker."

"She is definitely that. She is also a nurse—super smart, very caring, but she can also be a little bossy. She's very good at calling the shots, so we usually follow."

"Hannah didn't like me at all. I have a feeling there was some trash talking done at some point."

"That point being fourteen years ago. I may have mentioned that you broke my heart."

"May have?" he asked with a raise of his brow. "Hannah looked like she wanted to put a dagger through my heart when I said my name."

"It wasn't that bad. But Hannah can be protective."

"That's a good trait in a friend. I do wonder what happened to your locket, though, since I didn't take it."

"I don't know. I rarely took it off, but that day I did when I went to take a shower, and it disappeared. There was a point when I actually wondered if Rebecca had done it. She was jealous that we were hanging out, that you weren't interested in her at all. Which is why it's still so odd to me that you and she ended up together."

"Like I said, she was different as an adult, at least I thought she was. Who knows?"

"Why do you think she got into drugs?"

"She used to say that there was a darkness in her soul that terrified her. When it got to be too much, she drank, and then the drinking escalated into taking drugs. Having Hailey forced Rebecca to clean herself up for a while, but then it got hard again. Or maybe she was unhappy with me and didn't know how to get out of it. That's what the Carvers think."

"Is it true?"

"I don't think I was the reason she did anything. In retrospect, I suspect that Rebecca liked me for Hailey more than she liked me for herself. I think that's why she clung to me. I was a good father for her kid. But there were problems in our relationship that were probably insurmountable."

"Why did you stay?" she asked curiously.

"I didn't want to leave until she was clean, until she could be a good mother."

"So, you were both hanging on for Hailey."

"I guess we were. I made some mistakes," he said heavily.

"Join the club." She gave him a commiserating smile. "But all we can do is move forward, right? We can't change the past, no matter how much we want to."

"It's hard to let the guilt go. I feel like I could have done more."

"I know," she said softly, wishing she could ease the pain in his eyes. "You've always carried more emotional weight than anyone ever knew. On the outside, you were the funny, charming, outgoing guy who everyone wanted to hang out with. But there was a lot more to you than most of the kids realized. You were torn up about your dad when we were at camp. You were worried about your little brother and your mom. You blamed yourself for not talking your dad into quitting his commission and coming back home."

"I forgot about that. I did blame him. He put his job before us."

"It wasn't just a job to him."

"No, it was his calling." Zach gave her a long look. "I can't believe I told you all that. But you've always been easy to talk to."

"Likewise."

"It feels so good to have you here, Gianna." He shifted sideways, looking straight into her eyes. "I didn't expect that you would be in Whisper Lake, but I'm very glad that you are."

"It's only temporary until my aunt gets better. Probably for the summer."

He gave her a slow, sexy smile. "Well, summer is our best time together."

"We've only ever known each other in the summer. We could be terrible in winter or spring or fall."

"Who knows? But hot nights…those were always good for us."

Butterflies danced through her stomach. "You're flirting again. I told you not to waste your time."

"Because you're off men."

"Yes." Maybe if she said it often enough, she'd believe it, because right now, she felt herself leaning toward Zach—getting sucked into the magnetic, irresistible pull that had always made it really hard to say no to him. "I should go home."

"Or." He slid one hand around the back of her neck. "We could get our kiss out of the way."

"What are you talking about?" she asked breathlessly.

"You know it's coming, Gianna. You're curious. I'm curious."

"I'm not curious."

"You want to know if it would be as good as it once was."

"It's never as good as you remember," she said, but his fingers were stroking her neck, and he was so close now his hot breath brushed her cheek.

"Let's find out," he said huskily, his mouth coming down on hers.

His lips were warm, firm, teasing, sexy…and as she slid into the kiss, heat ran through her, the same delicious, thrilling desire that she'd felt a very long time ago.

Her brain was telling her to end this now before all the old feelings came back. But her body wasn't listening to her brain. Her senses were tingling, her nerves were firing, and one kiss turned into two, then three. As they angled their heads one way, then another, her world became completely about Zach. She wanted the kisses to go on forever, wanted to explore his mouth, run her hands down his body, breathe in when he breathed out. She wanted to feel completely connected to him in every way, and that was a terrifying thought.

Because being together now wasn't anything like she remembered; it was much, much better.

Finally, she found the strength to break the kiss.

They stared at each other in the late-night shadows, their breaths swirling in the cooling air. There were fiery lights in Zach's eyes. And the desire in his gaze nearly sent her back into his arms. But this couldn't go anywhere…

She couldn't allow herself to fall…not again…not with him.

She slid down the bench, putting some distance between them, then she got to her feet.

Zach stood up, his gaze turning troubled. "Do you want me to apologize?"

"No."

"Good, because I wasn't going to. That was something else, Gianna."

"We've always had chemistry," she mumbled.

"Undeniable sparks," he agreed. "From the first time we kissed. They're still there."

"So, we'll put them out," she said ruthlessly, folding her arms across her waist. "Our curiosity is satisfied. It's done. Let's walk." She turned and started strolling down the path before she could change her mind.

Zach fell into step alongside her. He didn't say anything, and that surprised her. He'd always been good at persuading her to do what she was reluctant to do. But he was strangely quiet. Maybe he realized what had just happened was a big mistake.

When they reached the antiques store, she paused beside the door that led up to the apartment from the street and pulled out her keys.

Zach stepped in front of her, blocking her way. "I know you don't want to feel anything toward me, Gianna, but you do."

"I told you—"

"I know. You're taking a break from men and relationships. I understand that."

"And you're here for a little girl, not for me," she reminded him. "So, this—whatever this is—is not going to happen. It's too complicated. We can't go back in time. We can't be those impulsive, free-spirited, reckless teens again."

"That was one good summer."

"Until it ended. And this would end, too. I can't handle another ending, especially not with you," she said honestly.

His gaze darkened. "I'm sorry I hurt you, Gianna."

"I'm sorry, too. I'm not giving you a chance to do it again. I also don't want to hurt you, and my history should tell you that that would be a good possibility. So, let's say good-bye."

He shook his head. "I'll say good night, but that's as far as I'm going. I still want to be your friend."

"You want more than friendship."

"I want whatever you have to give." He swooped in and stole another kiss before she could protest, the action so fleeting, it just left her lips tingling.

"Who said I wanted to give you another kiss?" she challenged.

He gave her the cocky grin that had always turned her heart over. "See you tomorrow, Gianna."

She unlocked the door and stepped inside, her heart beating way too fast. She never should have let that kiss happen.

On the other hand...

Zach had always been one hell of a kisser.

CHAPTER ELEVEN

As ZACH SAT down across from Mitch Carver at the Big Sky Café on Sunday morning, he felt a mix of emotions. While he was happy to keep the lines of communication open with Mitch, the person he really wanted to see was Hailey, and that opportunity didn't seem to be getting any closer.

"Coffee?" the waitress asked him.

"Please," he said, as she poured him a cup.

"Thanks for coming," Mitch said. "I heard you had a run-in with my father yesterday."

"He came out to the camp and threatened to stop the project if I don't leave town."

Mitch's lips drew into a grim line. "I would expect him to make good on that threat, Zach."

"Oh, I do. But I don't run from bullies and neither does Hunter Callaway, the owner of the camp, so your father will have his work cut out for him."

"I tried to tell him that last night, but he wasn't listening. He was more concerned with the fact that my mother was packing her suitcase."

Mitch's words gave him a jolt. "Your mom is leaving town? When? Is she planning to take Hailey?"

"I think that was her thought, but my dad talked her out of it. He said they're not running anywhere. That if anyone is leaving town, it's you."

Relief ran through him. "Then it looks like we're all staying. I have to say that if your mother tries to run and hide Hailey, I will find her."

Mitch stared back at him with a frown. "This war needs to end, Zach."

"Then set up a peace summit, Mitch. You're the only one who can do that."

"Believe me, I've suggested it more than once. They cut me off every time."

He picked up his coffee and took a long sip. "I feel like there's something else going on here. I'm not a threatening, violent person. Why are your parents so afraid of me? Did Rebecca make up stories about me?"

"Not that I know of."

"I understand why your parents want custody of Hailey. I know they're grieving for their daughter. And I can even see why they need to make me the villain, but their hatred, their fear of me, is over the top."

"I have to say I agree. Here's another odd thing. When I was at the house yesterday, I noticed that someone had gone through Rebecca's room. All the drawers were open. There were clothes on the floor. Honestly, it almost looked like someone had ransacked the room."

He leaned forward, resting his arms on the table, as he gave Mitch a speculative look. "You think your mom did that?"

"Or my dad. He's been on a spring-cleaning binge lately. He wanted to put Hailey in Rebecca's room, so he moved some furniture out of there, but my mom had a fit. Rebecca's room has always been sacred. My old room has been a sewing room, a gym, and now it's Hailey's room. They've had no problem purging themselves of all furniture and items related to my childhood, but Rebecca's room has always been kept ready for her to return, even when she was living with you. Since she died, it's where my mom has spent a lot of her afternoons. To see it in that state was weird."

He didn't know what to make of Mitch's comments. No matter what he thought of the Carvers, he'd always believed that Hailey was safe in their care. Now, he wasn't so sure. "That sounds odd."

"I agree."

"I need to see Hailey, Mitch, and soon. With your mom thinking of leaving town, and your dad sending cops to talk to me, everything is coming to a head."

"I can't believe he went that far. I keep hoping that when they calm down a little, they can listen to reason."

"I think you're being overly optimistic."

"Maybe. You need to give them a couple of days of breathing space. Let me keep working on them. Let them get used to the idea of you being in town."

He wanted to tell Mitch to screw it, that he was going to go to their house and demand to see Hailey, but he couldn't, because the last thing he wanted to do was give the Carvers real ammunition against him. As frustrating as it was, he had to play the waiting game. He had to be patient, and that had never been his strongest trait.

"All right," he murmured. "I'll wait—a little while longer. Can I buy you breakfast?"

"No, thanks. I'm not very hungry."

"Are you sure?" He felt a little guilty about making Mitch the middleman. Rebecca had always wanted to protect her younger brother and maybe he should be respecting that more. He was just desperate.

"Yes. I'll be in touch," Mitch said, as he got to his feet.

"If you want out, Mitch, I can take it from here. I don't want to put a wedge between you and your parents."

"I still want to help. Give me some time."

"Okay." As Mitch left, Chloe came over to the table.

"I was going to take your order earlier," she said. "But it appeared that you and Mitch were having an intense conversation, and I didn't want to interrupt."

"Thanks for that. What's good?"

"The spinach omelet is awesome."

"Then I'll go with that." He handed her his menu. "You look tired this morning. Do you ever take a day off?"

"Not very often. Work keeps me distracted. I promised Kevin when he left that I'd keep this café going. His parents were the original owners. They retired to Florida three years ago. My mother-in-law has asthma and needed a warmer climate."

"That sounds like a lot of pressure, especially when you're about to have a baby."

"The stress comes more from missing my husband. I'm looking forward to Kevin getting home. He has been gone so much the past five years, I sometimes feel like a single woman. But I shouldn't complain. My husband is serving his country. He's a hero. I'm just serving coffee."

"Don't do that," he said. "Don't downplay your own sacrifice."

She was taken aback by his sharp words. "I—I'm not making a sacrifice."

"Yes, you are. I don't know if Gianna told you, but my father was in the army, too. He spent most of my life away on deployment, and I watched my mom struggle to raise me and my brother on her own. She used to tell me the same thing you just did—that she had no right to complain, because her husband was doing the hard work. But she was working hard, too. She was trying to hold our family together."

"I didn't realize," she said, sliding into the chair across from him. "You do know exactly how it feels."

"I do."

"What happened to your dad? Did he eventually retire?"

He really didn't want to answer her question. At his hesitation, her lips tightened.

"He didn't come back, did he?" she asked quietly.

"No. He was killed in action right before my sixteenth birthday. I was really angry about that for a long time."

"I'm sorry," she said softly. "And you had every right to be angry. It wasn't fair."

"I wasn't just mad at the universe, I was upset with him. I felt like he'd chosen the service over us. He'd had times to get out, but he never took that opportunity. My mom said I couldn't blame him for loving the life he'd chosen. But I still did. I blamed her, too, for not making him quit. And sometimes I blamed myself for the same reason."

"It was his choice."

"It was."

"I've had those same thoughts and feel guilty about them," Chloe confessed. "I knew Kevin wanted to be a military man when I married him. His dad, his grandfather, and his uncle were all in the army. It was his path, and I chose to be his wife. I love him. I'm proud of him. I shouldn't be complaining or feeling sorry for myself."

"You're pregnant and alone. You can complain a little, especially to me. I get it."

She met his gaze. "It is nice to talk to someone who knows how I feel."

"I'm around if you ever want to vent. No judging."

"Thanks." She gave him a thoughtful look. "Can I ask what's going on with you and Gianna? Hannah told me that you're the guy who broke her heart at summer camp. I didn't realize you were that Zach."

"*That Zach* sounds bad," he said with a grimace.

"You stole her locket."

"I didn't, and she now believes me about that. She also wasn't the only one who ended up with a broken heart. But it was a long time ago. We've decided to put that in the past and be friends."

"Just friends, huh?" she asked with a doubtful raise of her brow.

"That's the plan."

"I know that you're both coming off some heartache, so I can see why you'd make that plan, but I wonder if it's sustainable."

He gave a helpless shrug. "I wonder that, too."

Chloe smiled and got to her feet. "Well, you're honest; I'll say that for you. I'll get your order in, Zach."

"Thanks."

As Chloe left the table, his thoughts turned to Gianna, to the passion they'd shared the night before. Trying to recreate their teenage romance was probably a stupid idea, but it sure would be fun...

Gianna used her aunt's truck to drive to Keira's lake house, which was a few miles out of town. Keira had grown up in the house and when her mother had suffered a traumatic brain injury in a car accident, she'd moved back in to help out. She'd also taken over her mother's real-estate business. Keira's father had died when she was young, so it had always been Keira and her mother; they had an incredibly close bond.

After parking in front of the house, Gianna grabbed the platter of brownies she'd made earlier. She wasn't much of a cook, but she did like to bake. Unfortunately, she also liked to eat, which was why she didn't bake too often.

She made her way up to the front door and rang the bell. Then she turned the knob and stepped inside.

Keira was coming out of the kitchen. She was a dark brunette with deep-brown eyes and her jean shorts and tank top revealed her curvy figure. Her eyes lit up when she saw Gianna.

"You came," she said happily. "I'm so glad. I was bummed when I couldn't make it to the bar last night."

"I missed you."

"I missed you, too, and not just last night. It's been what—a year since I've seen you?"

"Probably about that," she admitted.

"Well, come on into the kitchen. My mom is keeping an eye on my chili. The Lawsons are here—Jessica and Tom and their daughter Laura. They're out by the pool with one of the agents from my firm—Brenda Allen—and her boyfriend."

"Sounds like you're going to have a big crowd."

"I hope so. It's my annual barbecue, and it seems to keep

getting bigger and bigger. It's actually nice to see the pool and the dock and the lakefront being used. My mom and I don't spend much time outside anymore."

Gianna followed Keira into the large farmhouse kitchen. Keira's mother, Ruth, was standing by the stove, stirring the chili.

"It looks done," she told Keira.

"Thanks, Mom," Keira said, taking the spoon from her hand. "Do you remember Gianna?"

Ruth turned to her with a quizzical gleam in her eyes. Seeing the woman she'd grown up with and sometimes considered a second mother looking confused and frailer than she would have expected sent a wave of sadness through her. Ruth and her mom were probably close in age, but Ruth was a pale shadow of the vibrant woman she'd once been, all because of a drunk driver.

Forcing a smile, she said, "Hello, Mrs. Blake."

"Jill," Ruth said. "It's good to see you again. Your blonde hair is so pretty."

"It's Gianna, Mom," Keira said gently, giving her a helpless, apologetic smile.

"No, it's Jill. Tammy's friend," Ruth insisted. "You used to follow us around, didn't you?"

She had no idea who Ruth was talking about. "It's nice to see you again," she said simply.

"Why don't you sit down, Mom?" Keira urged. "You've been working hard all day."

"Well, there's a lot to do for the party."

"Yes, and I need you to put the cookies on the platter." Keira urged her mother toward the kitchen table where several Tupperware containers of cookies were ready to be put on display.

"Oh, right, I almost forgot," Ruth said, taking a seat at the table.

"Sorry about that," Keira muttered.

She shrugged, sliding onto a stool at the island as Keira moved around to the other side to cut up some vegetables. "How are you doing, Keira? I know you're busy working, but what about your personal life? Any men I should know about?"

"I've been dating but no keepers. I'm sorry about your engagement. Or should I be happy you escaped a bad marriage?"

"It just wasn't right. And now that I'm back home, I'm realizing that the problem isn't the guys; it's me. I'm floundering. I need to stop looking for someone else to make me happy, to give me direction. I need to find that for myself."

"That sounds mature and self-aware."

"It's about time," she said dryly.

Keira laughed. "You have had a tendency to fall fast."

"I think I've been in too big of a hurry to get to the next stage of my life. It's like when I read a book and I have to skip to the end to know what's going to happen. I need to learn to stay in the moment, to not think so far ahead."

"When you figure that out, let me know. So, what's next? I know you're here to help your aunt and run the antiques store, but what happens when she's better?"

"I look for another job. In the meantime, I also have some freelance art projects to work on." She paused. "And there's something else…"

Keira raised a brow. "Okay, this sounds interesting."

"I'm thinking about looking for my biological mother."

"Really? I thought you'd put that idea aside a long time ago."

"It came back to me. In fact, a lot of my past has been coming back to me."

"What do you mean?"

"I had to go up to the camp to pick up some furniture for my aunt's store, and I ran into Zach."

"Zach who?"

"Zach Barrington."

Keira paused. "Wait—your camp boyfriend? That Zach?"

"Yes. He's the architect on the camp project."

"That must have been some meeting."

"You can't even imagine. I was actually standing out on the pier, looking at the lake, and when I started to walk back, the pier broke apart and I landed in the water. Zach was just driving in, and—"

"He rescued you?"

"Yes. He didn't know it was me at first."

Keira's eyes lit up. "That's quite a story."

"It was shocking."

"Were there any sparks?"

"That's not important."

"That means there were sparks," she said with a knowing gleam. "How long will he be in town? Is he single? What's his story?"

"You don't know?"

"Know what?"

"That Zach was living with Rebecca Carver in San Francisco the last several years. I'm surprised you wouldn't have heard that."

"I did hear that Rebecca passed away in a fire, but I hadn't heard details about her boyfriend. I certainly had no idea it was *your* Zach."

"He hasn't been *my* Zach in a long time."

"How long will he be in town?"

"I'm not sure."

"Do you think you'll see him again?"

"Yes. He's coming to your party as a guest of Lizzie Cole's. The new owner of the camp is Hunter Callaway, Lizzie's cousin. He's coming, too."

"Right. She mentioned she was bringing some guests, but I didn't get the details. This should be fun. Is Zach still impossibly handsome?"

"Yes. But before you get all worked up—I'm not interested. I'm on a relationship hiatus."

"That sounds boring."

"I could use some boredom. I've had a little too much excitement the last year."

"Well, if Zach is back, I think more excitement is on the way."

"Can we change the subject?"

"Do you have something more interesting to talk about?" Keira teased.

"I might. I was going through one of the boxes I picked up at the camp and I found a photo of a girl who kind of looks like me, and she also happens to be wearing a locket exactly like the one I lost." She opened her bag and took out the photo she'd impulsively brought with her. "What do you think?"

Keira studied the photo, her brows knitting together. "Well, she has blonde hair and brown eyes and that does look like your locket... Who is she?"

"I don't know, but I need to find her. This picture was in a pile of photos from thirty or so years ago. This girl would probably be about the same age as my biological mother."

"Oh, whoa, wait...I didn't know that's where we were going. You think this girl could be your mother?"

"I'm sure it's a long shot, but there's something about her. Anyway, I thought I'd show the photo around and see if anyone recognizes her."

"What about your mom? How does she feel about this? You were always afraid of making her feel bad."

"I have her blessing. She doesn't think I'll ever be satisfied until I try to find my biological mother."

"So, you're really doing it."

"I'm taking it one step at a time. This is the first step."

"What are you girls looking at?" Ruth interrupted, wandering over to the island.

Keira showed the picture to her mom. "Gianna is wondering who this is. I don't suppose you recognize her, Mom."

Ruth gave Keira a confused look, then turned her gaze to Gianna. "That's you, Jill. Don't you recognize your own picture?"

Gianna's heart skipped a beat. *Was Ruth confusing her name?* Gianna and Jill sort of sounded the same. "What is Jill's last name?"

"You don't know your own name? Goodness, you're as crazy as I am."

"Mom, do you remember Jill's last name?" Keira asked.

"I'm not sure." Ruth squinted at Gianna, then frowned. "Maybe you're not Jill."

"Did you grow up with Jill? Were you friends?" Gianna asked.

"She was Tammy's friend. Or maybe she was Joan's friend. Goodness, I'm not sure of anything." She looked at her daughter. "I'm doing it again, aren't I? I thought I was getting better."

"You're fine, Mom," Keira assured her. "There's the doorbell. Do you want to let our guests in?"

"All right," Ruth said, then shuffled off.

"I'm sorry, Gianna. Mom has memory lapses. She has been getting better with therapy, but she still gets confused."

"Do you think the girl in the photo is this person she calls Jill?"

"I honestly don't know."

"But it could be a clue."

"Maybe. It looks like you're going to have more to do this summer than sell your aunt's antiques. You can look into this photo of a girl who might be your bio mom, and then there's Zach..."

"I won't be busy with him."

"We'll see. I can't wait to see him again. And no matter what you say, I bet you feel the same."

"You'd lose that bet."

"No, I wouldn't," Kiera said with a laugh. "You might be able to lie to yourself, but you can't lie to me."

CHAPTER TWELVE

SHE WAS A LIAR. When Zach arrived at the party with Hunter and Lizzie a half hour later, butterflies danced through Gianna's stomach, and she felt ridiculously eager to talk to him again. She could barely concentrate on the conversation she was having with her third-grade teacher, Miss Baker, who had apparently bought a house through Keira several weeks ago.

She thought at any moment Zach would interrupt them, but he was caught up by the crowd in the living room. Breaking away from Miss Baker, she made her way out to the pool area, sitting down next to Hannah, who was sunning on a lounger, her fair skin lathered in sunscreen, a floppy straw hat on her head.

"Hey, Hannah," she said, pulling over a chair. "I didn't know you were out here. I must have missed you come in."

"You were busy chatting when I arrived."

"It's fun catching up with everyone. Is Chloe here? I haven't seen her yet."

Hannah frowned. "She's not coming. She said the café was really busy this morning, and she's tired, so she's going to lay low."

"That's probably wise. I really hope Kevin gets back in time for the baby's birth. Chloe seems fragile right now. She's trying to tough it out, but I can tell she's scared."

"I know. I wish she'd take it a little easier with work. On the other hand, the café keeps her too busy to worry about Kevin." Hannah picked up her phone as it buzzed. "Sorry. I need to text my brother back. He's trying to plan a surprise party for my parents' anniversary, but we're having trouble connecting."

"Sure. Go ahead."

As Hannah occupied herself with her text, Gianna couldn't help noticing that Hunter and Zach had made it to the pool deck. Both men were in board shorts and T-shirts, and they were clearly an instant hit, especially with the ladies.

Watching Zach work the crowd, she couldn't help thinking that she'd seen this show before. The first day of camp, he'd been doing the same thing. All the kids had been drawn to him. All the girls had been smitten. And she'd thought to herself there was no way this guy was ever going to look in her direction.

But he had looked in her direction. Somehow, he'd managed to see past the paint on her fingernails and the braces on her teeth and the freckles splattered across her cheeks. Somehow, he'd seen her in a way that no one else had.

Her heart turned over as his gaze caught with hers now, and like so many years ago, she felt the same foolish, reckless wave of desire—a desire that was now being fueled by memories of the night before. Kissing Zach as an adult had been even better than kissing him as a naïve, insecure girl. Not that that hadn't been great, too. She just hadn't been emotionally ready for that teenage relationship.

Which reminded her that she wasn't emotionally ready for an adult relationship with Zach, either. She needed to get her life together. And she needed to do that on her own.

"Earth to Gianna…"

"What?" she asked, turning back to Hannah.

"I've been talking to you for five minutes. But you've been distracted by a certain handsome guy with incredible green eyes."

"Sorry. What did you say?"

"It doesn't matter. What happened last night after you left the bar with Zach?"

"Nothing," she said quickly. "He walked me home."

"And he just left?"

"Obviously, he left."

"Did you kiss him?"

"We don't need to talk about Zach," she said, heat running through her face.

Hannah laughed. "That's a yes. Wow."

"It's not a wow."

"Really? It was disappointing? Because you used to say he was incredible."

"It wasn't disappointing. I don't want to talk about it. It was a moment of madness. It won't happen again."

"Are you sure about that?"

"I would like to be," she said candidly.

Hannah met her gaze with a sympathetic smile. "Zach always got under your skin. I was so jealous of you that summer. I was supposed to go to camp, but I came down with mono and I missed out on all the fun you and Keira had. Then I had to listen to your stories for the next six months. It made me crazy."

"Sorry about that. Camp was fun," she admitted. "Until the end."

"When Zach hurt you. You thought he stole your locket, but obviously you've forgiven him."

"I now believe he didn't take the locket. So, there's nothing to forgive. Actually, I probably need him to forgive me, because my accusations got him kicked out of camp."

"If he kissed you last night, I'd say he's forgiven you."

"We were just curious."

"And it wasn't wow?"

"Okay, maybe it was," she admitted. "But I was a little drunk, and it was a hot night, and there was a full moon."

"You are coming up with a lot of excuses," Hannah said with a laugh.

"I called off an engagement three months ago. I need to be on my own and not get tangled up with another man. Nothing is going to happen with Zach."

"Time will tell. By the way, he's headed over here."

She turned to see Zach making his way around the pool. She drew in a breath, steeling herself against the wave of attraction already running through her.

"I'm going in the pool to cool off," Hannah said, swinging her legs off the lounger. "You might want to do the same."

"Maybe later." She'd put on her bikini under her sundress, but she wasn't that interested in swimming.

Hannah smiled at Zach as she moved past him and into the pool.

"Hey," he said with a sexy smile. He sat down on the lounger Hannah had just vacated. "Not swimming?"

"Not yet. But feel free to go ahead."

"I'd rather talk to you."

She sucked in a quick breath, reminding herself that Zach's attention was not a good thing. "It looked like Lizzie was introducing you around."

"I've met a lot of people in the last thirty minutes; I don't remember any of their names."

"That's understandable. It's a big crowd."

"I did speak to Keira—I'd forgotten how fun she is."

She nodded. Like Zach, Keira had a way of becoming the center of any social circle with barely any effort. "She's great. And she's an incredibly generous person. She was working in fashion in New York when her mom got in a car accident. She gave it all up to come home and take care of her and run the real-estate business that still supports them."

"That's quite a sacrifice. I met Keira's mother, too. She seemed a bit bewildered by all the people."

"I guess there are memory issues, especially when it comes to faces. You know what's weird, though?"

His gaze narrowed. "No. Tell me."

"When I first came into the house, Keira's mom called me Jill. I figured she couldn't remember my real name. But when I showed Keira the photo of the girl from camp, Ruth took a look at it and said it was me—Jill. I don't know if this girl really is named Jill or if Ruth just got confused."

"Interesting. Maybe that's a place to start. How old is Ruth?"

"Well, Keira is twenty-nine, same as me. I think her mother is in her early fifties, so she would probably be older than my biological mother. Ruth also mentioned that Jill had a friend named Tammy or maybe it was Joan."

"That's a few more names for you to research."

"I was thinking I should go by the library tomorrow. If Mrs. Gibbs is still working there, she might remember their names. She's been the town librarian since before I was born."

"Good idea."

"Is it? Am I about to go down a path that could lead to pain for more people than just myself?"

"I honestly don't know. But there's only one way to find out. You have to roll the dice, take the leap, jump off the cliff."

She smiled. "Do you have any more clichés to throw at me?"

"I think I've run out." He paused. "Gianna…"

The way he said her name made her stomach tighten. "Do you want to go swimming?" she asked.

"I thought you said you didn't want to."

"Well, I've changed my mind." She pulled her dress over her head. Only then did she realize in her effort to stop him from saying whatever he'd been about to say, she'd now put her bikini-clad figure right in front of him.

His appreciative gaze swept her form. "You're beautiful, Gianna."

She couldn't help but feel flattered by his words. She'd been skinny as a board back in camp, but thankfully she'd developed a few more curves over the years.

As she got to her feet, Zach stood up, and took off his shirt. The scars on his chest reminded her of what he'd been through.

He met her gaze. "I can't run away from the past, even with my shirt on, so I don't even try."

"I know. I just wish you hadn't had to go through what had to be a very painful experience."

"I survived. Let's go swimming."

He reached for her hand, and she couldn't help but slide her fingers around his. They exchanged a long, hot look. "I know you said we were over," he murmured. "But—"

"There can't be a *but*," she said firmly.

"And yet there is."

Before she could utter another protest, a wave of cold water hit her in the side. She looked down at Hannah's smiling face.

"It looked like you two needed to cool off," she teased.

Gianna let go of Zach's hand and jumped into the pool. While she normally preferred to take a slower, more controlled, approach to entering a body of water, she needed a jolt, something to get her out of the dream world she was creating in her head, where she and Zach got a second chance…

Zach landed in a cannonball splash not far from her, sending another wave of water over her head. He laughed and then swam away, heading toward Hunter and a bunch of other guys who were shooting a basketball through a hoop at the far end of the pool.

Hannah came over to her. "Well, I don't know what your definition of *wow* is, but I gotta say seeing the two of you together —*wow*."

"What am I going to do about him?" she asked.

"You know what you want to do."

"But I need to stop doing what I want and start doing what I should. And that needs to begin with Zach."

"Good luck, Gianna. If I had a guy that hot looking at me the way Zach looked at you, I'd be taking him home and making him breakfast."

"I'm off men," she said rather desperately.

"That's almost always when the best ones show up."

Gianna managed to avoid Zach for the rest of the party, although she had to fight off ridiculous waves of jealousy every time she saw him chatting up some other woman. She had a feeling he'd decided to avoid her as well, or maybe he was finally accepting the fact that she wasn't interested in him.

Only, she was. But she wasn't going to do anything about it.

Still, there was only so much she could take, and she left the party a little after ten. She had a long day ahead of her tomorrow, and after a lot of sun and too much food, she was ready for bed.

As she entered the store through the back door, she was startled by a crash and a beam of light from the far corner.

"Who's there?" she demanded, as she hit the light switch.

"It's just me," a woman said, stepping out from behind a large armoire.

She was shocked. "Mrs. Carver? What on earth are you doing here?"

"I'm looking for Becca's desk. There's something inside. I didn't know Ron was going to give it away. I have to find it."

Helen wore white pants and a long, silky top. Her hair was tousled, and her eyes were wild. As she moved around another piece of furniture, she stumbled and bumped her leg.

"Be careful," Gianna warned.

"I need my desk. Where is it?"

Helen's words were garbled and slurred, surprising her even more. "Are you all right, Mrs. Carver?"

"I am perfect," she said in a drunken sing-song voice. "I just have to find the desk. Where is it? You must know. Are you trying to hide it from me?"

"I'm not trying to hide it. It's in the showroom. I moved it in there earlier, so we could get it on sale."

"I didn't see it."

"Well, it's there. I can show you."

"Thank God you found it." Helen paused, looking confused. "Did you find it? Was it in the desk? I thought it was with Rebecca, but maybe it's been in the house all these years."

"I didn't see anything in the desk."

"She used to hide it," Helen rambled on. "She was so secretive. I guess she had to be." Helen reached for a wine bottle she'd apparently brought with her and took a swig. "It wasn't my fault, Gianna. You believe me, don't you?"

"I think I should take you home," she said slowly.

"But it's in Rebecca's desk. I think it is. I don't know. Maybe it's not." Helen suddenly swayed, then sank to the floor like a broken doll.

Gianna rushed forward. She dropped to her knees and put a steadying hand on Helen's arm. "Let me take you home, Mrs. Carver."

"Can't go home like this. Ron will be mad. Don't tell him. Promise me, you won't tell him. It's a secret. Please," she begged. "He'll hate me."

"I won't tell him anything, but you can't stay here."

"I'll just take a little nap." Helen stretched out on the floor and tucked her hand under her head, letting out a snore as she passed out.

Gianna blew out a breath. *What the hell was she going to do now?* Mrs. Carver was too heavy for her to move. She supposed she could call her parents, but it was late. They were probably asleep. And she didn't want to bother her aunt, either. She could call the police, but that seemed rather extreme.

She was still baffled by Helen's cryptic words. She'd broken into the store to look for something in Rebecca's desk. It had to be something significant. *Was it something Zach should know about? Would it affect Zach's ability to connect with Hailey?*

She needed to look in the desk again. She walked into the showroom and checked the drawers for a second time, but everything was empty. Whatever Helen was looking for wasn't there.

Tapping her foot on the floor, she debated her options, then made an impulsive, probably bad decision. Pulling out her phone, she texted Zach and asked him to call her when he was alone. She didn't want to catch him in the middle of a conversation at the party.

Her phone rang a moment later.

"Gianna?" Zach asked. "I'm surprised to hear from you. I thought you weren't talking to me."

"Something has happened."

"What? Are you okay?"

"I'm fine. But Mrs. Carver broke into my aunt's store. She was clearly drunk, and now she's passed out on the floor of the storeroom."

"Are you serious?" he asked in shock. "Why would she do that?"

"She was rambling about something of Rebecca's, something that might still be in the desk her husband put on consignment last week along with some other items. I'm sure she'll hate that I'm calling you, but I don't know what to do. She made me promise not to contact her husband. Should I leave her on the floor? I don't think I can move her. Or maybe you could call Mitch," she said. "He can come and get her. That's probably the best solution."

"I'll be there in a few minutes, Gianna. We'll figure it out."

"I'm probably making things worse by bringing you into it…"

"You couldn't make things worse."

"I really hope not," she said. But as she set down the phone, she wasn't so sure.

CHAPTER THIRTEEN

ZACH DROVE AS FAST as he could to Gianna's store, his mind racing with what he'd just learned. The fact that Helen was drunk was shocking enough. He'd never seen her sip more than one glass of wine, but maybe she had secret problems like her daughter.

But breaking into the antiques store? What the hell was that about? Gianna had said that Helen was looking for something of Rebecca's in a desk that they'd sent to the store to sell. *What on earth would that be?*

He couldn't come up with one remotely possible answer.

Pulling into the back lot behind the store, he threw the car into park and jogged over to the door. Gianna must have been watching for him, because she opened the door and quickly pulled him inside.

"Where is she?" he asked.

She led him around some furniture, and he saw Helen on the floor. The sight of the very prim and proper woman sleeping on the floor like a baby made his jaw drop. Helen was always put together, in control, but she was not in control now.

"I tried to wake her," Gianna said. "But she's in a deep sleep."

"I can see that. Where is the desk?"

"It's in the showroom. Did you call Mitch?"

"Not yet. Show me the desk first."

"I already looked in it," she said, as she led him into the other room. "All the drawers are empty."

As she pointed out the desk to him, he checked the drawers for himself, but she was right; there was nothing there. "What exactly did Helen say?"

"She wasn't making a lot of sense. She said that she had to find it—but she didn't say what *it* was. I got the feeling the item belonged to Rebecca. She said Rebecca was secretive, and she probably hid it. But she had to find it. She hadn't known Ron was going to give Rebecca's things away. She begged me not to tell him she was here, that she was looking for it. Then she passed out. Does any of that make sense to you?"

"Not even a little bit. Although..." He paused, thinking about the conversation he'd had earlier with Mitch. "Mitch did say that when he was at the house last night, it looked like Rebecca's old room had been ransacked, and he was shocked, because his mom had turned it into a shrine for her daughter. She wouldn't even let Hailey stay there. So why would she tear it apart?"

"Maybe Helen started her search in Rebecca's room."

"But what is she looking for?"

"Perhaps Mitch will know."

"He didn't have a clue this morning."

"Well, you need to call him. We can't leave Helen on the floor all night."

"Maybe we can get her up to your apartment."

Gianna frowned at that suggestion. "I'd rather get her out of here, get her home."

"It's late. And you said she didn't want her husband to know what she'd done. He'll know if we take her home now."

She stared back at him, a suspicious gleam entering her eyes. "That's not the reason you want to keep her here. You want to talk to her when she wakes up. But she will not want to talk to you."

"She won't have a choice. I'll finally have an advantage. She'll be embarrassed and feeling guilty about what she did, what she might have said. Maybe I can get her to open up to me. I've always wondered why they hate me so much, why they're afraid of me. It doesn't add up. And I'm thinking that there's something else at play...something about Rebecca, something I don't know." He paused, seeing the uncertainty in Gianna's eyes. "This might be my best shot at getting Helen to talk. I have to take it."

"Even if we can get her upstairs, when she wakes up, she'll run out the second she sees you."

"Not if we let her know you're going to call the cops and report her break-in if she does that." He felt a rush of excitement. For the first time in forever, he felt like he had some leverage. "Please, Gianna, I need this."

"I don't want to do anything to put my aunt's business in jeopardy. Helen and Ron Carver have a lot of influence in this town. They have power."

"Right now, she has no power. She's a drunk who broke into your store. Let's not forget that. She can't smear you without smearing herself."

"Good point. I don't know how she got in here. I thought I had locked everything up. She scared the crap out of me when I came inside."

"I can imagine." His gaze returned to the desk. It was white with a center drawer and three drawers running down the right side. He squatted down and looked underneath the desk, but there was nothing there, either.

"How many times are you going to look?" Gianna asked. "There's nothing there."

"I was remembering how Rebecca used to hide her pills in the apartment. After she went to rehab, I found them in all kinds of crazy places—the toe of a sock, inside a pasta box."

"She was that secretive?"

"Yes. So, if she hid something from her mom, it could be somewhere you wouldn't expect it to be."

"Well, it's not in this desk."

"It's somewhere."

"Unless she had it with her—in the apartment that burned down."

He frowned at that comment, because that was most likely what had happened. "You're right. It probably was in the apartment. Rebecca told me more than a few times that she was haunted. I thought she was talking about her own personal demons, but what if she wasn't? What if there was a secret? Maybe a family secret. I have to know what it is."

"I want to help you, but I'm walking a fine line here."

"You're in the power position, Gianna. Helen broke into your store. You can destroy her reputation."

"I suppose. But I don't want to do that. It could backfire. Her friends could boycott the store."

He understood that she had to protect her aunt and her business, but he needed her to realize the precarious position he was in. "I'm not trying to destroy Helen, either. She's Hailey's grandmother. And I respect their relationship. But if I can use her actions to force her into allowing me into Hailey's life, I will do that. I don't want us to be at odds, but I need you to see that I'm not just fighting for myself but also for Hailey. Helen's behavior tonight is crazy and reckless. I need to know what's going on so that if Hailey needs protection in some way, I can provide it."

"Helen was drunk, not dangerous."

"I would have never thought she was capable of breaking in here. Who knows what else she would do?"

Gianna's resolve weakened. "That's a fair point. I do want to help you, Zach."

"Then let me stay until Mrs. Carver wakes up."

"I have a feeling I couldn't kick you out even if I wanted to," she said dryly.

"Still, I'd prefer if we were on the same side."

"I'm trying to be Switzerland here."

"I'll take neutrality as long as you let me stay." He moved back into the storeroom, suddenly worried that Helen might have woken up and taken off. But she was exactly where they'd left her. He shook her shoulder, said her name quite loudly, but she just snored away. Taking out his phone, he took several photos of her for insurance. Helen's word would count for more than his, so he needed proof.

"I think we should try to get her upstairs," Gianna said. "Maybe she'll wake up if we move her."

With Gianna's help, he was able to pick Helen up and carry her up the stairs to the apartment. He set her down on the couch, and she stirred for a brief moment, then slipped back into oblivion. She reeked of liquor. He had no idea how much she'd drunk, but it had to have been a lot.

"You can go to bed, Gianna. I'll sit here with her."

"Are you going to stay awake all night?"

"Yes. I don't want her to leave while I'm asleep."

"Then I'll make you some coffee."

"If you don't mind."

He followed her into the kitchen, and as she started the coffeemaker, he leaned against the counter next to her. "Thanks for calling me."

"I'm not sure I should have. But I couldn't seem to stop myself."

"I'm glad you did. I'm a little surprised, though. You made a real effort to stay away from me at the party."

"Things were getting too…"

"Hot?" he suggested.

"You had plenty of company without me," she said, ignoring his pointed comment.

"Jealous?"

"Not for a second." She pulled a mug from the cabinet and filled it with coffee. "Hopefully, this helps keep your eyes open. I feel like I should join you. I don't know what Mrs. Carver is going to think waking up here in a strange apartment with you waiting for her. I feel like I should be the buffer, although, to be honest, she doesn't like me much, either."

"Why not?"

"Because Rebecca and I never got along. Her daughter didn't like me, so why should she? My family wasn't part of the Carvers' social circle, either. Whisper Lake may be a small resort town, but it has its share of politics. And the Carvers always preferred to spend time with the wealthy homeowners in the Highlands or at Sandy Point," she added. "That's where the big homes are."

"Rebecca could be pretentious, but once she got away from her parents' influence, she was much more normal. I wish you could have known her as an adult."

"Well, I am sorry she died so young. I feel for her daughter, and I feel for you, too, Zach. I know you mentioned that your relationship had its problems, but I'm sure you cared deeply about her."

"I did. It was a complicated situation."

"I understand."

He appreciated her words more than he could say, because his feelings about Rebecca were all over the map, and while there had been love, there had also been anger and disappointment. He took his coffee over to the table and sat down. Gianna poured herself a cup and then joined him. "Won't that keep you awake?" he asked her.

"I hope so. Because there's no way I'm going to sleep with you two enemies waiting to do battle."

"I'm not Helen's enemy."

"She thinks you are." Gianna took a sip, then set her mug down. "Tell me more about your life, the years after camp and before you met Rebecca. What were you doing?"

"I was really angry when I got home from camp, not just because you'd accused me of being a thief and turned your back on me, but also because I was back in the house where my dad should have been but wasn't. My mom was angry, too. She'd thought I'd come back a changed kid, that I wouldn't be the same pissed-off boy she'd sent to camp. We were constantly at odds."

"That's strange. I would have thought you'd be even closer after your dad died."

"She was mad at him, too, for not leaving the service, for dying, for leaving her alone. She used to rant about how he had to be everyone's hero but hers. I didn't disagree with her; I felt the same way. But I also still loved my dad."

"I'm sure she did, too."

"Probably, but she started dating a year later, which was even more weird. My dad had been gone so much, I hadn't even seen them together much. Seeing her with another man felt wrong. But she was moving on. She said she'd wasted too many years being alone. She wanted a life. It was her turn."

"That makes sense."

"It does now, but as a teenager, I felt like she was rejecting the family she'd had with my dad. It was different for my brother, because he was five years younger. He was still her baby. I was a thorn in her side. I was getting into trouble at school. My grades were sucking. We were just done with each other. After high school, I went to community college for two years and during that time my mom got engaged to her now husband. He was a hotel manager, and he ended up getting transferred from Denver to San Diego. They got married, and she and my brother moved to California. They formed their own family."

"I can't believe they didn't want you to be a part of it."

"I didn't want to be a part of it. I didn't think I needed a dad, and while this guy was okay, I didn't connect with him. It probably wasn't his fault."

"So, you were in community college in Denver? It's weird that we didn't run into each other, because I was there, too."

"I wasn't hanging with the university kids at that point, but I was starting to get my act together. I took an intro to architecture class, and it changed my life. I suddenly felt like I knew what I wanted to do with my life. I liked the idea of creating something out of nothing. I wanted to build homes that would last. I wanted to put my mark on the world. I was never that interested in commercial projects. I was always more focused on residential. Homes were personal. People would actually live in my creations."

"I can completely relate. Although, no one lives in my art, except me."

He smiled. "My new passion got me into a more academic frame of mind. I worked on getting my grades up, and I ended up transferring to San Francisco State and then going to grad school at UC Berkeley."

"Did you have any girlfriends during your college years?"

"I had a girlfriend at SF State. We ended right after we graduated. She went on to law school at UCLA. After her, there were some short relationships, but nothing that lasted more than a few months. I ran into Rebecca a little over four years ago. I think in some ways she brought a sense of home with her. At heart I was a Colorado kid, and so was she. And I fell in love with her daughter —maybe even before I fell in love with her. Hailey needed a dad."

"And you remembered that feeling," Gianna murmured, an understanding light in her eyes.

"I did," he admitted. "I liked being part of a family again." He'd never told anyone that before, not even Rebecca, but with Gianna, he seemed to have no boundaries. "Let's talk about you. Tell me about your work."

"Well, as much as I dreamed of being a master painter, I had to become a commercial artist in order to pay rent and buy food. I've done web design, logos, book covers, ads—anything that needs a graphic touch. I've liked my work. It's fun to bring someone's creative vision to life. I don't always get it right, but sometimes I give them something wonderful and unexpected, and that's even better."

"Your last job was at an ad agency, with your ex?"

"Yes, and it was also my least favorite position."

"So, you're not going back into advertising?"

"I'm not sure what I'll do. I have some freelance jobs. I did some book covers for a fantasy author about six months ago." She reached for her computer on the counter behind her. "Do you want to see?"

"I absolutely do."

She opened up her computer and tapped a few keys, then turned the monitor around. "This is a trilogy set in Egypt. What do you think?"

He was flat out amazed by the colors, the details, the impact. "The cover is great, Gianna, really good."

She gave him a beaming smile. "I think so, too. It took multiple tries to get to this design. I combined some hand drawings with digital manipulation and coloring, and this is where I ended up. The author was very happy. He has already referred me to several of his friends. I figured I could do those this summer when I'm not working in the store, although I have to be honest—I haven't done anything artistic in months, not since I broke up with Jeff." She tipped her head to the blank canvas on her easel. "Every morning, I think about painting, but I can't seem to pick up a brush. I feel like I've lost my mojo. And that scares me because whenever I've been unhappy or scared in the past, I could always turn to art. It was my escape, but now I have nowhere to go."

He met her gaze and saw the shadows in her eyes, reminding him that she'd been through some emotional heartbreak as well. "Your mojo will be back. Probably faster if you don't stress over it."

"I hope so. It's funny to me that you turned out to be an architect, although, it also makes sense, because you were always interested in my drawings, in how I came up with a picture. Maybe there was a seed planted even before you took that basic architecture class."

"I might owe it all to you."

"It's also interesting that you design homes—that you're creating places for families to thrive."

"Playing armchair psychologist?"

"There are no arms on this chair."

He smiled. "You're not the first person to make that point. I went to a therapist when Rebecca went to rehab. I thought maybe there was something I needed to change to make her better. The therapist mentioned that I might be trying to hold on to my image of the perfect family, because mine had crumbled. That my architecture is one more way for me to hold on to my ideals, my optimism that that perfect family exists. But I'm not sure I'm that deep."

"I think you are. And as a creator, of course, your feelings, your emotions, and your personal history play into what you design. It's the same for me. In my art, I tend to play around with themes of freedom, adventure, and fearlessness, probably because I wish I could be freer and more fearless."

"I think it's gutsy to call off three engagements. Maybe you're not as fearful as you think."

"You could read it that way or you could say I'm too afraid of marriage to make it all the way down the aisle."

"How do you read it?" he asked curiously.

"I honestly don't know. I haven't been very good at analyzing myself. But I have figured out that being who I am and living honestly is the only way I'm going to be happy."

"I want you to be happy," he said, wishing he could take the shadows out of her eyes.

"You're a fixer. You want everyone to be happy."

"I'm just not that good at making that happen." He sipped his coffee. "I couldn't fix Rebecca no matter how much I wanted to. She had to do that herself. I could only encourage and support her."

"Would you have stayed with her if Hailey wasn't in the picture?"

"No. And I feel bad for saying that, but it's true. I didn't see it for a while. Or even if I saw it, I didn't want to acknowledge it. I didn't want to face the fact that I loved her kid more than I loved her."

"She didn't make it easy to love her. She cheated on you."

"She did," he said heavily. "She was a slave to her addictions and she lost her life because of them. I can't change that. But I can try to make sure that Hailey has a good life."

"It's too bad the Carvers can't see their daughter for who she was and see you for who you are."

"I'm trying to show them a way to compromise, but they want to put all of Rebecca's past away and out of sight, and I'm part of that."

"Then we have to change their minds."

He glanced over at Helen, who shifted onto her side and then started snoring again. "Should I try to wake her?"

"You can try. Or we can keep talking."

"All night long?" he asked, remembering another night a very long time ago.

She met his gaze and smiled. "We did it once before."

"You were afraid we were going to get caught by our counselors for sneaking out."

"There was a good chance of that, or of one of the other girls turning me in."

"But no one did."

"Keira thought we messed around that night more than we did. She was the only one who knew I'd left the cabin after lights out. She was going to cover for me if anyone asked. She kept asking me afterward for the details, and I told her we just talked and kissed and talked some more until the sun came up. She thought I was lying. She thought we did it."

"I wanted to do it, but—"

"I wasn't ready," she finished. "And you didn't push."

"I was as nervous as you were. It felt like…" His voice drifted away. He couldn't quite find the right words.

"Like it would be important," she said, meeting his gaze. "Maybe *too* important for a fifteen-year-old and a sixteen-year-old."

"Did you ever have regrets?"

"Not about that night. I was just sad when it was over. I missed you, even when I was hating you."

"I felt exactly the same way."

"I wonder what did happen to my locket."

"I doubt we'll ever know. But you have another clue to the girl in the picture. That's something."

"It is," she agreed, stifling a yawn.

"You should go to bed, Gianna. You have to work tomorrow."

"I'm hoping Mrs. Carver wakes up soon."

"Is there more coffee?"

She nodded and got to her feet. "I'll get it for you."

"Thanks."

She refilled his mug, then pulled out a deck of cards. "Let's play. What's your game?"

"I think I beat you at Spit about two dozen times."

A smile spread across her face. "I haven't played that game since camp."

"Let's do it."

"It's better with two decks." She got back up and rummaged through the drawer. She returned with a second pack. "I noticed these the other day. Apparently, whoever lived here before liked to play cards. Okay, so remind me what we do?"

"We each turn over four cards and then we say *Spit* and start trying to get rid of the rest of the cards. You can only play one up or one down on either pile. If we get stumped, we spit again."

"It's all coming back to me. You're really fast and you play ruthlessly."

"That's the only way to win."

"There is such a thing as fun, you know. Winning isn't everything."

"It's a lot more fun to win than to lose," he pointed out.

"But winning at Spit doesn't get you much."

"How about dinner out somewhere? Loser buys."

"You seriously want to compete for a date?"

"I said dinner, not date."

She gave him a suspicious look. "I don't believe you, but I have wanted to try Gulliver's—a new restaurant in town. My mom said it's wonderful."

"Gulliver's it is." They laid out their cards. "Ready?" he asked.

"Spit," she said.

The cards flew, their hands crashing into each other, as they reached for the same pile. He might have lost a little speed since his youth, but he was still faster than she was. He took the win with a happy, gloating smile. "I hope Gulliver's has a good steak."

"Two out of three."

"You want to buy me two dinners?" he teased.

"That was a practice game."

"No way. You have to call practice before you lose. And what happened to the joy of just playing?"

"Fine, I owe you dinner," she grumbled. "Let's play again just for fun."

"I'll still win."

"We'll see."

They played another six games, filled with competitive smiles and a lot of laughs. He felt like he was sixteen again. And it wasn't only the cards he was enjoying; it was Gianna. She looked happy, too—carefree, distracted from her problems and the questions about her birth. She was in the moment, and it was a moment he wished he could keep going for a very long time.

Then Mrs. Carver groaned, shifted, and fell off the couch with a heavy thud.

They both jumped to their feet.

He made it to the couch first.

Helen looked up at him with confusion and alarm. "You? What are you doing here?" She looked around. "Where am I? What's going on?"

"That's what you need to tell us, Helen. Why did you break into Gianna's store?"

Her face whitened, and fear ran through her eyes.

He needed to find out what she was so scared of, because as much as she wanted to pretend it was him, he thought it was someone else. And he needed to know who.

CHAPTER FOURTEEN

HE EXTENDED his hand to help Helen up, but she ignored him and awkwardly made her way onto the couch, her gaze darting toward the door, as if she were weighing her chances of escape.

"Mrs. Carver," Gianna said quietly, drawing Helen's attention to her. "You broke into the antiques store. This is the upstairs apartment. Zach and I brought you here after you passed out."

"I—I'm so embarrassed," Helen stuttered, her hands going to her hair as she smoothed down the wild strands. "I don't know what to say."

"You can say why you needed to get into the shop after hours, what you thought was hidden in Rebecca's desk," he said.

Helen's eyes widened. "Who told you about the desk?"

"Gianna told me. You told her."

Helen's gaze swung back to Gianna. "I told you there was something in the desk? Did you find it?"

"The desk was empty," Gianna replied.

"Are you sure?" Helen asked, fear and worry in her eyes.

"She's sure. I also looked in the desk," he said, wanting Helen to feel the shift in power. She and Ron had been calling the shots since Rebecca's death, but that was about to change. "What were you looking for?"

"It doesn't concern you."

"Oh, but it does, because you were looking for something from Rebecca's past, a secret the two of you share, a secret you don't want to get out, something I might already know about."

"She told you?" Helen breathed in horror.

He had no idea what Helen thought Rebecca had told him, but it was in his best interests to keep her off-balance. "She told me a lot of things. You really should be embracing me as part of the family and not trying to keep me out of it. I've tried to work with you. I've offered many suggestions for compromise, but you blew me off each and every time. That's changing now."

"What—what are you going to do?" Helen asked warily.

"Well, that depends on you." He pulled out his phone and showed her the photos he'd taken of her sprawled on the storeroom floor. "I'm sure you don't want these to get out."

"Oh, God," she said, putting her hands over her face as she hung her head. "What have I done?"

He squatted down in front of her. "Helen, look at me."

She slowly dropped her hands.

"We can make a deal," he said. "You can let me see Hailey, and I can make sure that no one sees these photos."

"You're blackmailing me?"

"Let's call it a negotiation."

"Ron won't allow you to see Hailey. He doesn't trust you. And he loves Hailey. So do I."

"I love her, too. That's what we have in common, and we need to put her first."

"She's my granddaughter. She's all I have left of Rebecca."

"And I took care of her for four years. I was basically Hailey's father."

"You're not her blood."

"I'm still her family, and you need to let me see her. I'm not trying to take her away from you. I'm trying to share her with you."

"You won't stop there. Once you get in, you'll want her back. I lost Rebecca. I can't lose Hailey, too."

He drew in a breath, choosing his words carefully. "You don't really have a choice, Helen. I think you know that."

She stared back at him, her face white, her mouth tight. "I told you—Ron won't allow it."

"Then you're going to have to convince him. Otherwise, I'll tell him about all this."

Helen turned to Gianna. "How can you stand there and let him threaten me?"

"You broke into the store, Mrs. Carver. I could have called the police. This could be a lot more public than it already is."

"I don't understand why you called him."

"Well, it doesn't matter if you understand. I know Zach. He's a good man. And your granddaughter could only benefit by having him in her life. I feel for that little girl. She lost her mother and she lost the man who was taking care of her."

"She's fine. We are taking care of her."

"Why can't you all take care of her?" Gianna questioned.

"Because…" Helen's voice drifted away. "Zach hurt Rebecca. He got her into drugs."

"Stop with the lies," he ordered. "And that's not why you're keeping me away. It has something to do with Rebecca's secret, about what I might know."

"You don't know anything. You would have used it already if you did."

"Maybe I would have, or maybe I'm trying not to let things get down to that level. But you need to understand that you're no longer in charge."

Helen licked her lips. "Maybe we can work something out."

"No *maybe* about it. I want to see Hailey tomorrow. If you don't want to involve Ron just yet, then meet me at the park."

"He'll be angry if I go behind his back."

"He knows I'm in town. I could run into you accidentally."

A hopeful light entered her eyes, and he almost wanted to dash it, because he didn't want her to feel anything but fear. But he had to walk a fine line, not overplay his hand. Once he saw Hailey again, once he told her that he'd never meant to abandon her, that he would always be there for her, he could shed the weight of guilt and frustration that he'd been carrying around the past six months. Then he could look further into the future.

"I suppose Hailey and I could stop at the park after I go to the market," Helen said slowly. "We'd probably be there around noon. But what would you say to her?"

"I'd tell her that I missed her, that I love her, and that I'm not leaving her again."

Helen blew out a breath. "She'll be confused."

"We'll talk it out."

"You'll let her live with us?"

"Unless I have reason to believe she's not safe or happy there. You still haven't explained your wild and reckless behavior tonight."

"I thought that Rebecca might have left something in the desk that was personal. I wasn't around when Ron decided to ship her furniture over here. I didn't have time to check."

"And you couldn't do that during business hours?" he challenged.

"I—I should have. I was upset. I've been distraught since Rebecca died. I'm not myself. I'm sorry, Gianna."

"How did you get in?" Gianna asked.

"The window in the bathroom of the storeroom was unlocked."

He couldn't believe the usually reserved Helen had gotten drunk enough to climb through a bathroom window.

"I want to go home now," Helen added.

"I'll drive you," he said.

Indecision moved through her eyes, but she didn't want to talk to anyone in her family and calling for a cab or a ride at this time of night wouldn't be easy.

"All right," she said.

He stood back as she got to her feet.

Helen looked over at Gianna. "I trust you will keep this private as well."

"As long as you make good on your promise to let Zach see Hailey."

He was more than a little happy to hear Gianna's words and see the steel determination in her eyes. It had been a long while since he'd felt like someone had his back. "Thank you," he murmured, giving her a grateful look before ushering Helen to the door.

"I'll follow you downstairs," Gianna said. "I want to lock the window and the door behind you."

"Did you drive here?" he asked Helen, suddenly wondering if she'd driven drunk. Maybe Hailey wasn't safe with her at all.

"My car is at Walker's Tavern," she said, mentioning a bar a few blocks away. "I walked over here."

"Well, you can get it tomorrow." He ushered her through the storeroom and into the parking lot, turning back one last time to say good-bye to Gianna. "I'll be in touch."

"Good luck," she said.

He opened the door to the truck for Helen and then went around to the driver's side and slid behind the wheel.

"I'm not normally like this," Helen said, as he drove toward her house. "It's because Rebecca died. I haven't been myself."

"It has been a difficult time. For all of us."

"Rebecca was with another man the night of the fire. I assumed you were breaking up, that she didn't want you in her life anymore. I assumed that you wouldn't want to continue seeing Hailey. You were in the hospital. It made sense for us to take her home."

"And have the funeral without me?"

"Well, we couldn't wait forever, and you were in bad shape."

He shot her a quick look. "Maybe in the beginning you had reason to believe you would be the better caretakers for Hailey, but when I got better, and I told you I did want to be in Hailey's life, you and Ron shot me down and shut me out. You called the police on me when I got here, and Ron came by the camp and threatened the project if I didn't abandon it and leave town. Those are very drastic actions, considering all I want to do is see Hailey, be in her life. So, what aren't you telling me?"

"I—we just think it's better for Hailey to move on without any reminders of the past. She's young. She'll forget what happened, and that will make it easier for her. She has nightmares now. I want them to go away."

His heart ached at that piece of news. "Maybe she has nightmares because she wants to see me, because she doesn't know where I went."

"This isn't all about you," Helen said tartly, which made him really happy he had the photos, because Helen was not going down without a fight.

"What is it about? What were you looking for in Rebecca's old desk?"

"Did she really talk to you about her past?"

"Yes, of course. We lived together for four years. I saw her at her best and at her worst, when words were streaming out of her in a rambling, half-conscious state."

"Rebecca had a big imagination. She used to make up stories— lies, really. She always had a play going on in her head where she was suffering some tragic problem and she had to be her own hero- ine. The stories weren't real. They didn't actually happen. You can't think that whatever she might have told you about us is true. We're good people."

His stomach twisted at her odd words, and he gave her another speculative look. "What does that mean? What do you think she told me?"

"Probably nothing, but Mitch said you'll fight us with every- thing you have, and when I realized it was missing, well, I didn't know if you had it."

"What is *it*?"

"If you don't know, then you don't have it." Helen seemed relieved by that thought. "I loved Rebecca more than I loved anyone else in my life. She was everything to me—my beautiful daughter."

"And yet you saw her so infrequently. It was only in the last two years that you showed up at all, and she never came home. Why is that?"

"Well, she lived far away. We spoke, though."

"Not that often."

"That wasn't my choice." Helen turned her gaze out the window. "Like I said, Rebecca made up stories that didn't happen."

He tried to remember what Rebecca had told him about her parents, her mother especially, but she'd spoken in as many cryptic riddles as Helen was doing now.

Rebecca had mentioned fighting demons in her head, the feeling that she couldn't run away, that she could be trapped. She'd told him she couldn't sleep, and he knew she was terrified of utter darkness. She'd always insisted on a night-light. The few times they'd gone to a hotel, she'd kept the drapes open, so she wouldn't wake up and not be able to see. He'd asked her if something had happened to make her so afraid, and she'd always said no. He'd thought her demons were inside her head, but he was beginning to wonder.

"Someone hurt Rebecca," he said, taking a guess.

Helen immediately shook her head. "No, that didn't happen. We protected her."

"She was afraid of the dark."

"That's because she used to sleepwalk and when she'd wake up, she'd be very confused and disoriented. That's why she liked to leave the lights on."

It was a perfectly logical explanation, and one Rebecca had used as well, but he didn't think that was the whole story. "Rebecca kept a journal when she went to rehab. Did she ever share it with you?"

Helen's eyes widened. "No. I didn't know that. Do you have it?"

"I don't. It was lost in the fire, as far as I know. But she did tell me that she always felt better when she wrote things down. She mentioned that she used to have a diary when she was a kid. Is that what you were looking for in her desk?"

"That diary disappeared years ago."

"Then why were you worried it might still be in the desk?"

"I wasn't thinking clearly. Ron took the furniture from Rebecca's room without asking me. I didn't have time to look through it, and I started wondering if she might have left something personal in there. I didn't want it to fall into the wrong hands."

"Okay, but why didn't you just ask Gianna to let you look in the desk?"

"She didn't even know where it was when I saw her on Thursday. It was bothering me, and I was drinking. I shouldn't have been. I'm a lightweight. It goes right to my head. I made a bad decision. If you loved Rebecca at all, you won't do any digging into her past. Let her rest in peace."

He didn't think it was Rebecca who wanted peace; it was Helen. But as much as he was curious about the secret, Hailey was his main priority. Maybe Helen had given him another tool to wedge his way into their lives. "I'm more concerned about rebuilding my relationship with Hailey than digging into the past. If you don't come to the park tomorrow at noon, I will come to the house. And I will show Ron the photos and anyone else who needs to see them, including the police. You could be arrested for what you did. You could end up in jail."

"Stop," she cried, putting up her hand. "Please, stop. You've made your point."

He pulled up in front of her dark and quiet house. "I'm surprised everyone is asleep. Wouldn't Ron wonder where you are?"

"We don't sleep in the same room anymore. He has a terrible snoring problem. I usually stay in Rebecca's room. I'm sure he doesn't know I'm gone. But I didn't leave Hailey alone. She was asleep, and Ron was there," she added defensively. "It was all good. I was going to have one drink and then go home. I thought it would help me sleep. I've been having trouble."

"That's what Rebecca used to say when she took whatever she was taking. She just wanted to sleep, but it always eluded her."

"I have to go. The neighbors will wonder why I'm sitting out here in your truck."

"It's three o'clock in the morning; I don't think anyone is looking."

"Janice Peters is always looking, and she doesn't sleep much either."

"I'll see you tomorrow at noon," he said, as Helen opened the door.

She didn't respond, just got out and quietly closed the door, then walked quickly up to her porch. He waited until she got inside and then drove back to the inn, his mind racing with a dozen different thoughts. There was still something he didn't know about Rebecca, something that happened to her, some secret her mother wanted to keep.

But whatever the secret was, it wouldn't bring Rebecca back or change what had happened. He needed to look forward.

Hopefully, Helen would show up at the park tomorrow with Hailey.

What other move could she make?

He had her over a barrel. She would never want the photos to get out. But there was still a wild card in the mix, and that was Ron.

He couldn't help wondering if Ron was involved in the secret. Or if he was the reason Rebecca couldn't sleep at night. She'd always said she wasn't close to her father and that she knew she was supposed to love him but half the time she didn't even like him very much. He hadn't found that difficult to believe since Ron could be a self-righteous asshole. *But was there more to Rebecca's dislike?*

Maybe he did need to figure out the secret, because his brain was going down a very bad path, and it was one thing to leave Hailey with loving grandparents who hated his guts than to leave her with two people who might not have done right by their own daughter.

Gianna knew she should not go down to the park at noon on Monday. It was not her business, but she really wanted to see Zach and Hailey reunite. As the clock moved closer to twelve, she turned to Nora, who was scheduled to work at the store until three. "I'm going to take lunch. Will you be all right on your own?"

"Of course. Mondays aren't very busy. Take your time."

"Thanks."

She grabbed her purse from behind the counter and headed out. It was another hot day, and she was happy to be wearing a sleeve-less dress and wedge sandals. The park was close by, and it only took her about five minutes to get to the children's playground. She didn't see Helen, but Zach was pacing back and forth by the basketball court on the other side of the swings.

Surprise flashed across his face when he saw her. She hoped it was a welcome surprise, but if it wasn't, she'd wish him luck and take off.

"Hi," she said. "I probably shouldn't have come, but I wanted to see how this was going to play out. I also thought you might want some support, but if you'd rather do this alone, I will go."

Indecision played through his eyes. "I'm glad you're here, but…"

"But you'd rather I wasn't."

"I don't want to confuse Hailey any more than she already is."

"I understand. Could you text me later and tell me how it went?"

"You don't have to leave yet, Gianna, but when they get here, I need to talk to Hailey alone."

"Of course. Did Helen say anything to you in the car on the way home last night?"

"Not really. She claimed her behavior was an aberration. That she hasn't been sleeping well since Rebecca died."

"That's understandable. She lost a child—the worst thing that could happen."

"I know. But there's something else going on. She kept asking me what Rebecca had told me about her past. There's a secret that Helen is worried about getting out. I think Rebecca had a diary that went missing years ago and Helen suddenly thought maybe it was still in the desk."

"What would Rebecca have said in an old diary that would make Helen break into the store?"

He shrugged. "I don't know."

"Well, whatever happened, it's in the past."

"Yes, and I probably would leave it at that if it wasn't for Hailey. If something happened to Rebecca as a child, if the Carvers did something wrong, how can I leave Hailey with them? I need to know if there was a reason Rebecca left home at eighteen and never went back. And she certainly didn't encourage her parents to have much contact with her daughter. They visited a few times when we were together, but it wasn't a lot. Helen also mentioned that Mitch told her I'd fight her and Ron with everything I had. I got the feeling that triggered her night of drinking. She's afraid I know more than I do or that I'll figure it out." He checked his watch, his mouth drawing into a tight line. "She's late."

"She has to show up. She doesn't have a choice."

"Unless she runs away and takes Hailey with her."

"I don't think the Carvers can just run away. Ron is a city councilman."

"Helen could go on her own. Mitch told me yesterday she'd already started packing but Ron had talked her out of it. What if she left this morning? Was I crazy to just drop her off last night?"

"Give it a few more minutes."

"Damn!" He ran a hand through his hair. "I feel like I'm so close and yet so far away."

"Have you thought about what you're going to say to Hailey?" she asked, hoping to distract him from checking his watch again.

"I haven't been able to think about anything else. I have a lot I want to tell her, but I also don't want to overwhelm her."

"It's going to be fine. And don't forget—you have always been good with the ladies."

He gave her a faint smile. "Thanks for the reminder. And thanks for coming. You're the reason this is even happening. If you hadn't called me last night…"

"I'm glad that I could help. I know how much this means to you."

He suddenly stiffened and grabbed her arm. "There she is."

She turned her head to see Helen walking toward the playground holding the hand of a little girl wearing shorts and a T-shirt, her brown hair up in a messy ponytail. "Go," she said.

He let go of her arm and started walking toward the swings. He was about ten feet away when Hailey saw him. Her eyes widened and then she released her grandmother's hand and ran to Zach. He fell to his knees and gathered her up in his arms.

Moisture filled Gianna's eyes at their loving reunion. But when she looked past them and saw Helen watching with a wary, angry gaze, she knew the fight wasn't over yet. Helen had done what she had to do, but she wasn't happy about it.

Hailey, on the other hand, was thrilled. She was all smiles in Zach's arms, and Gianna could see the poignant emotion on his face. Feeling very much like an intruder now, she turned away. This moment belonged to Zach, and she was going to let him have it.

CHAPTER FIFTEEN

ZACH COULDN'T LET GO of Hailey, even when she protested he was squeezing her too tight. But he did ease up on the embrace as he gave her a happy smile. She looked good, healthy, and her brown eyes were filled with sparkle. "I'm so happy to see you," he told her.

"Grandma said you had to go away."

"I came back as soon as I could."

"Mommy went to heaven; she can't come back." The light in her eyes faded.

"I know, baby," he said, sliding his hands down her small arms. "But she's still keeping watch, making sure you're okay."

"I miss my room. I miss Piggy," she added, referring to the stuffed pink pig he'd given her for her sixth birthday. "Piggy went to heaven, too, after the fire. How come I didn't go?"

His heart twisted at the question. "Because you are meant to be here. You're going to have a long, happy life. Have your grandparents been taking good care of you?"

She nodded, then darted a quick look at her grandmother before dropping her voice down a notch. "Grandma doesn't like you. Neither does Grandpa. I heard them fighting about you coming back. I was afraid you wouldn't come."

He heard the worry in her voice and hated that she'd overheard anything. "It's all going to work out."

"Are you going to live with us?"

"Not in your grandmother's house, but I'm staying in town. I'm going to get my own place."

"Can I live there with you?" she asked eagerly.

He saw Helen flinch at Hailey's question. She'd moved closer, clearly wanting to hear every word. He didn't want to disappoint Hailey or send Helen into a panic, so he decided to play it very carefully. "We'll talk about it later. Do you want to go on the swings?"

"Will you push me?"

"Absolutely." He straightened as Hailey ran toward the swing. He met Helen's gaze. "Thank you for bringing her."

She seemed surprised by his words. "Well, I had to. But you can't let her think she's going to live with you. That's not the deal."

He didn't bother to answer. There would be plenty of time to talk to Helen. Now, it was all about Hailey.

He moved over to the swings, laughing as Hailey pleaded to go faster and higher. Once they were done with the swings, it was on to the slides, and then the small rock wall that she easily climbed. Hailey had always been athletic and fearless, nothing at all like her mother.

It was nice to see her playing and laughing. Maybe the Carvers hadn't been all that bad for her. She seemed to be okay. But Rebecca's problems had all been under the surface. He couldn't judge Hailey's true feelings after a few minutes in the park. He needed to be with her more often. He needed to talk to her every day.

Helen had been right about one thing. Seeing Hailey once was not enough. He did want more—a lot more.

Hailey jumped off the rock wall and ran back to him, throwing her arms around his waist and looking up at him with an adorable smile. "Can we get ice cream?" She pointed to the nearby vendor, who was walking through the park selling ice cream sandwiches and popsicles.

He turned to Helen who had been hovering nearby for the past hour. "What do you think about a Popsicle?"

"I suppose it will be all right, but we'll need to go after that."

Hailey's smile turned down. "I don't want to leave, Grandma. I want to stay with Zach."

As much as he wanted to say he would take her home with him and never let her go, he couldn't do that. Even with his ammunition against Helen, she and Ron had legal custody, and they needed to work things out.

"I'm still looking for a place to live," he told Hailey. "But you and I are going to spend time together. Your grandparents will make sure of that. They love you very much. And so do I. Now, how about we get a Popsicle?"

"Okay," she said, taking his hand. She skipped alongside him until they reached the vendor, then chose a raspberry Popsicle. He grabbed an orange one, offering to buy one for Helen, who quickly refused and sat down on a nearby bench.

He and Hailey took a seat at a picnic table a few yards away. He wanted to keep his time with Hailey as separate from Helen as he could. "Do you have your own room at your grandparents' house?"

She nodded. "It used to be Uncle Mitch's room. Grandma said I can't stay in Mommy's room, because she sleeps in there."

"How do you and Grandpa get along?"

"Good," she said, raspberry juice dripping down her chin.

He smiled and used his napkin to wipe it off. "Do you have any friends?"

"Maddie is my friend. She sat next to me in school. I finished the second grade. I'm going to be in third next year."

"You're getting so old."

"Where did you go on your trip? Why didn't you call me?"

"Different places. And I wanted to call you."

"How come you couldn't?"

"I just needed a little time."

"Grandma said you were hurt after the fire and that you had to go away to get better. Are you okay now?"

He was happy that that was the excuse Hailey had been given. "I'm all better."

"I missed you, Zach. You didn't even say good-bye."

His heart tore at the pain in her voice. "I really wanted to. Do you think you can forgive me?"

"As long as you don't go anywhere else," she told him.

He wanted to make her that promise, but he couldn't. "You better eat your Popsicle; it's melting fast."

She giggled as more juice flowed down her face, but she managed to finish the Popsicle in the next two bites.

"Hailey, we have to go," Helen said, walking over to them.

"Can you come with us?" Hailey asked Zach.

"I'm sorry, but I can't. I have to go to work now. I'm building a new summer camp in the woods. You're going to like it. It's going to have a train you can ride."

"Can I go there?"

"When it's done, sure. But right now, you have to go with your grandmother." He stood up and pulled her to her feet. "I'll see you soon."

"When? Tomorrow?" she asked, worry in her eyes.

"Your grandmother and I will work it out," he assured her.

At his words, Hailey turned to Helen. "Grandma, when can I see Zach again?"

"I don't know, honey. We'll talk about it when we're home."

Hailey got a stubborn look in her eyes, one that reminded him very much of Rebecca. He had a feeling a blowup might be on its way.

"How about I call you tonight before you go to bed?" he suggested. "I'm sure your grandmother won't mind."

Helen hesitated, then gave a tight nod. "You can call my phone at eight. I'll make sure she's available to talk to you. I'll give you the number."

He put her number into his phone, noting that she clearly didn't want him talking to Ron.

"I'll talk to you tonight, Hailey." He opened his arms and

Hailey ran into them again. He hugged her for a long minute, wishing he didn't have to let her go, but he did.

He forced a smile on his face as she said good-bye and left the park with her grandmother. He watched them until they got into Helen's car and drove away. Then he blew out the breath he hadn't realized he was holding.

He was happy that he'd seen Hailey again, that he'd had a chance to tell her he loved her. *But where did they go from here?*

There were still obstacles in the way, the main one being Ron. But the wall the Carvers had built around Hailey had cracked, and he was going to tear the whole damn thing down, one brick at a time.

Gianna yawned as she put on a T-shirt and PJ shorts and climbed into bed just after nine on Monday night. With only a few hours of sleep the night before, and a long, busy day in the store, she was exhausted.

She was about to put her phone on the nightstand when it buzzed. Zach was calling, and her heart leapt happily at that realization. He'd texted her briefly in the afternoon that things had gone well at the park and he'd call her later.

"Hello?"

"I hope it's not too late to call," he said.

"It's not. How did your time with Hailey go?"

"It was great. I thought she might be angry or not even care that I had come to find her. But she was as loving as she always was. It was like no time had passed. We spent an hour playing in the park together before Helen pulled the plug."

She settled back against the pillows. "I'm surprised Helen gave you that much time. Did she interact with you?"

"No, she hovered nearby. She was definitely listening to our conversation, though. Hailey said she wanted to come and live with me, and I could see Helen flinch."

"Wow, Hailey said that? That's interesting."

"She doesn't understand why she can't live with me since we were together for as many years as she can remember."

"What did you say?"

"That I was looking for a new place and that I'd be nearby in the meantime."

"That was diplomatic."

"She was sad when Helen made her leave. It broke my heart —again."

She felt a rush of sympathy for him. "Well, you're in her life now."

"Only because Helen got drunk and broke into your store. But I'll take it. And I'm not above blackmailing Helen if she tries to stop me from seeing Hailey again."

"It doesn't sound like she's going to do that."

"I hope not. She did let me say goodnight to her on the phone."

"That's something."

"She had to promise Hailey she would do that or there was going to be a tantrum at the park. Hailey can be stubborn."

"Does Ron know you saw Hailey?"

"I don't think so. Helen asked me to call her on her phone. After answering, she immediately gave the phone to Hailey. I'm not sure if she stayed in the room with Hailey or not, but we didn't talk about anything groundbreaking. Hailey was telling me about her day, and her friend Maddie, and the puppy that the neighbors got."

"It sounds like she's happy enough."

"She's doing all right, and that's a relief."

"Did she talk about her mother at all?"

"Not much. She told me at the park that her mother had to go to heaven along with the stuffed pig I bought her. She wondered why she hadn't gone to heaven, too."

"That's rough."

"Yeah, it is," he said, a dark note in his voice. "But tonight she didn't say anything about her mother."

"Maybe it's good that she's so young. She's not as aware of everything."

"Helen told me Hailey has nightmares, though. Her fears may come out in the night." He paused. "Do you think it's crazy that I love this kid so much when she's not even mine?"

"I actually think it's amazing and wonderful that you love her the way that you do. I know families aren't just about blood. My parents had no biological tie to me, but they love me, and I love them. That's what matters."

"Thanks."

"Did you really have any doubts?"

"Not exactly. But my younger brother and my mother did mention once that maybe it would be better for me to move on with my life, make my own family, and let the Carvers raise their grandchild."

"Well, your family is probably worried about you. They don't want you to be hurt any more than you already have been." She paused. "I thought you said you don't have a relationship with them anymore."

"They came to see me when I was in the hospital. I was going out of my mind at the time, wondering where Hailey was and wanting to see her."

"I'm glad they were there for you."

"They do try on occasion, but it's hard to breach the distance after so many years. That's partly why I'm so desperate to get Hailey back now. I know what time can do to a relationship."

"I think the way the Carvers handled the situation was terrible. But I know they were grief-stricken, so I'm trying not to judge them too harshly."

"I've also tried not to judge them. But as time has passed, it has become more and more difficult."

"Have you spoken to Mitch about his mother's adventures last night?"

"No. I told Helen it was between the three of us. Unless something changes, that's where it stays. If you're okay with it, of course."

"I'm okay with it." She stifled a yawn.

"I'm keeping you up," he said.

"I was about to go to bed. I know it's early, but I've been fighting to keep my eyes open since about six o'clock this evening."

"I'm beat, too. Neither one of us slept much last night. But I'm also hyped up."

She smiled to herself. "I can hear the energy in your voice. Maybe you should take a run or practice yoga."

"A run is a better idea than yoga. I'm the most inflexible person on the planet."

"I highly doubt that."

"It's true. Do you like yoga?"

"I've taken some classes. I like the meditative quality of the moves, staying in the moment, feeling grounded and in balance."

"That does sound very Zen."

"I create better when I'm not stressed."

"Have you done any creating yet? Or is that canvas still blank?"

"I thought about it tonight, but I couldn't bring myself to start anything. I don't know what's wrong with me. I've always been able to lose myself in art. But I haven't painted in months. And the digital art isn't the same, not that I've done much of that, either." She snuggled deeper into her bed. She should hang up and go to sleep but saying good-bye to Zach was getting to be more difficult with each day. "What else did you do today?"

"Hunter and I had a meeting with a guy from the building department. He seemed to be acting normally, so apparently Ron hasn't tried to put any pressure there yet."

"That's good. But I wouldn't get too comfortable. He might still try to screw you over once he knows you have leverage on Helen."

"Believe me, I'm not overconfident when it comes to that situation. But enough about me. What about you? Did you talk to anyone about the photograph?"

"I asked a few locals who came in. No one knew the girl in the photo or seemed to know a Jill or Tammy from that time period. I didn't have a chance to go by the library. I still need to do that. But I was pretty busy selling antiques and trying to answer everyone's questions. I really need to learn more about what we're selling."

"Did anyone buy Helen's desk?"

"I took the price tag off it and put it on hold just to make sure the other cashier wouldn't sell it when I wasn't there. I feel like I need to hang on to it."

"Why?"

"Just a gut feeling. Maybe Helen will want it back. It sounded like her husband brought it in without her blessing, and it was Rebecca's. I'll give it a week and if she doesn't ask to get it back, then I'll put it on sale again."

"That's a good idea. I'm sorry your aunt broke her leg, but I'm very happy you came back to Whisper Lake when you did."

She had to admit she was feeling pretty happy about it, too. She was also happy that he'd come back as well. "So, you're at the inn right now?"

"Yes. I'm sitting in a very comfortable over-sized armchair, and I grabbed one of Lizzie's chocolate chip cookies on my way upstairs."

"Lucky you."

"What about you? Are you in bed?"

"I am."

"What are you wearing?"

"Who says I'm wearing anything?" she asked with a teasing laugh.

He groaned. "Oh, man, that brings an image to my mind."

"You've never seen me naked."

"I've seen you in a bikini."

"Not the same thing."

"I have a good imagination. But I don't believe you're naked. I think you've got on a long nightgown with long sleeves, and it's buttoned up to your neck. Or maybe you're in PJs, something colorful. It might even have unicorns on it."

"Ha-ha," she said. "I haven't had PJs with unicorns on them since I was fifteen."

"I remember."

She smiled at the memory. "What do you sleep in?"

"Not much, especially in the summer."

"I don't believe you're not wearing any clothes, either."

He laughed. "I just wanted to give you something to think about."

"This is a pointless conversation, Zach."

"Not everything has to have a point. I like talking to you, Gianna. It's strange to think that fourteen years went by without us talking."

"We've lived a lot since that teenage summer."

"But no one has ever been as easy to talk to as you," he said.

"You don't have to say that."

"I'm not making it up."

"Rebecca wasn't easy?"

"No. She was a very complicated person."

"But you loved her."

"For a while I thought I did. Like I said, I think I fell for Hailey before I fell for Rebecca. Or maybe Hailey just showed me the family I could have, and I liked the picture. But that wasn't fair to Rebecca."

"Or to yourself," she said quietly. "But I'm not judging you, Zach. I've made too many of my own mistakes."

"What do you think you're looking for that you haven't found in the men you were engaged to?"

"The thing is—I don't even think it's about the men; it's me. I need to find myself before I can be with someone else."

"Which is why you need to find that girl in the picture."

"What if that doesn't help? What if it's just me that I can't find?" It felt a little scary to say it out loud, but she found Zach easy to talk to as well.

"You'll find her. And I think you're being too hard on yourself. Your twenties are a time for introspection, figuring things out. That's what you've been doing."

"I hurt people along the way. I'm sorry about that."

"I know you are. I hurt people, too. The problem is that when two people don't feel the same way about each other, someone ends up in pain. That's why love is a risk."

"Not one I'm going to take again."

"You say that now, but—"

"I mean it, Zach. I can't fall in love again. I can't mess up for a fourth time."

"Who says the next one won't be the right one?"

"Me. There is no right one. I will be single forever."

"That's dramatic," he said lightly.

"Fine. Then I'll be single for a while."

"Better."

"What about you? How do you feel about taking another risk on love after Rebecca?"

"I haven't thought about it much. But I don't want to have regrets. Life is for living, mistakes and all. It's part of the journey."

"Maybe you don't need yoga. You're already Zen."

"I wouldn't go that far." He paused. "You need to paint again, Gianna. You should let your art remind you who you are."

"The girl with the paint-stained fingers?"

"The girl who could imagine a magnificent picture and bring it to life."

Her heart skipped a beat at his words. "My pictures haven't been magnificent for a long time. As I got older, I became more critical. All I could see were weaknesses and flaws. Nothing was ever the way I saw it in my head."

"I doubt the art is any less magnificent; it's your perception that's changed."

"It had to change. Making a living at art means making compromises. I don't create for myself. I do it for other people."

"Then paint something for yourself. Close your eyes and let your imagination run free."

"Right now?"

"Yes. What do you see?"

She turned off the light and closed her eyes. All she could see was Zach. But she couldn't tell him that. "I don't see anything. My mind is blank."

"You're lying."

"I am not," she protested.

"You're thinking about me, about us, that summer at the lake, making out at the pond, running through the trees, snuggling under the blanket at the campfire."

His words brought all those images into her head. "It was a magical time," she murmured. "We were so young, so carefree. Everything seemed possible."

"Maybe it still is."

Her gut tightened. "You need to stop, Zach. We can't go back in time. We can't be those kids again."

"I don't want to be them; I want to be us."

"I don't even know what that would look like."

"Why don't we find out?"

"I told you I'm off men."

"Right. I forgot. I have to wait until your hiatus ends."

"That will be a very long time. I'm going to say good night now."

"I wish I could kiss you good night and then kiss you again in the morning."

Her stomach did a crazy little flip-flop at his husky words.

"It's not just the talking that comes easy to us," he added.

"I'm ending this call, Zach."

"When am I going to see you again?"

"I don't know. Whenever we run into each other, I guess."

"Let's make that soon."

She forced herself to disconnect. Then she set the phone down on the nightstand.

As she closed her eyes again, Zach's image came back into her head, but she wasn't seeing the boy from her youth; she was seeing the man he was now. She could taste his kiss on her lips. She could see the laughter in his eyes. She could feel the heat of his desire.

But he was the wrong man at the wrong time.

Or maybe he was the *right* man at the wrong time.

Either way, it was the wrong time…

CHAPTER SIXTEEN

ZACH WAS on his third cup of coffee when he drove up to the camp around eleven on Tuesday. He hadn't fallen asleep until two or three in the morning, unable to get his brain or his body to quiet down. Talking to Gianna had been great, but then he couldn't stop thinking about her, imagining her in his head, reliving all of their times together from when they were kids to now.

He felt like he'd been in hibernation since Rebecca died, and even before that he'd been numb, living in a world where he was trying to help a woman he cared about but didn't really love anymore and wanting to make things right for Hailey by getting her mother back on track.

It had all been so complicated, so wrong…

But he'd been deep in it and he hadn't been able to see that forcing a relationship to work was a futile exercise and one destined to end in pain. He couldn't have foreseen the fire or Rebecca's death, but he could have predicted some sort of tragic outcome. In fact, he'd told Rebecca that on more than one occasion. She'd agreed with him. When she'd been sober, she'd always been apologetic, and she'd told him many times that she wanted a better life. She wanted to be a good mother. But then she used, and everything changed. She couldn't see outside of herself, her problems, her worries, her everything...

The sadness of her life hit him hard, and he swigged down another gulp of coffee. It wasn't his fault, but sometimes he still felt the guilt.

The idea of getting involved with another woman should be unthinkable. But it had become a lot more thinkable since he'd run into Gianna again.

Talking to her last night had felt good. He'd felt like himself again. And suddenly there was a future with possibilities and hope...

Not that Gianna was interested in that future.

Actually, he thought she was interested; she was just scared of making another mistake.

He was uncertain, too.

And there was Hailey to consider. If he could get her back into his life, how would she fit with Gianna? He knew they would like each other but putting Gianna in the middle of his very antagonistic relationship with the Carvers might not be good for her, or for Hailey, or even for himself.

He needed to put the brakes on, which was exactly what Gianna wanted him to do.

Finishing off his coffee, he pulled up in front of the lodge. Hunter and his fiancée Cassidy Ellison were standing on the porch.

He smiled at the happy grin on Hunter's face. Hunter was so taken with the beautiful blonde Cassidy that he could barely see straight.

Hunter and Cassidy met him as he got out of the truck.

"Zach," Cassidy said. "It's good to see you again."

"You, too," he said, giving her a hug. "I'm glad you made it."

"It took some doing, but I am finally here. Hunter has been telling me about your plans. They sound good. I can't wait to see the lodge transformed."

"And I can't wait to see your landscape plans."

She gave him a sheepish smile. "I have so many ideas; I keep changing my mind."

"I can relate to that."

"I told Cassidy about the train," Hunter said. "She's a fan."

"I love trains," she said. "I'm trying to think of ways I can incorporate the landscaping in that area around the train, maybe a small depot or some water features."

"Just remember, you two, we have a budget," Hunter put in. "And I have other investors whose money needs to be carefully spent. Since they're all family, I have to take care of them."

"Especially your grandfather," Cassidy put in. "That old man is scary."

Hunter laughed. "He's just gruff. He's a marshmallow on the inside. My grandmother twirls him around her little finger."

"How is your grandmother?" he asked. Eleanor Callaway was suffering from Alzheimer's, which was very hard on the family.

"She's the same, maybe a little worse," Hunter admitted. "But we cherish the good days."

"I actually saw her right before I flew to Denver," Cassidy said. "She was visiting with Hunter's mom, Sharon, his sister, Kate, and his cousin Emma. Those women talk a lot. I got quite a bit of family gossip," she added, smiling at Hunter. "Did you know that Dylan and Tori are expecting a baby?"

"No way. Dylan hasn't said a word."

"They were waiting for the three-month mark, which was yesterday. I told them I'd let you in on the big news."

"That's great," Hunter said. "I'll be an uncle again."

"Congratulations," he said. "The Callaway family keeps getting bigger."

"It's always fun to welcome a new member." Hunter paused as a car came down the drive, blowing up a wave of dust. "Who's this?"

"That's Mitch Carver," he said, his pulse speeding up. "I'm sure he's here to talk to me. I saw Hailey for the first time yesterday."

Surprise flared in Hunter's eyes. "I didn't think that was going to happen."

"I'll fill you in later. Can I meet you inside?"

"Take your time," Hunter said, as he and Cassidy headed toward the lodge.

Mitch got out of his car. "What the hell happened?" he asked, as he took off his sunglasses and gave him a perplexed look. "You were at the park with Hailey yesterday?"

"Your mother told you?"

"Hailey told me first and then my mother confirmed it. Apparently, my dad is still unaware, but that won't last long. Hailey can't stop talking about you. I heard all about how you're moving to Whisper Lake and getting a house and how she's going to live with you again."

"That's not exactly how it went down."

"Well, that's what Hailey took away from your conversation. My mom looked physically ill during the discussion. When I asked her about it, she just said something about how she couldn't stop you from seeing Hailey. What's going on?"

"Your mother agreed to let me meet Hailey at the park."

"How? When? Why?" Mitch planted his hands on his waist, confusion in his eyes. "When I saw you on Sunday, everything was the same. What changed yesterday?"

"Your mother had a change of heart. We're still taking things slow. She wants time to get Ron on board."

"What aren't you telling me?"

"Look, she decided it was in Hailey's best interests to see me. I would think you'd be happy about it."

"I'm trying to be happy, but I feel like I'm missing something."

"If you want to know why your mother changed her opinion, you should talk to her."

"Like I said, I did, but she wasn't talking back."

"Did she mention anything about looking for Rebecca's old diary?"

Mitch's gaze narrowed. "No, but that would explain her ransacking of Rebecca's room. Why does she care about an old diary?"

"I think she's afraid Rebecca wrote something down that doesn't reflect well on her or your father."

"Is that what she said?"

"It's what I inferred. What do you think?"

Mitch stared back at him, an uneasy look in his eyes. "I don't know."

"Seems like there's something on your mind, Mitch."

"Rebecca and my mom were tight as could be when we were really young. But when Becca got into her teens, they argued over everything. They seemed to hate each other at times. I thought it was just teenage rebellion, but maybe there was more to it than that. When Becca left home after high school, she pulled me aside and said in a very serious voice that I should call her if I ever felt scared. It didn't matter what time it was, or who I was afraid of, I could always call her, and she would come. I didn't know what she meant. I wasn't feeling scared about anything."

His gut tightened at Mitch's words. "It sounds like she was trying to warn you about something or someone."

"Or she was just being a protective big sister."

"I know she cared about you a lot, Mitch."

"I cared about her, too, but Rebecca was a mystery in so many ways. I don't know that I ever knew her, or that anyone did. Sorry if that sounds harsh, since you lived with her…"

"It's not harsh. I don't think I knew her, either. But that's because she didn't want me to know her deepest secrets."

"I wish she'd felt free to talk to me. Maybe she'd still be alive."

"Don't go down that road, Mitch."

"Too late. I've been down and back a million times," he said with a sigh. "Anyway, Becca is gone, and her secrets died with her. They don't matter anymore."

"They might matter, Mitch. I don't want your mother doing the same number on Hailey that she did on Rebecca."

"I don't think she did anything that bad. It wasn't like Rebecca never spoke to my mom or dad. They didn't see each other often, and Becca never came back to Whisper Lake, but they weren't completely estranged. Anyway, it appears that you don't need my intervention anymore. I'm actually happy not to be in the middle."

"I hated putting you there. Any thoughts on whether your mom will be able to get your dad on board with me being in Hailey's life?"

"None whatsoever. But if she doesn't talk to him soon, Hailey will. One way or another, he's going to find out, and then who knows what hell will break loose?"

"I've figured out your mystery," Keira told Gianna as she set her purse down on the front counter at the antiques store a little before five on Tuesday.

"What mystery is that?" she asked warily.

"The girl in the photo wearing your locket—what else would I be talking about?"

"Oh, right. What about her?"

"My mom said her name was Jill. Well, I pressed my mother a bit more today, and she told me that the girl's name was Jill Harper. Her mother was Theresa Harper."

"Theresa Harper?" she echoed in surprise. "The dining hall director from the camp—that Theresa Harper?"

"Yes. She lives on the north shore, and I found her address." Keira slid a piece of paper across the counter.

"This is amazing," she said, her heart racing. "What about Jill? Do you know where she is?"

"I couldn't find her anywhere in this area, but I'm sure her mother knows where she is. You can start with her."

She stared down at the address, feeling emotionally torn. She'd wanted a clue, but now that she had one…

"Is something wrong?" Keira asked.

She lifted her head to meet Keira's inquiring gaze. "I never thought I'd actually get a lead."

"This is what you wanted, isn't it?"

"I think so. I'm scared."

"I can understand that. But I also know this question has been plaguing you your entire life."

"It has always been in the back of my mind," she admitted.

"Then talk to Theresa Harper. You may find out her daughter has nothing to do with you."

"You're right. Just because she had a similar locket doesn't mean anything."

"Exactly. Or Jill could be your mom. Either way, you have to know, Gianna."

"I will look into this tomorrow. Thank you, Keira. This is huge. I owe you one."

"I'm glad you said that, because I need a favor. It's not really for me, but I need your help."

"With what?"

"An intervention. I want you to go to the café with me now and convince Chloe to stop working. I went by there at lunch and she was practically asleep on her feet. She looks horrible, and she said something to me about not having heard from Kevin in the last few days. I tried to talk her into going home, but she wasn't listening. I say we kidnap her, take her out to dinner, get her mind off Kevin, and encourage her to start taking it a little easier."

"I'm on board, but what about the dinner rush at the café? Is Chloe the only one there? Maybe she can't leave."

"Marina is working today, and she told me she has the café covered, but Chloe won't stay home."

"Then let's go get her," she said, grabbing her bag.

"Great. My car is outside. I'll drive."

Minutes later, they got into a sleek, white BMW, and Gianna couldn't help but appreciate the gorgeous leather detail. "This is very luxurious."

"It helps my street cred as a successful real-estate agent," Keira said with a grin. "I sometimes drive clients around, and I want them to think I'm good at my job."

"From what I hear, you are good at your job. But is Whisper Lake big enough for you?"

"There are quite a few new houses going up these days, especially at Sandy Point and on the west shore. But I also work properties in Chambers and Paxmore," she said, referring to the new housing developments in nearby suburbs.

"You must be extremely busy."

"I am. I like my job. It was never my dream, you know that. But since Mom's accident, I had to step up and take over her business, and I discovered I'm good at it."

"I'm really glad, Keira. I felt bad that you had to give up your dreams of being a fashion designer. You worked so hard to get your degree and then you had your dream job in New York. I really admire you for being willing to give it all up for your mom."

"It's been her and me against the world for as long as I can remember. And it will always be that way. I just want her to be completely better."

"So do I."

"And I'm not the only one willing to sacrifice for family. You're doing that for your aunt."

"I'm not as selfless as you, Keira. There was a big part of me that jumped at the chance to help Aunt Lois because it got me out of LA. The last three months have been difficult. I was looking for a new job, but nothing was right. My friends—well, a lot of them were really Jeff's friends, so they were gone. I lost my coworker friendships, because they're still at Jeff's company. I was floundering."

"I'm sorry. What went wrong with Jeff? You've never told me much."

"It wasn't one thing; it was a lot of things. I felt like I was compromising a lot, and he wasn't compromising at all. I had to fit into his life; it wasn't going to work the other way."

"Which is why he never made time to see me and Hannah when we visited you last year."

"He had trouble making time for my friends, my needs." She sighed. "I have made so many mistakes when it comes to men. I don't know what is wrong with me. I keep picking the wrong guys."

"We've all done that."

"Yes, but you figure out they're wrong before you get engaged."

"Why do you think you don't?"

"Because I've been too impatient to get to the next part of my life. I've always wanted to skip ahead, so I ignored the little things, the nagging doubts. But when the wedding date became real, when deposits were put down, that's when my brain woke up. So that's it. I'm done with love."

Keira smiled. "Sure you are."

"I mean it. I'm not going to fall again."

"Have you told your face that? Because the way you looked at Zach Barrington the other day..."

She frowned. "I didn't look at him in any particular way. Jeez, you sound just like Hannah."

"And probably anyone else who saw you together."

"We were hardly together at your party."

"That's right. You tried like hell to avoid each other. I swear I thought I was back at camp, watching the two of you dance around each other the way you did in the beginning of your relationship. You couldn't trust that the cutest boy at camp was interested in you."

"And he probably didn't have a clue why he wanted to hang out with the most awkward girl there," she said dryly.

"He saw the real you."

"He did," she admitted with a sigh.

"You saw the real him, too. Until you convinced yourself that he'd stolen your necklace and everything about your relationship was a lie."

"I had solid evidence—or I thought I did at the time."

"No, you had fear. I didn't see it then, and I'm sure you didn't either, because we were stupid girls, and you were caught up in your first real love. But I think you jumped on the missing necklace as a way to push Zach away."

"In retrospect, that might be true. But, like you said, I didn't know it at the time."

Keira shot her a look. "So, what now?"

"Nothing. I'm busy with the store and Zach has his work and other issues to deal with."

"Is one of those issues Rebecca's daughter? I heard he's trying to get the Carvers to let him see the child."

"Yes, he is, and he deserves to be in that little girl's life. He adores her. He really just wants to do right by her. The Carvers need to get over their own egos and let him in."

"Wow, you have changed your mind about him."

"He's a good guy, and I'm impressed with how hard he's fighting for this kid who's not even his."

"It does seem admirable. It also sounds like he's going to be in town awhile, as are you," she added pointedly.

"Stop trying to make this more than it is."

"You should stop trying to make it less than it is, Gianna."

"It's not the right time."

"You can have fun with him without getting engaged."

"Apparently, I can't," she said with a wry smile.

Keira laughed. "If he proposes, just say no."

"It's not going to get that far."

"So, it's going to get somewhere?"

"I don't know. You are so pushy," she complained.

"I like to close deals."

"Well, this deal is not even open."

"Sure it is. But I will back off—for now," Keira added, as she parked the car. "I'm glad to have you home, Gianna. I've missed you. Maybe you should think about staying here permanently."

"My life is in LA."

"Your life *was* in LA. It could be anywhere now. But enough about you. Let's go butt into Chloe's business."

"Yes, let's do that," she agreed, eager to get herself off the hot seat.

Keira grinned. "It's what friends do."

―――――――

"I'm fine. I'm working," Chloe protested, as Gianna and Keira each grabbed one of her arms. "Let me go."

"Nope. This is an intervention," Keira said firmly.

"It's a kidnapping," Chloe complained. "And I need to get my purse."

"I've got it," Gianna said, as Marina handed her Chloe's purse.

"Traitor," Chloe told Marina.

"You need a break," Marina said.

"It's the dinner rush. I can't leave," Chloe replied, waving her hand toward the dozen tables that were all filled.

"I have everything under control," Marina assured her.

"So, you're coming with us," Keira said, as they walked Chloe out the front door to a handful of applause from the locals, who all urged Chloe to get some rest.

"I have my car. I can drive myself home," Chloe said with annoyance, as they moved down the street.

"I'm driving," Keira said, opening her car door for Chloe. "Get in."

"You're so damn bossy. I'll take the back."

"Just to be contrary?" Keira asked, as Chloe got into the back-seat. Keira rolled her eyes at Gianna. "The hormones have made her crazy."

"I'm not crazy; I'm annoyed," Chloe retorted, as Gianna and Keira got in the car. "This kidnapping intervention better involve food, because I was just going to make myself a sandwich."

"You need to eat something you didn't have to prepare or serve," Keira said. "We're going to Delmonico's."

"Ooh, pizza," Gianna said, happy at that thought.

"Hannah is going to meet us there," Keira added.

"Another traitor," Chloe muttered. "I guess Delmonico's is fine, although, they are one of my competitors."

"Your café is always packed," she said, turning in her seat so she could see Chloe. "I don't think you have to worry."

"It's packed because I work hard. When I'm not there, things slack off."

"You're not going to be there once you have this baby—at least not for a few months," she pointed out. "Right?"

"I don't know. It depends on how much leave Kevin gets." As

Chloe finished speaking, she started blinking her eyes really fast, and then her mouth crumpled.

"Chloe, what's wrong?" she asked in alarm. "Are you crying?"

"It's the hormones," Chloe said, between short little sobs.

"I'm pulling over." Keira stopped on the side of the street.

"We can keep driving," Chloe said, dabbing at her eyes with her fingers. "The waterworks will pass soon enough. I'm just feeling emotional because… Oh, it doesn't matter."

"What's going on?" Gianna asked.

Chloe stared back at them. "I haven't heard from Kevin since Saturday. It's been three days. He rarely stays out of touch this long, especially now when I'm so close to my due date. He has to be on a mission. That's the only reason he wouldn't call or text or email. I just don't know when he's coming back. And I'm freaking out."

Gianna's heart went out to Chloe. She always seemed to have her life together, but there was obviously a lot going on underneath the surface. "I'm sorry, Chloe. I'm sure he'll call as soon as he can."

"I want it to happen already. The longer he's out of touch, the worse my imagination gets."

"He's going to be fine," Keira said firmly. "And so are you. You need to stop being so stubbornly independent and let us be there for you. You're not alone, Chloe. We're here. And half the damn town would drop everything to help you."

Chloe gave them a watery smile. "Everyone is being really nice. I shouldn't complain."

"You can complain," Gianna said. "You can go off on a really long rant about how unfair it is that you have to be nine months pregnant and all by yourself because of the damn army."

"The damn army," Chloe echoed. "Unfortunately, Kevin loves everything about it."

"He doesn't love it more than you."

"Sometimes I'm not so sure. He sees his team more than he sees me. But I knew what I was getting into, and I love him." She drew in a breath and let it out. "I'm okay. We can go to the restaurant now. Besides being emotional, I am actually hungry. And, by the way, you guys are lousy kidnappers, but you're really good friends."

"We're not that lousy—we got you in the car," Keira said, as she pulled back onto the roadway.

"Only because I didn't want to make a scene at the café."

"Everyone cheered us on for getting you out of there," Gianna reminded her.

"That's because people are too worried about me. I'm fine—most of the time."

"Well, when you're not fine, you should tell us."

"I don't want to bother anyone. You all have your own lives, your own challenges."

"That doesn't matter," Keira assured her.

"Let's talk about something more cheerful," Chloe said. "I heard the barbecue at your house was amazing, Keira."

"It was great, but we missed you."

"I know. I'm sorry."

"You don't have to apologize, although you did miss Gianna flirting with her camp boyfriend."

"Really?" Chloe asked with interest. "Let's talk about that."

"I know I'm a good distraction," she said. "But let's not talk about Zach."

"Gianna likes him," Keira said, ignoring her.

"I saw that the other night at the bar," Chloe replied. "When Zach arrived, neither one of you could look anywhere else."

"That's how they were at the party. I can't blame Gianna," Keira said. "Because Zach is even hotter now than when we were teenagers. My God, that man is mouthwatering. I bet he's a great kisser."

"Stop," Gianna said, feeling her cheeks heat up. "Nothing is going to happen between Zach and me. We're just friends."

"Friends who want to have sex," Keira said.

Gianna leaned over and turned on the radio full blast. "I think we need some music," she yelled.

Keira laughed. "You can drown me out, but it doesn't make what I say any less true."

CHAPTER SEVENTEEN

THE TRUTH WILL SET you free. Gianna stared at the framed, needle-pointed saying that a customer had just placed on the counter, feeling like the message was meant more for her than the elderly woman who'd handed her ten dollars for it.

"Are you all right?" the woman asked.

"Sorry. Here's your change."

"Thank you. This will go perfectly in my grandson's bedroom. He tends to bend the truth a lot. I think he could use a reminder every night before he goes to sleep."

Somehow, she didn't think the woman's grandson would appreciate the homespun art, but that wasn't for her to say.

As the woman left, she glanced at her watch. It was three o'clock on Wednesday afternoon, and she was quickly running out of time to make the decision that had been rolling around in her head all day. She pulled out the piece of paper with Theresa Harper's address on it. If she wanted to get to the other side of the lake, now was the time to go.

"Do you have somewhere else to be?" Nora asked, as she joined her behind the counter with a quizzical smile. "You've been checking your watch all day."

"I have an errand to run. Are you okay to stay until closing?"

"I was planning on it. Feel free to leave whenever you need to."

"Thanks." She'd just grabbed her purse when the door opened, and Zach walked in. A happy wave ran through her. Keira was right. She didn't just want to be friends with Zach. And even if she kept lying to everyone else, she needed to be honest with herself. She hadn't seen him the day before, and she'd missed him way too much. She didn't know what she was going to do about that, but maybe admitting that small truth to herself would set her free.

"Hey," he said, giving her a warm smile.

"What are you doing here?"

"I was in the neighborhood. How are things going?"

"Not too busy today. I was actually just about to leave." She was very aware of Nora's interested smile. Nora was a fantastic part-time employee, and also a fantastic gossip. Whatever conversation she was going to have with Zach she didn't want to have in front of Nora. "I'll see you tomorrow," she told the older woman.

"I'll be in early," Nora said. "I have to leave at one, so why don't you come in a little later if you like?"

"That sounds good. Thanks." Her truck was in the back, but she'd finish her conversation with Zach and then get it.

"Where are you headed?" Zach asked, as they reached the sidewalk.

"Well, I'm still debating…"

He gave her a curious look. "What does that mean?"

"Keira believes the girl in the photo is Jill Harper, Theresa Harper's daughter."

"Harper?" he muttered, his brows knitting together. "That name sounds familiar."

"That's because Theresa Harper was in charge of the camp dining hall when we were there. We called her the Dragon Lady, because she was always spitting mad at someone, often you."

"Right," he said with a grin. "I remember her. She did not like my opinion of the mashed potatoes."

"Which were always lumpy."

"She's the mother of the girl in the photo?"

"I think so, but I need to talk to her. She lives on the north shore. Keira got her address for me. I just have to decide what I want to do."

"What you want to do?" he echoed. "You're going to go there and ask her if Jill is your mother."

She sucked in a quick breath. "You make it sound easy."

"It's not easy, but it's necessary, and I'm going with you. In fact, I'll drive."

"I don't know, Zach."

"I have time, and I owe you a favor for helping me with Helen."

She hesitated. It would be nice to have support. But bringing Zach along was the opposite of putting distance between them.

"Come on, Gianna. What's the problem?" he asked.

"There's more than one actually."

"Well, give me the first one."

"There's a chance that we'll get to Theresa's house and I'll chicken out, and this whole trip could be a waste of time."

He nodded. "If you want to bail, I won't judge you."

"Really? You won't encourage me to get past my fear?"

"I didn't say I wouldn't encourage you; I said I wouldn't judge you on whatever decision you make. But this is ultimately up to you, Gianna. What else are you worried about?"

"You."

He gazed back at her with his warm green eyes. "Nothing will ever happen that you don't want to happen."

"That's the problem. When you're around, I want things to happen that shouldn't."

He smiled. "As far as I'm concerned, we're just going for a drive, one that could potentially change the course of your life, but just a drive."

"Thanks for that added bit of pressure."

"My truck is right here. Are we going?"

"Yes, but if I decide not to go through with it, you will keep your mouth shut."

"Deal. But I think you have more courage than you think."

"We're going to find out."

It was another beautiful summer afternoon and as they drove the winding two-lane highway around the west side of the lake, Gianna rolled her window down and let the warm air blow through the truck. She was nervous about what was to come. And she wasn't sure she had nearly as much courage as Zach thought she had.

Was she really ready to change her life in a profound way?

That question ran around in her head for a good twenty minutes.

Zach seemed happy enough to let her wallow in her thoughts, but eventually she needed a distraction. "Did you see Hailey today?"

"No. I haven't seen her since Monday at the park. I talked to her last night before she went to bed, but it wasn't an easy conversation. She kept asking me when she was going to see me again, and I had no answer for her. When I got Helen back on the phone, she said to call her today, and she would speak to me about another visit. But she didn't answer my call today. I left her three messages."

"What do you think is going on?"

"I think she doesn't want to tell Ron she has changed her mind about me, but he needs to be on board, or this won't work."

"Have you threatened to tell Ron about what she did?"

"I'm trying to avoid any more threats, but it might come to that."

"I wish I could do more to help."

"Thanks. I just have to be patient, one day at a time. It's damn hard to do."

"I know."

"Did you tell your mom about Theresa Harper and her daughter Jill?" he asked, flinging her a quick look.

"No. I thought about it. I spoke to my mom earlier today, but I couldn't get the words out. And she was busy with work, so it didn't seem like the right time."

"I walked by your parents' store the other day. It was packed with people."

"Summer is their busiest season with all the lake activities. They rent boats, kayaks, Jet Skis, canoes, paddleboards and they sell all the gear needed for a great day on the lake."

"We should take a boat out sometime. I haven't been on the lake since camp."

"You'd enjoy it."

"Maybe this weekend."

"Maybe," she said, not wanting to make any more plans at the moment. "Adam is taking a big crowd out on the Fourth of July. I'm sure you and Hunter will be invited."

"That would be cool."

"Nothing better than seeing the fireworks from the water."

"I'll bet."

She gazed out at the view, tall trees framing beautiful images of the lake as they drove along the bluff high above the water. "Sometimes I forget how big the lake is."

"I've never driven all the way around it. In fact, I've never even been to the north shore."

"It's quieter, especially in the summer, when there's no snow. Most people who live there love the access to the north shore ski slopes. While the beaches are still beautiful, there aren't as many restaurants or shops, although there is a great steakhouse that my father loves. We often go there on his birthday, although I haven't actually been here on his birthday in a few years."

"Do you ever think about moving back permanently?"

"I've been thinking about it more often since I came home. I do miss my friends, the town, the feeling of community. I always thought I needed to be in a bigger city doing bigger things, but maybe that's not really what's going to make me happy." She sighed. "Honestly, I have no idea what I want to do with my life. I keep making plans, but they just don't work, and then I have to change them."

"Maybe you don't plan; you just live. Roll the dice, see where the numbers fall."

"That's a good way to end up broke," she said with a smile.

He grinned back at her. "You can always freelance or paint... any chance there's some color on that canvas yet?"

"No. I'm still not feeling inspired."

"Maybe it's the apartment. No offense, but it's kind of depressing. Why don't you go outside? In fact, why don't you go up to the camp? You can set up your easel in the meadow by that quiet cove, the way you used to."

She smiled at that memory. "That is a beautiful place, but I'm sure Hunter wouldn't want me wandering around up there."

"And I'm certain he wouldn't care at all. Think about it."

"I will." She sat up a little straighter as they turned off the main highway, her thoughts moving ahead to Theresa and what was coming next.

"According to the GPS, we're four minutes away," Zach said.

"Four minutes to decide," she muttered, tapping her fingers restlessly on her thighs. Then she picked up her bag and pulled out the photo. Jill Harper felt so familiar, and the locket was just like hers. *Was she really going to come this far and not ask the question?*

As Zach pulled up in front of a small A-frame house in a modest neighborhood of single-family homes on extra-large lots, she drew in a shaky breath. Her heart was pounding against her chest, her palms were sweaty, and when she saw the silver coupe in the driveway, she had a difficult time catching her breath.

She looked at Zach, feeling a wave of panic. "Can I really do this?"

"Do you want me to go with you?"

"I don't know. I should do this alone, right? She's my mother."

"Theresa Harper isn't your mother. She might be your grandmother, but not your mom."

"Jill could be here, too."

"She could be. I'm happy to wait in the truck. It's your call. Everything about this is your choice. I said I wouldn't judge, and I won't."

She licked her lips, the photo clutched in her hand. Then she turned her gaze to the house, but she couldn't seem to make herself move.

"You can do it," Zach said encouragingly. "The first step is the hardest. Just open the door. Then stand on the sidewalk. Small goals."

She opened the door, then turned back to him. "Will you come with me?"

"Of course." He got out of the truck and came around to her side, extending his hand. "Ready?"

"No, but I feel like it's now or never." She took his hand and stepped onto the sidewalk. They walked up to the door together, and she forced herself to press the bell.

The moment it took for Theresa Harper to answer the door felt like an eternity and a thousand doubts ran through her mind, each one making her want to run.

But then the door swung open, and she found herself face-to-face with the woman they'd once called the Dragon Lady. Theresa Harper's red hair was now streaked with gray. Her face was round and pale, and she'd put on a few pounds in the last fourteen years. But her dark eyes were still as cold and irritated as they'd always been when confronted with someone she didn't want to talk to.

"I'm not buying anything," Theresa said briskly.

"Uh, we're not selling anything," she said, stumbling over the words.

"Then what do you want?" Theresa's gaze darted from her to Zach, and then she frowned. "Do I know you?"

"Zach Barrington," he said.

"I remember that name. You were a troublemaker at camp. Tom had to kick you out." She turned to Gianna. "And you—you were the girl who accused him of stealing something."

"Yes, I'm Gianna Campbell."

"What are you both doing here?"

At Theresa's unfriendly glare, she found it difficult to find the words. "Uh, I'm trying to find someone, and I thought you might be able to help."

"I can't see how. I'm busy."

"Wait," she said desperately, as Theresa started to close the door. She pulled out the photograph. "Is this girl your daughter, Jill?"

Theresa didn't even look at the photo. "Why are you asking about Jill?"

"Because she has a necklace very much like one I used to have—the one I got from my biological mother." She drew in a shaky breath, surprised she'd actually gotten the words out.

"Where did you get this?" Theresa demanded.

"It was in the boxes I picked up from the camp for my aunt's antiques store. Is this Jill? Did she have a baby when she was a teenager? A child she gave up for adoption? Was that baby me?" Now that she'd found her voice, she couldn't stop talking.

Theresa's lips tightened as she met her gaze. "No. Jill didn't have a baby. I don't know who told you that. Jill was a good girl."

Her heart fell at Theresa's words. "You're sure she didn't have a child?"

"I would have known if she was pregnant. She was my only daughter. Whoever told you she had a baby was wrong. I'm sorry I can't help you." Theresa stepped back and shut the door.

"What the hell?" Zach muttered.

"It's not her," she said, staring at the door. "Jill isn't my mother." She turned to Zach. "The picture didn't mean anything."

"I don't know, Gianna."

"What don't you know? You heard what she said."

"I did. I'm just not sure I believe her."

"Why would she lie?"

"I can think of a few reasons. Want me to ring the bell again?"

She hesitated. "No. I don't think she'll suddenly change her answer. Let's go." She walked back to the truck, her mind racing as she got inside and fastened her seat belt.

Zach made no attempt to start the engine, his worried gaze fixed on her.

"You can drive," she said.

"I don't think you should give up so easily."

"What else can I do? Theresa probably won't answer the door

again, and if we stay here too long, I wouldn't put it past her to call the police. I asked my questions. She gave me answers. They weren't the ones I wanted, but it is what it is." She felt overwhelmingly disappointed. She'd really thought down deep in her gut that she was connected to the girl in the picture.

"You could go around Theresa," Zach said. "Find Jill. See if she has a different answer."

"I wouldn't know where to start."

"We'll figure it out together. The internet makes it easy to find people. And we have Jill's first and last name. We know who her mother is. We can find people who know both of them. Whisper Lake isn't that big."

He made good points. "Do you think it's worth it, Zach? Shouldn't I take what Theresa said at face value? If she's determined to keep Jill and me apart, maybe I should respect that."

"Why? This isn't between you and Theresa; it's between you and Jill. And, frankly, Theresa acted like she had something to hide. If she'd said it differently, maybe I would have believed her. But she was hostile and defensive, and she couldn't wait to get rid of us."

"True. But even when she was just the Dragon Lady, she was hostile and defensive. I think it's her personality."

"Only one way to find out."

"But do I have the right? Theresa could have lied because she's worried I'll disrupt Jill's life."

"Possibly. That's why you need to find out more about Jill."

"If she's married with kids and doesn't want anyone to know about the child she gave up, I need to respect that. I don't want to hurt anyone."

"I know you don't."

She blew out a breath. "I feel so frustrated and restless…this was a wasted trip."

"No, it wasn't. You just have to change directions, that's all."

"Let's go home."

He started the engine and drove down the street. They'd only gone a few blocks when she realized the last thing she wanted to do was sit in the truck for the next forty-five minutes. She had too much adrenaline coursing through her body.

"I've changed my mind," she said. "Can you turn right at the next light?"

He shot her a questioning look but gave a nod. "Sure. Where are we going?"

"I need to walk. There's a beach path along the lake. Do you mind? I can't sit right now."

"No problem. I wouldn't mind a walk, either."

A few minutes later, she directed Zach into a parking lot near a public beach. Then she jumped out of the truck and started walking. Zach caught up quickly with his long, athletic strides.

They strolled along the lakeside path for a good forty minutes, the air losing its heat as the sun slipped over the mountains just before six. When her legs got tired and she ran out of breath, she left the path and flopped down on the sand a few feet from the water.

Zach stretched out next to her. "I was wondering if we were going to walk all the way back to the south shore," he said lightly.

"Sorry. I needed to burn off some emotion."

"Understandable. I know you're disappointed."

"Actually, I've gotten past disappointment."

"Oh, yeah?" he asked a questioning look in his eyes. "Where are you at now?"

"Determined to find Jill."

"Good for you."

"Jill might give me the same answer Theresa did, but the more I've thought about how Theresa acted, the more I think she was hiding something. And it's not uncommon for the mother of a teenage girl to hide her daughter's pregnancy, especially thirty years ago. Theresa might have been ashamed that Jill had gotten pregnant at sixteen."

"More than likely."

"Isn't it strange to think the Dragon Lady could be my grandmother? I hope Jill isn't like her."

"But even if she is, you're determined," he reminded her.

"I am. I've been so indecisive about this subject for years, but now I feel like I have clarity. I know what I need to do." She took a breath, then added, "Thanks for having my back today, Zach."

"Happy to do it, but you are going to have to buy me dinner, because I'm starving, and it's a long drive back. I'm thinking that steakhouse you mentioned might be a good choice."

"Jackson's is very good. I could go for a steak. But let's take a few more minutes. It's a nice evening, and we have the beach to ourselves."

"I'm in no hurry. I think you should breathe deep and let the lake work its healing magic."

She did as he suggested, feeling better, calmer. "Good call. How do you always know what I need?"

Her question came out far more seriously than she intended. Zach's gaze darkened. "We have an unquestionable connection, Gianna."

"I know. No matter how much I want to deny it, there's something between us. In my mixed-up world where almost nothing makes sense, one thing does—you."

"I'm surprised you're admitting that. You've been pushing me away since I pulled you out of the water."

"Because I'm on a break. Because of all the mistakes I've made." As she gazed at his handsome face, a reckless wave of desire ran through her. "But I'm thinking about taking a break from my break."

"Oh, yeah?" he asked softly.

"Just a short one. Just enough time for…this." She leaned forward and pressed her mouth against his. She'd meant the kiss to be quick, teasing, playful, but the heat of Zach's lips, the desire coursing through her turned it into so much more.

In their need to get as close as possible, she tumbled onto her back, pulling Zach on top of her. She ran her hands under his shirt, loving the feel and the heat of his skin. She didn't care that she was getting sand in her hair or that there was an uncomfortable rock beneath her spine. All she could focus on was Zach.

He filled her senses. He took over the night. Every breath was filled with the musky scent of his aftershave. Every touch took the heat higher.

Finally, he lifted his head, his green eyes glittering in the twilight. He gazed down at her with so much emotion that her heart ached.

He was looking at her. He was seeing her—*the real her*, not just the woman she was now, but the girl she used to be.

She'd missed this connection, this very special, intense, one-of-a-kind connection.

Every other guy in her past faded deep into the background.

There was only Zach.

Maybe it had always been him. Maybe he was the one she'd been looking for in everyone else.

CHAPTER EIGHTEEN

ZACH COULD LOOK at Gianna forever. He'd thought that when he was sixteen, and he thought it even more now. Gianna's face had always been interesting—the curve of her brows, the tilt of her nose, the sweetness of her lips, and the stubbornness of her jaw. And her eyes were amazing—her beautiful brown eyes filled with gold sparks, that came alive when she was caught up in passion— for painting and for him.

There was passion in her gaze now, a very adult awareness that he really wanted to follow up on. But even as that thought crossed his mind, he heard voices in the distance. Turning his gaze away from Gianna, he saw a group of teens walking down the path, and within minutes they'd be upon them. Probably best not to give them some X-rated scene for them to pop on to social media.

He was disappointed by their arrival, but maybe it was better this way. He didn't want to just fool around with Gianna on the beach; he wanted more—a lot more, probably more than she wanted to give, maybe more than he had a right to want.

He moved off her and pulled down his shirt, wishing Gianna's hands were still heating up his skin.

Gianna sat up, running her fingers through her hair, releasing fine grains of sand. They scrambled to their feet as the kids passed by, and then by silent accord began walking back the way they'd come.

As the silence went on for a while, he wondered if Gianna was having regrets, even though she'd been the one to start things up.

They were almost back to the truck when she finally said, "Do you think it's strange that we can still be attracted to each other after so many years?"

"I think it's very cool. So many things don't last; I like it when something does."

She shot him a quick look. "But that something...well, who knows what it is?"

"I know this. I want you. And you want me."

She sucked in a quick breath. "Maybe that's true. But the question is what would we want beyond each other, beyond one night?"

"We could find out."

"Or we could not take this any further and not complicate our lives."

"Is that what you were thinking when you kissed me?"

"No, I was thinking to hell with it. You're so damned attractive; it's not fair."

He caught her by the arm and made her stop walking long enough to look at him. "You're beautiful, too, Gianna. Not just on the outside but also on the inside. I saw that a long time ago."

Her gaze filled with emotion. "I don't know how you did, but it's what made me fall for you."

He tipped her chin up once more and gave her another kiss, just because he could, and because he knew all too soon he might not have the chance.

She kissed him back, then pulled away. "This is madness, Zach. We need to get back to reality. Maybe we should skip dinner and just head home."

"No way. You owe me a steak. I'm collecting."

"Fine. We'll eat, then we'll go home."

"I like how you call Whisper Lake home."

"It always was my home, but it was never yours."

"It might be now."

"Well, now my home is in LA."

"Does it have to be?" he challenged.

"It should be. I have more opportunity there."

"But you have friends and family in Whisper Lake."

"I haven't made any final decisions."

"Good. I like that answer."

She gave him a helpless smile. "You should stop liking everything."

He grinned. "I can't help it when you're around. You make me feel…optimistic."

"You make me feel that way, too, and that is bad."

"Why?"

"Because I'm supposed to be doing penance for all my mistakes in the past, not feeling happy or looking forward to the future."

"Is that really what you think?" he asked curiously. "That you need to be punished for the failed engagements?"

"I hurt people with my actions. I feel like I should hurt, too."

"Do you hear how crazy that sounds?"

"When I say it out loud, yes," she said, as they began strolling down the path once more. "But it is how I feel. I have a lot of guilt. It weighs me down."

"You have to let it go, Gianna. You ended a few relationships, maybe after the point where they should have ended. But you did what made sense for the long run."

"Logically I know that, but I'm still angry with myself for the mistakes I made."

"I get it. I've had to deal with a lot of my own anger at myself and even at Rebecca. But since she died, since that fire, I have realized one inescapable truth. Life is short, and you shouldn't waste it. We can't change the past. But we have today and hopefully tomorrow. We can make those days anything we want. We can learn from our mistakes and try not to make the same ones again." He paused as they reached the truck. "Being with you feels right, and it's not something I expected at all. I had some negative feelings about you for a long time."

"I hated you, too," she admitted, giving him a smile to take the edge off her words. "But I hear that love and hate are two sides of the same coin. I probably couldn't have hated you if I hadn't..."

"Loved me?"

"Yes. And you loved me, too. Even though you tried to deny it to your friends."

"You're right. I did love you, Gianna."

He had to bite back the crazy thought that he might love her now. That would terrify her. Hell, it scared him, too. He had Hailey to think about. He had a career to figure out. Falling in love was the last thing he needed to do. He opened the door for her. "Shall we get that steak now?"

She seemed relieved by the change in topic. "Let's do that."

Dinner was fun—too much fun, Gianna thought, as they drove home just after nine.

The food had been wonderful, but the conversation even better. They'd opted for lighter topics during their meal, and she'd had a chance to get a fuller picture of Zach's life. He was passionate about his work, something she hadn't quite realized during all their discussions about the Carvers and little Hailey. He'd shown her a few photos on his phone of some of his jobs, and he'd definitely downplayed the complexity of his designs. She'd been truly impressed by his creativity.

She'd also learned more about his friends, including Hunter and his fiancée Cassidy, who she had yet to meet, and the big Callaway family, several of whom had invested in the camp. Besides the Callaways, Zach had a good group of friends at work and from his college days. He didn't seem to have many couple friends from his time with Rebecca, but she'd stayed away from that subject.

In return, she'd shared more of her life with him, not only her job, but also how often she'd gone to art museums on the weekends, spending hours in admiration of the masters, and seeking her own inspiration. As she spoke about art, she realized how little she had to say about her life with Jeff or before that with Victor. In retrospect, neither of those relationships had offered her as much satisfaction as a few hours at the Getty Museum, which made her decision to say yes to both men even more baffling. But she was tired of kicking herself. She needed to move on, get back to what mattered most, and that was her art.

Maybe tomorrow she'd drive up to the camp as Zach had suggested and see if her favorite cove could inspire her.

"Are you falling asleep on me?" Zach asked, breaking into the quiet.

She gave him a smile. "No, but I could. I feel very relaxed after all that food and wine. Sorry you had to limit yourself to one glass as our designated driver."

"That wasn't a problem. I'm glad you're not as stressed as you were after we left Theresa's house."

She'd almost put that whole encounter out of her head, but now it was back. "Thanks for breaking into my happy buzz with the reminder."

"Forget I said anything."

"It's fine. It is what it is. I'm still determined to find Jill. I was so scared of going to Theresa's house, but I don't feel the fear anymore. I'm not sure why."

"Don't question it, just go with it."

As her phone buzzed, she dug into her purse to grab it. She frowned as she read the short text message.

"Everything okay?" he asked.

"No. Keira is at Chloe's house. Chloe is having a freak-out. Another day has gone by without hearing from Kevin. She hasn't talked to him since Saturday, and she's really worried about him." She texted back that she could come over in about twenty minutes.

Keira replied with a heartfelt thanks and a sad face emoji.

"Could you drop me at Chloe's?" she asked. "It will be faster. Keira can give me a ride home from there."

"Of course. Is there reason to be concerned about Chloe's husband?"

"I don't know. Chloe told me last night that he's always out of touch when he's on a mission, but they don't usually last more than two or three days. She's only weeks away from her due date, so I think she's starting to panic that he won't be back in time. She's had to do the entire pregnancy alone. She didn't find out she was having a baby until after he was deployed."

"That's rough."

"I'm sure if something had gone wrong, they'd tell her, right?"

"Someone would," he said grimly.

She noted the hardening of his profile. "I'm sorry. This conversation is reminding you of your father."

"It is. I remember very clearly the day that two men in uniform came to my house. I had just gotten home from basketball practice. My brother was watching TV in the kitchen. We were both having a snack. Mom was thinking about making dinner. It was like every other day, only my mom was a little more stressed out than usual, because, like Chloe, she hadn't heard from my dad in a few days. And then the doorbell rang. I still didn't think anything of it. It wasn't until she screamed that I got out of my chair and ran down the hall. She had collapsed in the chaplain's arms. She was crying like I'd never heard her cry before. I didn't even hear what anyone said. Seeing her like that, like her whole world had ended, told me all I needed to know."

"How awful," she breathed.

"My little brother came running down the hall. He grabbed my arm, asking me what was going on. I looked at the faces of the two men and saw the pity in their eyes."

A knot filled her throat as she pictured two confused, terrified kids holding each other on the worst day of their lives. She'd heard some of the story before when they'd first been together at camp, but she didn't remember him telling her so many of the details. "I'm so sorry, Zach. I can't even imagine what that felt like."

"You can't imagine, and you don't want to."

"I hope Chloe doesn't have to go through that."

"Me, too. I could see she was worried the other day when I saw her at the café. She was trying not to complain, desperately trying to be the stoic army wife, but when I told her that I'd grown up with a dad just like her husband, she let her guard down and told me how she really felt."

"Really? How does she feel?"

"Scared, mad that he's not with her, a little resentful that she's had to be pregnant alone, wondering if he loves her as much as he loves his job."

"Wow, you got a lot out of her. I guess that's not surprising. You understand better than anyone what she's worried about."

"I do. I lived her worst fear. I wasn't in the exact position that she and my mother were in, but I was part of it. But understanding doesn't help that much. It doesn't change anything for her."

"It probably helps more than you think. The rest of us have no idea what her fears are, but you do. When we get to the house, you should come in and talk to her."

"We'll see. This sounds more like a girlfriend thing."

"It's just a friend thing. And, clearly, you're friends."

"I'd like to think so." He paused. "It's great that you've stayed in touch with your childhood friends even though you've been gone."

"I'm lucky to have them. I wasn't the best friend the last couple of years, but everyone stuck with me."

"You were away. It's harder with distance to keep the relationships going."

"It wasn't only the distance. They were all asked to be bridesmaids in my first two weddings. When I broke off the first one, they'd already bought their dresses and thrown me a bachelorette party. For the second engagement, they'd bought yet another dress before I called things off."

"What about the third time?"

"I wasn't going to have a bridal party; I was just going to ask Chloe to be my maid of honor, but I was waiting until the last minute to do that. I never got that far. My one saving grace; I didn't waste anyone else's money or time with my last engagement. I wouldn't have blamed them if they'd decided to delete me from their friend list, but somehow they didn't."

"Good friends accept you for who you are. I'm sure you do the same for them."

"They haven't put me to the test like I've done to them."

"They may still do that." He paused as they drove into downtown Whisper Lake. "Do you want to give me directions to Chloe's house?"

"Yes. It's a few blocks from the café."

When they arrived, she said, "Why don't you come in for a minute? You don't have to stay if you're uncomfortable, but you might be able to comfort Chloe in a way that Keira and I can't—if you don't mind."

"I'll do what I can."

They walked up to the house together. When Keira opened the door, her relief was followed by curiosity as her gaze moved from Gianna to Zach.

"Zach was with me when you texted," Gianna quickly explained. "He gave me a ride."

"Sure. And I would like to hear more about that. But Chloe is crying, and I can't get her to stop. Hannah is at work, so she can't come over. I haven't been able to reach Lizzie or Chelsea. I'm at my wit's end. Chloe is spiraling, rambling on about every fear known to an army wife, and I don't know what to say."

"That's why Zach is coming in. His mom was an army wife, and his dad was killed in action. He knows what that fear feels like."

"I'm sorry. I don't think I ever knew that," Keira said. "Please come in."

When they entered the living room, her heart twisted at the sight of Chloe's tear-stained face. "Oh, Chloe," she said, moving over to the armchair where her friend was sitting. "What can I do?"

"Nothing," she said with a sob, twisting a soggy tissue in one hand. "I think something terrible has happened to Kevin. He's not coming home. He's not going to meet our baby. He won't be a father or a husband. He's just going to die a soldier, and I'll be alone." A flood of sobs followed her words.

Gianna looked back at Keira and Zach, not sure what to say.

Zach moved forward. He sat down on the ottoman facing Chloe. "Hey," he said softly.

"Did you come with Gianna?" Chloe asked, sniffing after every word.

"I did. I understand you haven't heard from Kevin."

"Not since Saturday—four days. It's rarely this long."

"You know that if something was really wrong, someone would call you."

Chloe stared back at him. "What if they don't want to tell me?"

"They'd still tell you."

"Like they told your mom?"

He nodded, his profile somber. "Yes. But there were other times when she felt just like you do now, and nothing bad had happened."

"I'm hoping this is like that."

"That's all you can do, Chloe. Keep the faith. I can't make you promises. You wouldn't believe them even if I tried. But I can tell you this. You will get through this night. The sun will come up. It will be a new day, and there will be hope again."

"I'd like it to be a new day. I'd like the sun to be up now. And I'd love to feel hopeful again."

"You'll get there."

"You really think I'm worrying for nothing?" Chloe asked.

"Not for nothing—for yourself and for your baby. But your child doesn't need you to worry. He or she—"

"It's a boy," Chloe interrupted. "But we don't have a name yet."

"Your son doesn't need a name right now; he just needs you. And you're here. You're protecting him. He's safe."

Chloe put her hand on her abdomen. "I know being upset isn't good for him. I can usually handle the loneliness, but it hit me hard tonight."

"Tell me about Kevin," Zach said.

"He's pretty amazing. We fell in love in high school."

As Chloe started to talk about happier days, Keira tipped her head toward the kitchen, and Gianna followed her down the short hallway.

"Wow," Keira said as they huddled by the kitchen island. "Zach is amazing."

"He is really good with her."

"He's like magic. I didn't think she'd ever stop crying."

"Well, he has been in her shoes."

"I think you told me his dad had died, but I don't remember hearing that he was a soldier."

"Zach didn't want anyone to know."

"But he told you."

"Well, we talked about everything. He was angry when he got to camp because he was reeling from his father's death. He didn't know what to do with all that emotion. That's why he was so wild."

"But his anger faded when he fell for you," Keira said.

"I think talking to me helped," she admitted.

"Keira tilted her head, giving Gianna a speculative look. "What were you doing with him tonight?"

"Oh, right. You don't know."

"Know what?"

"He went with me to see Theresa Harper."

Keira's eyebrows shot up. "You told him about Theresa? And you actually went to speak to her?"

"Yes to both questions. Zach has always known how much I've wanted to find my biological mother, and he came by the store just as I was leaving, so he offered to drive me."

"What happened? What did Theresa say?"

"She told me that Jill was never pregnant and I'm not her kid. She was angry and unpleasant, and then she slammed the door in my face."

Keira's mouth turned down into a disappointed frown. "I'm sorry. I was hoping for a different outcome."

"The thing is, Keira, I'm almost certain that Theresa was lying. Zach thinks so, too."

"Really? Why would she lie?"

"To protect the secret? I don't know, but I need to find Jill. Do you think your mother might be able to recall the last name of Jill's friend, Tammy?"

"I can ask her again. And I could help you dig a little deeper to find Jill." Keira paused. "I wonder if Adam Cole could help you. He's a cop. He has access to police files."

"Probably not to help me find my biological mother."

"He still might be able to give you a few tips on how to search for her on the internet."

"That's true. I'll ask him tomorrow. Should we get back to Chloe?"

"In a second," Keira said with a sparkle in her eye. "Did you kiss Zach again?"

"Keira," she protested.

"That's my name, not an answer."

"I don't kiss and tell."

"Yes, you do. I've heard about every first kiss you've ever had, and you've heard about mine."

"First kiss maybe, but not all the rest," she said with a grin.

"So there have been a lot more—I knew it. You two are smoking hot together. I shouldn't have called you. If I hadn't, you might be ending this night on a very different note."

"I was not going to sleep with him tonight."

"Not tonight, but maybe tomorrow…"

"Stop. I'm not thinking that far ahead."

"That far ahead?" Keira echoed. "Tomorrow is in like two hours."

"The truth is…" Her voice fell away as she ran out of words.

"What?" Keira prodded. "What is the truth?"

"I don't know what to do about him," she confessed. "I like him —a lot. But it's too soon after everything that happened with Jeff. I should be living like a nun for the next three years."

"Who says?"

"It just feels like I'm going to fall again way too fast."

"Too fast?" Keira challenged. "You fell in love with Zach fourteen years ago. That wasn't your time. Maybe it is now."

"Right now, I'm going to focus on Chloe. Let's get back to her."

"Fine. But while you can run away from my questions, you can't escape your feelings."

"Well, I'm going to try."

When they returned to the living room, Gianna was stunned to see that Chloe was laughing.

"What's going on?" she asked.

"Zach just told me a funny story," Chloe replied.

"Really?" she asked, turning a questioning gaze on him.

"It's funnier if you know the army," he said, as he got to his feet. "I'm going to take off now. Do you want a ride home, Gianna?"

"I'll hang out here for a while. Keira will drop me off later."

"All right. Chloe, I'll see you later."

"Thank you, Zach," Chloe said with heartfelt appreciation. "You helped a lot."

"Any time."

"I'll walk you out," Gianna offered. When they reached the front door, she said, "Thanks again, Zach. You were amazing and not just with Chloe. Having you with me on this quest for my biological mom meant a lot to me."

"I'm glad I could be there for you. Will I see you tomorrow?"

"Maybe. I'm thinking I might paint in the morning, or at least try."

"At the cove?"

"We'll see. What about you?"

"I'll work my way up to the camp at some point, but I want to stop by the Carvers' house in the morning and try to see Hailey."

"Good luck."

He gave her a quick kiss. "I'll talk to you soon."

"Bye." She closed the door after him and walked back into the living room.

"Did he kiss you good night?" Keira asked, with a mischievous smile.

"You're acting fourteen again, Keira." She sat down across from Chloe. "I'm glad you're feeling better."

"Zach is very easy to talk to."

"He is. I'm happy the two of you could connect."

"I'm sorry you both had to run over here. I clearly interrupted something between you and Zach."

"You really didn't. Don't give it another thought."

"You can both go home. It's late. And I'm tired," Chloe added with a yawn. "I'll be okay. I'll feel better tomorrow."

"I know you will," she assured her, hoping that tomorrow would bring Chloe a call from Kevin. She glanced at Keira. "Should we go?"

Keira nodded. "But we're both just a phone call away, Chloe. Remember that."

"I will. I do need one more favor before you go," Chloe said.

"What's that?" Gianna asked.

"Help me to my feet." Chloe extended her arms.

She laughed and grabbed Chloe's hand, helping her up. Then she gave her a hug, and Keira did the same.

"No more Zach talk," she said, as she and Keira walked out to the car.

"I wasn't going to say anything more about him."

"Good."

"But I did want to say that I'm glad you're back, Gianna. And I think you should consider staying. I've missed you."

"I've missed you, too. I don't know what I'm going to do yet."

"So, Whisper Lake might be an option?"

"We'll see."

CHAPTER NINETEEN

ZACH DROVE TO THE CARVERS' house on Thursday morning, waiting until after nine, hoping that he'd catch Helen and Hailey on their own once Ron was off to work. Besides being on the city council, he also worked as an insurance broker, with an office on Front Street.

He rang the bell, hoping that Helen would let him in, but he was nervous that his leverage was slipping. He hadn't talked to Hailey at all yesterday and he hadn't seen her since Monday. That was too long.

The door opened slightly, and Helen peered out, frowning when she saw him. "What are you doing here, Zach? You can't just show up without calling first."

"I called you twice yesterday; you didn't call back. I want to see Hailey."

"She's sleeping."

"No, she's not. She never sleeps past eight."

As if on cue, he heard Hailey's voice. "Grandma, who are you talking to?"

He pushed his way into the house. Hailey's face lit up when she saw him. She ran forward, jumping into his arms. "Zach," she said with delight. "You're back. Grandma said you went away on business."

"Really?" he asked, shooting Helen a pointed look. "Well, I'm here now. Why don't you show me your room?"

"Okay," she said, taking his hand as she led him down the hall.

While Hailey was apparently living in Mitch's old room, he had to give the Carvers' credit for making the room suitable for a little girl. There were pink and purple pillows on the bed as well as plenty of toys and books. As Hailey showed him her favorite things, he felt a mix of emotions. He wanted to be happy that she was thriving with her grandparents, but it didn't make the pain of her absence any less.

He'd already lost six months with her, and she'd changed in that short time. She was bigger. She was more verbal. She was almost a third grader. He could remember when she'd started kindergarten, how she'd held his hand and refused to let go, so he'd spent the first two hours of class sitting with her, feeling like a giant in a sea of five-year-olds and tiny little chairs.

"Zach?" Hailey asked. "Are you listening?"

"Sorry. What did you say?"

"I want to see your new house." A gleam of stubborn determination entered her eyes.

"I don't have one yet. I'm staying at a hotel in town."

"Which one?"

"It's called the Firefly Inn."

"I know that place. It has a pretty garden."

"It does," he agreed. "Do you like living here with your grandparents?"

She nodded. "Yes, but I miss you."

"I miss you, too," he said, as she gave him another hug.

"I made you a picture," Hailey said, running over to the desk, then returning with a piece of paper. "It's me and you."

He glanced at the drawing. It was messy and colorful and incredibly touching. Hailey had drawn stick figures of a man and a little girl and surrounded them with hearts and the word *love* written a half-dozen times. "This is great."

"You like it?"

"I do. You're a wonderful artist." As he said the words, he wished he could take Hailey to meet Gianna. He had a feeling they would immediately hit it off. Hailey had always liked to color, and while she might not be the artist Gianna was, she had enthusiasm and a love for blurring the lines.

Helen cleared her throat as she came into the room. "Hailey has a play date with her friend Maddie. I need to take her over there. You should have called first."

"I want to stay with Zach. I'll play with Maddie later," Hailey said.

"It's okay," he said quickly, not wanting to disrupt her life. "I have to go to work anyway."

"Will you come back tonight?"

"I'll call you before you go to bed."

Hailey's bottom lip turned down. "I want to see you. Why won't Grandpa let you come over?"

"We're working things out, honey."

"What things?" she asked in a plaintive voice.

"Grownup stuff. But I'll call you, okay? You have fun with Maddie."

"Get your things together," Helen told Hailey. "I'll walk Zach out and then I'll take you over there."

He hugged her again and then followed Helen out of the room and down the hall. He urged her to step onto the front porch with him. "What's happening with Ron? Did you tell him I saw Hailey?"

"Hailey told him. He was very angry. I said we just bumped into you, but I don't know that he believed me. He insisted that I do everything I can to avoid you."

"That's not going to happen. We need to sit down and talk, all three of us. In fact, maybe Mitch should be there, too."

"You can't tell them what I did," she said pointedly.

He gave her a direct look. "I won't—if you help facilitate a meeting. Hailey isn't going to stop wanting to see me. You know that."

"I have to say I didn't quite realize how attached she was to you."

"We spent a lot of time together, especially when Rebecca was in rehab. Then it was just the two of us for a month at a time."

"I would have been there if I had known, but no one saw fit to tell us."

"That was up to Rebecca. She didn't want you to know, and I had my hands full just convincing her to stay at the clinic and work on her sobriety. I couldn't fight your battle, too. Talk to Ron. I'm around tonight or tomorrow. I'll expect a call from you. If not, I'll be back."

She sighed and went back into the house without offering him any assurance she would do what he'd asked. But she would do it, because she had to. Hopefully, if he could get them all together, they could hash things out and find a workable compromise, because the current situation was not sustainable. He didn't want to hurt Hailey more by being around but not really in her life. That would only be more confusing.

As he got in the truck, he looked down again at the picture Hailey had drawn for him, and his heart ached. There had been times when he'd thought meeting Rebecca had been the worst day of his life, but out of that troubled relationship had come an incredible one with a special little girl.

And despite the anger he and Rebecca had sometimes felt toward each other, she'd been really happy with the way he'd taken care of Hailey. She would want him to continue doing that. She would want him to fight her parents for that right.

That's exactly what he was going to do.

Her muse had woken up. Gianna couldn't believe the drawing taking shape on her canvas. After weeks of nothing, she was suddenly filled with ideas, and she had Zach to thank for her sudden burst of creativity. She'd followed his suggestion that she come to the meadow and paint by their favorite cove, and since arriving she'd been inspired.

Five hours had passed since she'd set up her easel at seven a.m., wanting to catch the quiet, the early rise of the sun. It was now almost noon. It had been months since she'd been able to lose herself for so long in her art. And it felt good. She'd finally found a way to shut down her critical brain and just paint.

But while she was happy with her burst of creativity, she was a little less excited with the subject of her painting. Being at the camp had taken her back in time and the teenage couple running through the meadow, their hands almost touching, were definitely an homage to Zach and herself. She could almost feel Zach's fingers brushing against hers as they'd playfully chased each other through the meadow and the trees, ending up at the cove where they'd kissed for the first time.

She told herself to stop being such a sap, but she couldn't seem to stop.

The sound of an engine coming down the road made her pulse leap. She'd heard the sound a few times, but up until now no one had ventured in her direction. The lodge and cabins were about three-quarters of a mile away, and she'd parked off the main road, so it was doubtful anyone would know she was here.

A door slammed.

Except for Zach, of course. She'd told him she might come to paint this morning.

And here he was.

He strode through the trees dressed in worn jeans and a short-sleeved maroon T-shirt, aviator glasses covering his eyes, giving him an even sexier look, if that was possible.

"You're painting," he said with a happy grin, removing his glasses as he drew close.

She stepped in front of the easel, blocking her art. "It's a work in progress. No peeking."

"Seriously? You always used to show me your painting, no matter where you were in the process."

"That was then. This is now."

He gave her a speculative look. "You painted us, didn't you?"

"Why would you say that?"

"Because you have an embarrassed, guilty look on your face."

"It's not really us; it's just the spirit of us."

"Let me see."

She reluctantly stepped to the side.

Zach stared at the painting for a long moment.

"What do you think?" she prodded.

"I think you're even better than you used to be. And I also think I was one handsome kid."

She laughed. "Don't pretend you didn't always know you were attractive."

He grinned back at her. "You said this wasn't us, but I think I see braces on that girl."

"Fine. It's us. It's our past. Our story. It's because I was here. And the memories felt very vivid. Anyway, I'm happy to be painting again."

"It's part of who you are, Gianna. You have to keep doing what you love, no matter who you love."

His words were incredibly wise, but his tone was weary, and she wondered if he wasn't talking to himself as much as he was talking to her. "You look tired, Zach."

"It was a rough morning. I stopped by the Carvers' house to see Hailey, which was great, but she's asking me questions I can't answer. She wants to know when she's going to see me again, when she can live with me."

"That can't be easy."

"It's not. I told Helen she has to set up a meeting with Ron and me and her. We need to work this out."

"Does Ron know you've seen Hailey?"

"Yes, and he's angry, which is why Helen is stonewalling. I reminded her that she doesn't have the power—I do. We'll see if she acts, or if I have to force things."

"I hope she'll do what's best for all of you and that has to be talking."

"I agree."

"Speaking of talking...I wanted to thank you again for working your magic on Chloe. She went from tears to laughter in like fifteen minutes."

"That was probably the pregnancy hormones. Have you spoken to her this morning?"

"We've texted. She's back at work, of course. But she said you were right about a new day bringing a new attitude. I also hope the day brings a phone call or an email from her husband."

"That would be great," he agreed. "How long are you staying here?"

"A little while longer. I told Nora I'd be in around two, so I have some time."

Zach's gaze moved back to the picture. "God, we were young...and happy."

"We were."

He turned back to her, giving her a long look that he followed up with a hard embrace, and a kiss filled with both desire and restraint. It confused her a little.

"Are you okay, Zach?"

"I don't know."

"Is there anything I can do?"

"Fast-forward and show me everything turns out the way I want it to."

"I wish I could."

He gave her a half-hearted smile. "I'm fine. Don't worry about me."

"I don't think you're fine. But I do think that you'll find a way into having a relationship with Hailey. I don't know how or when, but I'm sure it will happen."

"I hope so." He paused, his gaze darkening. "What about us? What do you think is going to happen with us?"

His words drew a shiver down her arms. She wanted to say *nothing*, but the way her heart was racing made that seem like a very big lie. "What do you want to happen?" she asked softly, not sure she was ready to hear the answer.

"I want you back in my life, Gianna."

She took a quick breath at the bluntness of his words. "I don't know what that would even look like."

"Don't you?" He tipped his head toward her painting. "It looks like that. Those kids weren't afraid of anything. They followed their hearts, their passion."

"Because they didn't know what was ahead—how much could go wrong, how difficult life could be. And they broke up, remember?"

"They were scared to face their feelings. I lied to Tony about mine, and you were quick to believe I was a thief, because that made it easier for you to walk away from me. But before they let fear win, they were happy. I think they could be again—as adults."

She swallowed a knot in her throat and turned her gaze back to her painting. She'd like to be that happy and joyous again. *But could they really recreate what they had?*

"We can't go back in time," she murmured. "And how do we know things wouldn't end up exactly the same way?"

"We don't. We'd have to take a risk—the risk those two couldn't take." He paused. "But maybe it's not the right time. Maybe we're still not ready. I'm going to head up to the lodge."

As he turned away, she said, "Wait." The impulsive word came out of her mouth before she could stop it.

"What?" he asked, a question in his gaze.

"Is anyone else at the lodge today?"

"Not right now. Hunter and Cassidy are having lunch in town with Lizzie and her siblings. Why? Do you want to come down to the lodge with me?"

"No." She licked her lips, nervous excitement bubbling within her. *Did she dare to speak the words running around inside her? Could she be that brave?* "I don't want to go to the lodge with you," she said slowly. "I want you to stay here. I want…"

His eyes glittered recklessly in the sunlight. "What do you want, Gianna?"

"I want us to be fearless again."

"You do?"

"Yes. Right now."

"Here?" he asked in surprise.

"Why not here? It's our place." She moved forward, putting her hands on his hips as she looked up into his eyes. "I always wanted to make love with you here in this meadow by our beautiful cove. I dreamed it a million times. Want to make one of those dreams come true?"

"More than I want to do anything else," he said, sliding his hands through her hair, trapping her face for a long, sweet, promising kiss.

"I've got a blanket," she said, tipping her head toward grass. "That's all we need."

He hesitated. "Maybe not all we need."

"Oh. Right. Protection." She felt like an idiot. "I guess I should be better prepared for spontaneity."

"That's the opposite of being spontaneous," he said with a small smile. "Fortunately..." He reached into his pocket and pulled out his wallet. Tucked in the billfold was a condom.

"Well, aren't you quite the Boy Scout."

"After last night on the beach, I had a hopeful feeling we might end up needing it, and I wanted to be ready. Are we really doing this? Are you sure this is what you want?"

"Yes," she said, feeling a certainty run through her that she hadn't felt in weeks. "I want to be fearless again, and I want you, Zach. Whatever happens afterward—I don't care."

"You will care, Gianna."

"Maybe, but that's for later. I just want to be in this moment with you. Please don't say no."

His jaw hardened, his eyes filling with emotion, as he wrapped his arms around her and pulled her up against his hard body. "I could never say no to you." He gave her one more hot look and then his mouth was on hers.

CHAPTER TWENTY

THIS KISS WAS unlike any other they'd exchanged. It was as if a dam had broken. All the pent-up feelings from the past flowed out in a surge of desire that could not be stopped—*would not* be stopped. Gianna felt like she'd been waiting for this moment for a lifetime, and part of her wanted to go slow, savor every second, while the other part of her was impatient, needy, filled with a sense of urgency to finally be with Zach—no barriers between them, no rules, no restraint.

Breaking free from their embrace, she pulled her top over her head, feeling not only the warm sun on her skin but also the heat of Zach's gaze. He had always made her feel beautiful, even when she wasn't.

She reached for the front clasp of her light-pink lacy bra, feeling nervous and excited, a little like that fifteen-year-old girl in the picture, who knew something amazing was almost within reach.

"You're killing me," Zach muttered, as her fingers fumbled with the clasp.

"Anticipation is good," she teased.

"I've been anticipating this for too long. Let me help you." He slid her fingers out of the way as he unhooked the clasp and pulled the edges of her bra apart, his gaze feasting on her breasts, and then his fingers swept across them. "Beautiful—everything about you," he said, raising his eyes to hers. "Not just now—before. You know that, don't you?"

She slowly nodded. "That's the way you always made me feel."

He pushed her bra off her shoulders, and she let it fall to the ground. She reached for the hem of his T-shirt, wanting to feel his chest against hers.

As she helped him pull it over his head, she saw once again the physical scars of his past. Her fingers traced the patchy, white lines, the slightly raised bumps of tissue that should have marred his male perfection but somehow only made him feel that much more real to her.

She leaned over and put her lips against one of his scars, wanting to ease the pain that still lingered within him. She thought she could take an hour or a day or a week to explore his body, to taste every inch of him. But as Zach's hands ran up and down her bare back, as he nuzzled her neck and flicked his tongue against the curve of her ear, a sense of desperate impatience took over.

She kicked off her shoes and shimmied out of her shorts while Zach did the same. Then they looked at each other in happy amazement. She would have thought she'd be nervous or shy in the bright light, but she wasn't.

"I think I'm the luckiest man in the world," Zach said.

"You always know the perfect thing to say. This feels right."

"So right," he agreed, pulling her into his arms.

As they kissed once more, her nerves tingled at every heated connection between them. She loved the power of his body, the urgency of his mouth. They stumbled over to the blanket she'd spread out earlier, never imagining that she'd be using it for this purpose.

Zach's hands were everywhere—her breasts, her stomach, the warm heat between her legs—and his mouth followed as he teased and tormented her with delicious desire.

She repaid the favor when he ended up on his back, and she took her time exploring his wonderful male body in every way she'd ever imagined. Touching him, kissing him, loving him in the bright warm sunshine felt freeing and joyful. It had taken forever to get to this moment, to be one with Zach, to be connected so closely, so deeply that she felt like they were two halves of a whole. With her heart pounding, and her body soaring, she knew it had been more than worth the wait.

Zach wondered how long it would take for his heart to slow down. But a better question might be how long it would be before he wanted Gianna again. He gazed down at the top of her head, her blonde hair lit up in the sunlight as she rested her face on his chest. He could feel the beat of her heart, too—in perfect rhythm with his.

Being with Gianna had filled all the empty spaces in his soul. He felt like himself again. And he didn't want to let go of the feeling—not now, maybe not ever.

But he wouldn't tell her that. They were living in the moment, and he planned on keeping that moment going as long as he could.

He turned his gaze up to the perfectly blue sky. There wasn't even a speck of a cloud above them. It was just an endless vista of beauty, of hope. Surrounded by the majestic mountains, and the lapping lake just yards away, he felt completely at peace.

As Gianna had said, this was their place, and he was glad they'd made love here, where the past and the present had come together, where they'd finally come together.

Gianna let out a sigh and then shifted, raising her head to look at him, as she rested her hand on his chest. "What are you thinking about?"

He gazed back at her with a smile, feeling a rush of tender possessiveness. He still had a hand on her back, so she couldn't completely move away, and there was a part of him that wasn't sure he could actually let her go. He didn't want to lose her again.

But that emotional thought was followed by all kinds of pragmatic questions that he had a feeling would be running through her head quite soon.

"Zach?" she questioned, a gleam of worry moving into her eyes.

"I was thinking that I wish I had brought two condoms."

A smile blossomed across her lips. "I was also thinking that. We were good together."

"Did you really have any doubts?"

"Maybe not doubts, but you've starred in a lot of my dreams, both past and present. I wasn't sure it would be as good as I always thought it would be, but it was better. It was real."

"We've always been real," he said quietly, reaching out to pull a twig from her hair.

She met his gaze. "We have. I've never felt like I had to be anyone else when I was with you. I can't say that about my other relationships."

"I can't, either. I've always been my best self with you."

As silence fell between them, her smile faded. "There's a but coming…"

"No, there's not," he denied.

"Yes, there is. You're thinking about what's next."

"I'm not. I didn't know this was *next* a half hour ago, and I'm happy, so I don't need to know what's next."

"I've always felt a need to look ahead," she said. "Except for my art, everything else in my life is planned, thought about, forecasted."

"How has that been working for you?"

"Not well at all."

"Maybe we change things up."

"We could do that. We could let this moment be what it is—a really perfect moment."

"I like that idea."

Her lips curved back into a smile. "You've liked a lot of my ideas in the past half hour."

"You've been quite creative," he agreed.

"You weren't so bad yourself." She paused as a bee buzzed by, ducking her head to avoid it. "We should probably get dressed before we get stung or sunburned."

"Either one would be worth lying naked in the grass with you. One of my best fantasies came true."

"Mine, too." She sat up as a rumbling sound came from the road. "Oh, my God, that's a car. I thought you said no one was coming up here." She scrambled off the blanket, searching for her clothes.

"I said Hunter and Cassidy were having lunch. Lunch might be over," he said, checking his watch before scrambling into his jeans. "Maybe they'll go straight to the lodge."

"Or they'll see your truck and wonder what you're doing out here." She pulled on her shorts and her bra, throwing her shirt over her head.

He grabbed his T-shirt off the ground and had barely gotten it on when he heard the slam of a car door, followed by voices. "Definitely Hunter and Cassidy," he murmured, looking over at Gianna.

Her hair was beautifully wild, her face a picture of panic. "You have guilt written all over you." He put on his shoes as she smoothed down her hair and tried to force a normal expression on her face.

"How's that?" she asked.

"Better," he said with a smile. "Just be happy they didn't come by when we might have been too busy to hear the car."

"That would have been fun to explain."

"Hey, there," Hunter called out with a wave, as he came through the trees with Cassidy. As he moved closer, he said, "What's going on down here? I saw your truck on the side of the road, Zach."

"Gianna came to paint, and I…I'm just enjoying her painting," he said, stumbling over his answer.

Hunter gave him a speculative look. "Okay." Then he turned to Gianna. "I'm glad you're here. This is my fiancée, Cassidy Ellison. This is Gianna. She's an old friend of Zach's and a local girl."

"It's nice to meet you," Cassidy said with a smile. "What are you painting?" She moved toward Gianna's easel. "This is pretty. It feels carefree."

"It's how I remember summers here at the camp," Gianna said.

"Are those teenagers supposed to be you two?" Hunter asked, a smile now lurking in his eyes when he looked at Zach.

"Don't ask me; I didn't paint it," he said.

"It's not anyone per se," Gianna answered. "It's just art. But Zach and I did come here a lot the summer we were at camp together. It was one of my favorite places to paint. I've been a little blocked when it comes to art lately, and I thought this meadow might inspire me again. It was actually Zach's idea." She gave Hunter a quick look. "I know I'm trespassing. I hope it's okay."

"It's absolutely okay," Hunter said. "You're really talented. Your picture is only half done, but it's already so detailed."

"There's a lot I still need to do."

"Well, feel free to come out here whenever you want," Hunter added.

"I can see why you were inspired," Cassidy said, sweeping her hand toward the view. "This area is beautiful. Every time I turn around, I seem to find a new place of beauty. I feel so lucky to be here." She walked back to Hunter, and he slung his arm around her.

"We're both lucky," Hunter said, exchanging a warm look with Cassidy. Then he turned back to them. "I don't know if Zach told you, Gianna, but Cassidy and I were high school sweethearts. It took us a long time to come back together."

"I didn't realize that," Gianna said.

"Second chances can be good, as long as you don't let them go by without acting on them," Hunter added, letting his words sit for a moment. "Anyway, we better get up to the lodge. Lizzie is on her way. She wants to give me some decorating and paint color advice."

"It's going to be a family affair," Zach said with a laugh. "I'll be right behind you."

"Take your time. And Gianna, please stay as long as you like."

"I actually have to get to work this afternoon, but thanks."

As Hunter and Cassidy moved out of sight, he gave Gianna a smile. "You can breathe again."

"That was a little too close."

"Most great moments come with risk. But don't forget it was your idea to get naked out here."

"I don't regret it, Zach," she said, looking him straight in the eye. "I'll never regret it, no matter what happens next."

He was very happy to hear that; he just hoped it was the truth. "I feel the same way. I hate to leave, but I should get up to the lodge."

"Go. I'm going to clean up and head out, too."

"Do you need help?"

"No."

He stepped forward and slid his arms around her waist. "One kiss for the road?"

She lifted her face to his, and he took a kiss that he really hoped wouldn't be the last one.

"Did you hear me?"

Gianna looked at the irritated elderly woman standing at the counter and realized she'd been daydreaming again. It had been happening all afternoon, ever since she'd come back from the camp. She might not still be with Zach, but she couldn't stop thinking about him, couldn't stop remembering how great they had been together.

"What is wrong with you?" the woman asked, tapping the counter with her wallet. "Are you going to sell me these candle-sticks or not?"

"I'm sorry. I'm a bit distracted today."

"Clearly."

She took the woman's credit card and wrapped up the candle-sticks, breathing a sigh of relief when that was done. There was only one other woman browsing in the store and it was almost five. As soon as that customer left, she was turning the sign to Closed.

She couldn't wait for the day to be over. Even though she'd only been at work since two, it felt like forever. She wanted to be alone. She wanted to be able to think and dream.

A smile crossed her lips as Zach's image flashed through her head, and her body tingled at the memories. She could still taste him on her lips, still feel his arms around her, and a surge of giddy happiness ran through her. She knew she was dancing on a dangerous precipice, but damn if it didn't feel good.

"I'll take this," the woman said, bringing a music box to the counter. "It reminds me of one I used to have."

"It's one of my favorite pieces. I'm glad you like it."

The woman opened the lid, letting the dancing girl inside do another twirl before she closed it. "I loved ballet when I was a little girl. Gosh, it was so long ago," she added with a helpless smile.

"It's never too late to dance."

The woman laughed. "My friend Jill always says that, but we're both middle-aged women now. What are we going to do—take ballet with a bunch of little girls in tutus?"

Her heart skipped a beat. "You said your friend, Jill. Would that be Jill Harper by any chance?"

Surprise ran through the woman's eyes. "Well, yes, she used to be Jill Harper. She's Jill Kenner now."

Gianna reached into her bag for the picture she'd been carrying around. "Is this her?"

The woman picked up the photo. "Oh, wow. This is from a long time ago. Where did you get it?"

"From the summer camp. After the owner died, we got some of the things left behind."

"The camp, of course. I should have recognized the background. Jill had a love-hate relationship with Echo Falls Camp. She loved being outdoors and all the activities, but her mother being there kind of weighed her down. She could never get into as much trouble as the other kids." The woman paused. "Is something wrong? You look funny."

She debated what to say and how to say it. But in the end, she decided it was time to be blunt. "Do you know if Jill was pregnant when she was a teenager? If she had a baby that she gave up for adoption?"

The woman's face paled. "Why—why would you ask me that?"

She pointed to the locket on Jill's neck. "I was adopted as an infant and the only thing that came with me was a locket like that one. I was told it belonged to my biological mother. But the adoption was closed, and the records were lost. I've been trying to find out if Jill might be my mother."

"Oh, God! I don't know what to tell you."

She saw the truth in the woman's eyes. "She had a baby, didn't she?"

"I can't say. I *shouldn't* say."

"Then don't. Just tell me where I can find her. I'll ask her myself."

"What—what do you want from her?"

"I just want to know who she is. I don't want to ruin her life or be a problem. I simply want to meet her." Her heart was pounding so fast, she had to force herself to breathe. "Can you help me out?"

"I'm not sure."

"Please. I really need this."

"Well, I suppose I can give her your name and your number, and then she can decide. That's all I can do."

She pulled a sheet off a nearby memo pad. She scribbled her name and number down and handed it to the woman. "What's your name?"

"Tammy Cooper."

"Tammy," she echoed. "I should have figured."

"What does that mean?"

"My friend's mother, Ruth, mentioned you and Jill were friends."

"Ruth was my sister's best friend."

"Thank you for helping me. I can't express how much it means to me."

"I don't know what Jill will say," Tammy said worriedly. "Maybe don't get your hopes up. Jill is married. She has two daughters. I don't think they know anything."

"Please tell her that I don't want to cause her any trouble, but if she'd be willing to talk to me, I'd love that."

"When were you born?"

"October second."

Tammy nodded. "And you're how old?"

"Twenty-nine."

Tammy put the paper into her purse. "Okay. I'll do my best." She started to leave, then paused. "Do you still have the locket?"

"No, I lost it a long time ago."

"Too bad. It was one of Jill's most treasured possessions."

"Mine, too," she whispered, as Tammy left the store.

After the door closed, she put both hands on the counter, feeling suddenly weak. She drew in a couple of deep breaths, but they didn't help much. Her mind was racing with questions.

Would Jill be shocked to know she was looking for her? Would she lie like her mother had done? Would she agree to see her? Was this the beginning or the end?

The door chime pealed once more, and she jumped, hoping Tammy hadn't come back to say she'd changed her mind. She was ready to tell whoever walked through the door that they were closed, but it was Zach.

His smile vanished when he saw her face. "What's wrong?"

She came around the counter and threw herself into his arms, needing his solid body to hang on to.

"What's happened, Gianna?" he asked worriedly.

"I think I might have found my mother."

CHAPTER TWENTY-ONE

"Your mother?" Zach echoed, gripping her arms as he looked into her eyes. "Who is she? Where is she? Did she just come in here? Because you look like you saw a ghost."

"Jill's friend Tammy was just here. She confirmed that the girl with the locket was Jill Harper. She said they were friends as kids and when I asked her if Jill had gotten pregnant, if she'd had a baby, she couldn't deny it. The more we talked, the more it became obvious that Jill did have a child that she gave up for adoption, even though Tammy was reluctant to say much about it. I told Tammy that I want to talk to Jill."

"And?"

"She took my name and number and said she'd pass it on to Jill. Her last name is Kenner now. She's married and has two girls. I have sisters." She swayed at that dizzying thought.

"Okay, slow down."

"I can't. My heart is racing."

"Completely understandable. Can you close up? Can we go upstairs and talk?"

"Yes. I was going to do that as soon as she left, but I wasn't sure I could walk as far as the door." She stepped out of his embrace. "I'm okay now. I'm just a little shocked, nervous, and scared." She moved over to the door and turned the bolt, then flipped the sign to Closed. "What if she doesn't call me?"

"Let's hope she does. And whatever happens, it's better to know than not to know. Even if she doesn't call, you have her last name now. It might not be that difficult to find her on your own."

"But do I have the right? She gave me up for a reason. Maybe she isn't interested in me turning up again. She made the decision to give me to someone else." She blew out a breath. "I'm spinning out a little."

"I can see that. Do you have plans tonight? Do you want to get some dinner? Maybe start with a stiff drink."

"I'm supposed to drop by my parents' house." She groaned. "How am I going to do that? They'll see that I'm upset. They'll ask why. My father will be angry if I tell him what's happening. I can't handle it."

"Is it a special occasion? Can you cancel?"

"I think I could. I left it kind of open-ended. Maybe I'll tell my mom I'm not feeling well."

"Whatever you want. But if you decide not to go over there, I'd like to have dinner with you."

"Aren't you supposed to be talking to the Carvers tonight?" she asked, as she turned off the lights in the showroom, and they took the back way up to her apartment.

"Helen asked me to come by tomorrow night. Ron has a meeting this evening."

"Sorry."

"It is what it is," he said, following her into the apartment. "Do you want to eat here or go out?"

"Let's stay in. I'm not really up for a night out, and I'm pretty sure I'm going to be glued to my phone all night, praying for it to ring. I have wine here, and while I don't have a lot of groceries on hand, if you like breakfast for dinner, I'm your girl."

He smiled. "I love breakfast for dinner. I also love that you're my girl."

"I only said that in the context of breakfast."

"I'll take what I can get."

Zach took a seat at the table while she opened a bottle of red wine and poured them each a glass. She set one in front of him and sat down. "I hope you like red wine with your eggs."

"I'm easy. What else did Tammy have to say? Anything of note?"

"She asked if I still had the locket. I said I'd lost it a long time ago. She told me it was Jill's most treasured possession." She paused. "I've been thinking about how the locket went missing, and I had a crazy thought."

"I know what you're going to say," he replied, a smug look in his eyes. "You think Theresa Harper took it."

"I do. But why would she have done that?"

"Because she didn't want anyone to link you with her daughter. I had the same thought earlier today. I was in the old camp dining room, and I was thinking about Theresa serving up food and always keeping an eye on us. I'm sure she noticed the locket hanging around your neck every time you went up to fill your plate."

"It still seems like a bold move to make."

"Lying to you last night was bold, too."

"I don't know why she did that. Did she really think I'd give up that easily?"

"She obviously doesn't know how stubborn you can be."

She made a face at the teasing smile on his face. "You're stubborn, too. You keep showing up even when I tell you we're done."

"After what happened earlier, did you really think I was going to stay away from you?"

She shook her head. "No, and I was hoping you wouldn't," she admitted. "Today was wonderful; I've been completely distracted ever since then."

"Me, too."

"I just don't know what happens next…"

"We don't have to know now. We'll figure it out." He set his wineglass down. "Do you want me to cook?"

"Do you know how to cook?"

"According to Hailey, I am the king of pancakes."

"Well, if you're the king, then I think you should do the honors. And you're in luck—I have pancake mix, along with eggs and bacon."

"Perfect."

"Do you want me to help?"

"No, you sit and relax."

"Okay, I'm not going to argue." She sipped her wine as she watched him move around the kitchen with quick and efficient movements. She could get used to him cooking for her. She could get used to a lot of things when it came to Zach.

As Zach mixed the eggs, she picked up her phone and texted her mother that she wasn't feeling well, and she'd catch up with her tomorrow. Her phone rang one second later.

"Hello, Mom," she said. "I'm fine. I just have a headache. I hope you weren't already cooking."

"I'm always cooking, but I'm not concerned about the food. I'm worried about you. You're not trying to avoid your dad, are you? Because I had a long talk with him, and he agreed to back off on criticizing your decisions."

"That must have been quite a discussion."

"He's had time to think things over. He knows it's your life, and you have to live it as you see fit. Plus, he appreciates the fact that you came home to help Lois."

"I'm not trying to avoid him. I just want to stay home and rest tonight. I didn't get a lot of sleep last night."

"Why not? What's going on?"

"Nothing really. I was at Chloe's. She hasn't heard from Kevin in a few days, and she needed some support, so Keira and I spent some time with her."

"That was kind of you. I hope everything is all right with Kevin."

"Me, too."

"Well, I'll let you go then. But let's make sure we get together soon. I can't believe you're living less than a mile away, and I've only seen you once."

"I'm going to be here all summer, so we'll have time."

"Take care, hon."

"You, too."

She set her phone down, feeling a little guilty for not being completely honest with her mother, but thankfully her mom hadn't asked about her search for her biological mother, so she hadn't had to tell a direct lie. She hadn't even been lying about her headache; there was an aching pain behind her temple.

"Dinner is almost ready," Zach said. "Unless you want to change your mind and head over to your parents' house; I won't hold it against you."

"No. My mom will be fine."

She got up and grabbed some silverware out of the drawer, setting the table as Zach put their meal together. Five minutes later, she was enjoying one of the best breakfasts she'd had in a while.

"Okay, you are the king," she said, stabbing her fork at a pancake laden with maple syrup. "The pancakes are light and fluffy, the eggs are perfect, and the bacon has just the right crisp."

"I'm glad you're happy."

"My headache is even starting to go away. I guess I needed to eat. I missed lunch."

"So did I," he said, exchanging an intimate look with her. "We were a little busy."

"Just a little."

"You surprised the hell out of me."

"In what way?" she asked curiously.

"In every way. Just the fact that you wanted to be together in the meadow, in the daylight."

"I wanted to be the girl in my picture again. Actually, that isn't even true, because the girl I drew wasn't me back then—it was who I wanted to be."

"That's probably true for the boy in the picture, too." He set down his fork. "In case you were wondering, I picked up a few more condoms."

"I wasn't wondering," she said with a small laugh, although she shivered a little at the look in his eyes.

"Well, just so you know."

"I'll keep it in mind, but I'm not sure we could do better than we did today."

He leaned forward, resting his arms on the table. "Challenge accepted."

She laughed. "It was not a challenge."

"Oh, I think it was." He paused as a hard knock came at her door.

She started in surprise. "I don't know who that is. I usually buzz people into the building."

"I'll get it," he said, getting to his feet.

"Gianna?" a male voice said, adding another knock. "It's me."

She caught Zach by the arm. "That's my dad."

"You better get it then."

She walked over to the door and quickly opened it. "Dad, what are you doing here?"

"Your mom said you're sick and you can't come to dinner. If that's because you're avoiding me, it's not necessary."

Her dad's gaze moved past her to Zach, to the kitchen table, and to their empty plates. His eyes filled with anger. "You're not sick at all. You're on a date."

"This isn't a date."

"Who are you?" He gave Zach a scathing look.

"Zach Barrington," Zach said evenly.

Her dad turned his gaze back to her. "You have another man already? I thought you were taking some time for self-reflection."

"I am. Zach is an old friend. We went to camp together."

"Zach," he murmured again, a new light in his eyes. "I've heard that name before. He was that kid you cried over for weeks."

She flushed, realizing how many people had experienced that heartache along with her. "That was a long time ago. We're friends now. He's designing the remodel of the camp. And I'm not avoiding you, Dad. I really do have a headache. Zach just stopped by. We made some eggs. It wasn't a big plan." She felt like she was sixteen again, defending her actions when she really shouldn't have to. "I'm sorry for the late cancel. I know it isn't going to make things better between us, but frankly I don't know what will. You're really angry and disappointed, and I can't change that."

"I'm worried about you, Gianna."

"I know, but I'm fine. I'm getting my head together. I'm taking actions that I need to take."

His gaze narrowed. "You're looking for your birth mother?"

"Yes, and I think I've found her. To be completely honest, I didn't want to tell Mom that tonight, and I was afraid she would ask. That's the real reason I cancelled."

"Who is she?"

"Her name is Jill Harper. She's Theresa Harper's daughter. I don't know if you know her, but she ran the dining hall at Echo Falls Camp."

"The biological mother wasn't supposed to be from Whisper Lake," he said. "Where does this woman live?"

"I'm not sure. Her mom lives on the north shore. I met one of Jill's friends today. She's going to have Jill call me. I don't know if she will, but I hope she does. I have to know the story of my existence, Dad. I don't need a relationship with her, but I need to know who gave birth to me."

"And you also want to know why she gave you up," her dad said heavily.

"I do," she admitted. "But it doesn't change the fact that I love you and Mom, that I consider you my parents."

"We love you, too," he said gruffly. "I'm sorry I came down on you so hard about your broken engagements. I do want you to be happy. I just don't know if your expectations are too high."

"They should be high, don't you think?"

He gave her a half-hearted smile. "You're right. They should be high. I'll leave you to your…whatever this is." He tipped his head to Zach, who had resumed his seat at the table. "Sorry for barging in."

"No problem," Zach said. "For what it's worth, I think you raised one hell of a good daughter."

Her dad gave a slow nod. "I know we did. Good night, Gianna. Call your mother tomorrow. Or better yet, come by the house."

"Are you going to tell her about Jill?"

"No, I'll let you do that, when you know something real, when you're ready."

"Thanks, Dad." She gave him a hug and then walked him to the door. "By the way, how did you get in the building without me buzzing you in?"

"I have a key. Lois gave me one years ago. Who do you think she calls when the sink gets clogged up?"

"Good point. Bye." She closed the door behind him and then walked back to the table and sat down. "So, that was my dad."

"He didn't like me at all."

"He doesn't even know you. That actually didn't end up as bad as I thought it would when he first got here. He got the wrong idea when he saw you and me having dinner. He thought I blew them off for a date. But he came around."

"Because you were honest with him, and he loves you."

"I love him, too."

"So, you cried over me for weeks?"

She rolled her eyes. "That's what you got out of the conversation?"

"It's the part that interested me the most."

"You already knew that you broke my heart."

His gaze turned more serious. "You broke mine, too, Gianna."

"Which begs the question, what are we doing now? Aren't we headed for more of the same, Zach?"

"I don't know. But I think we should find out—on a bed this time."

"I wasn't talking about sex."

"I know, but still." He got up and extended his hand. "It's time for me to make good on your challenge."

She slid her fingers into his. "It wasn't a challenge. And aren't you at all concerned that this is going to hurt a lot more if we keep doing what we're doing?"

"No. Because we've already jumped off the cliff. Only time

will tell if we land on our feet. But in the meantime, it will be a hell of a ride."

"Well, when you say it like that..."

CHAPTER TWENTY-TWO

IT WAS a night she'd always remember.

Gianna rolled on to her side and smiled with pleasure at the sight of Zach sleeping so peacefully in her bed. The covers around them were tangled from their passion, and Zach's hair was wild, long strands falling over his forehead. There was a shadow of beard on his jaw, and his slightly parted lips only made her want to kiss him again. She would have thought that making love three times would have satisfied her, but it had just made her want more.

She put her hand on his arm, feeling the heat of his skin. He stirred slightly but didn't wake up. She should really let him sleep. It was only seven. She doubted he had anything he had to get to, and she didn't have to be in the store until one. They could have some morning fun and then a big breakfast.

As her stomach rumbled, she wondered if food might have to come before the fun. But Zach had cooked most of what she had in her refrigerator. Maybe they could go down to the café, see Chloe, and order up some blueberry waffles or Chloe's famous veggie omelet. That thought made her even more hungry.

She snuggled up closer to Zach, resting her head on his shoulder, gently stroking the line of one massive scar across his chest. It still hurt her to think about how Zach must have suffered the night of the fire. Even though he and Rebecca had had problems, he'd loved her, and he'd lost her. He'd almost lost Hailey, too as well as his own life. But he'd made it, and hopefully he was on his way to getting Hailey back.

Which made her wonder how their relationship could possibly fit in with that one...

If Zach could get partial custody or even visitation, he'd be focused on rebuilding his relationship with Hailey, as he should be. Considering what she knew of the Carvers, she thought Hailey would be better off with Zach. Or at least with both her grandparents and the man she'd thought of as her father for the last four years.

Zach would be a great dad. She'd seen the way he and Hailey had hugged with so much love and emotion. And knowing how hard he was working to stay in that little girl's life impressed her beyond belief.

Any child would be lucky to have him as their father. Any woman would be lucky to have him as the father of her children.

A small sigh escaped her lips as she realized how far ahead she was getting in her thoughts. This was just supposed to be fun and spontaneous, a live in the moment fling. She did not need to be considering Zach for the role of dad to her future kids.

Moving away from Zach, she slid out of bed and grabbed her robe from the closet.

"Hey, where are you going?" Zach mumbled, blinking his sleepy green eyes.

Her stomach clenched as desire and love ran through her. *No, not love. Just desire*, she told herself.

"I'm hungry," she said. "I'm going to take a shower and then rummage around in the kitchen, but I'm thinking we should go to the café."

"Good idea," he said, sitting up in bed. "I used up most of your eggs last night."

"We can check on Chloe, too, although I'm hoping she's at home and not at the café. But knowing her, I doubt it."

He swung his legs off the bed and stood up. Her mouth watered at the sight of his very attractive male form.

"Let's shower together," he suggested, a wicked sparkle in his eyes. "It will be faster."

"Really? You and me in a hot, steamy shower, is going to be faster?"

He gave her a happy, sexy grin. "Well, it will be better."

"I don't know."

His smile faded, his gaze narrowing on her face, as he walked over to her. "What's wrong?"

"It's morning. It's time to get back to reality."

"This is reality, Gianna. It's not a dream."

"It feels like one. A very fast-moving dream."

"So, we'll slow things down."

"To what speed?"

"Whatever speed you want."

"What if I said I didn't want to do this again?"

"I'd think you were scared, or that you were lying."

She stared back at him. "Okay, that would be true."

"One day at a time, one moment at a time, remember? I'm not getting down on one knee. I'm not asking you to commit your heart forevermore. I just want to take a shower with you. Let's keep it simple. You can handle that, can't you?"

"I feel like we're postponing the inevitable, but—" She stopped abruptly as he nuzzled her neck with his very sexy mouth. "That does feel good."

"Wait until you see what I can do in a shower."

———————

Zach wasn't just good in a shower; he was good everywhere. Two hours later, Gianna watched him greet Chloe when they got to the café, then say hello to Lizzie and Chelsea, who were seated at the counter and had just finished breakfast. Every one of her friends was completely charmed by him. And every one of her friends also found a way to give her a very pointed look, no doubt wondering what the heck was going on with them, even though they could probably guess.

"I'll show you to a table," Chloe said, leading them across the room.

"You should be at home resting," she told her.

"Keeping busy is better for me. I'm only going to work for another hour, just through the breakfast rush and the lunch prep." She paused, her smile dimming. "And, no, there's no news."

"I wasn't sure if I should ask."

"I talked to the wife of another soldier in Kevin's unit. She hasn't heard anything, either, and she talked to two other wives. We're all in the dark."

"Maybe you can take comfort in that. The guys are all together. It's not just Kevin who is out of touch."

"It does make me feel a little less scared," Chloe admitted. "But I still need him to get home in time to see his son born. Anyway, same old song…sorry."

"Don't apologize, please."

"What are you two up to today?" Chloe asked.

"Work," she said.

"Me, too," Zach said.

Chloe laughed. "You two need to come up with a better story." She handed them menus. "Whatever you want is on the house. My thanks for the other night."

"Absolutely not," Zach said firmly. "You've got a kid on the way. We'll pay for our breakfast."

"He's right," Gianna agreed.

"If you insist, fine, but I still might throw in some extra home fries." She paused. "I almost forgot to ask, Gianna, have you progressed any further in your search for your biological mother? Keira told me that the Theresa Harper lead was a dead end."

"Actually, that dead end might have come alive. I don't want to jinx it, but I'll let you know if anything happens."

"And if I can help."

"Absolutely." As Chloe moved away, she picked up the menu. "Everything looks good. I'm starving."

"We worked up an appetite this morning," he said, giving her a small, intimate smile. "And last night."

"Stop that," she said. "People will start talking about us."

"Too late. Your friends are already wondering why we're so often together."

"I also wonder that," she said with a helpless sigh.

He laughed. "You don't have to wonder; you know why. You can't stay away from me."

"More like you can't stay away from me," she retorted.

"It's not a crime to want each other."

"Not a crime, but probably stupid. We didn't end well the first time."

"Maybe we don't end at all this time."

She took a quick breath at his words, at the look in his eyes, and she had no idea what to say. Fortunately, they were interrupted by a waiter wanting to take their order.

After a hasty look at the menu, they decided to split a waffle and a veggie omelet, along with a side of sausage, and two tall glasses of freshly made orange juice.

After the waiter left, a busboy came by to fill their coffee mugs, and Gianna took a grateful sip. "I love Chloe's coffee."

"It's good," Zach agreed. "Do you have an opinion on what I said before the waiter came over?"

"I think it's too soon to have an opinion."

"That's fair. What time do you have to get to the shop today?"

She was happy that he'd decided to pursue a less personal topic. "Officially one, but I'll go back to the store after we eat. I need to move items out of the storeroom into the showroom. We have some displays that need filling."

"How is your aunt doing?"

"Better. I spoke to her briefly yesterday. I think she's actually enjoying the time off now that she's not in as much pain as she was."

"Did you ever tell her about Helen's break-in?"

"No. I didn't want to worry her. And it's better for you if I keep that quiet."

"I appreciate that." He glanced down at his phone as it buzzed.

"If you need to answer that, go ahead."

"No. It's Hunter. He's going to drive down to Denver for the night and show Cassidy the city."

"That will be fun. She seems very nice." Another buzz had her reaching into her bag for her phone. It was a text from a number she didn't recognize. Her entire body stiffened.

"What's wrong?" Zach asked.

"I'm not sure. It's a text, but I don't know the number. Could it possibly be my mother?"

His gaze met hers. "Only one way to find out—open it."

Her fingers were shaking as she opened the text and read the message: *This is Jill Kenner. Tammy told me that I need to talk to you. I can meet you at Greta's Bakery in Paxmore between eleven and one today if that works. Let me know.*

"Well?" Zach asked impatiently.

"It's from Jill."

"Really?" he asked, a light in his eyes. "What does she say?"

She handed him the phone, so he could read the message. "What should I do?"

"Meet her. You just said you don't have to be at the store until one." He handed her back the phone. "This is what you wanted."

"I know, but I'm terrified."

"She wants to talk to you. That's a good sign. She could have blown you off."

"That's true." A seed of hope took root within her. "She is willing to meet me. But she obviously doesn't want to do that at her house or at my home or even here in Whisper Lake. Paxmore is ten miles away."

"Maybe that's where she lives. It's not that far, Gianna."

"I know." Her hand tightened on her phone. "If I do this, there's no going back."

"Nope," he agreed, meeting her gaze. "But if you don't do it, you'll have regrets forever. Whatever happens, you're strong enough to deal with it."

She didn't feel strong at the moment. "I guess."

"I'll drive you."

"I have to do this myself."

"You will do it yourself. I'll just get you there. I don't have anything pressing this morning. Let me support you."

She gave him a grateful smile. "Okay. I wouldn't mind the company on the drive." She drew in a breath and let it out. Then she typed in her answer: *I'll meet you at eleven.*

CHAPTER TWENTY-THREE

GIANNA WAS quiet on the drive from Whisper Lake to Paxmore. In fact, she hadn't said much since they'd finished breakfast. Not that she'd eaten much. Her hunger had evaporated after the text from Jill. Zach thought it was a good sign that Jill had gotten in touch so quickly and that she wanted to meet Gianna, but whether it would turn out to be positive in the long term was up in the air.

He glanced over at Gianna, who was drilling her fingers on her thighs as she gazed out the window. He had no idea what she was thinking, which felt wrong, because they'd gotten so close in the past week. He'd gotten used to being very much in sync, but she was on a solo daydream that did not involve him.

He didn't like it, but he could understand it. This was the moment she'd been waiting for her entire life. He really didn't want her to be disappointed. But there was nothing he could do to control the situation. She was going to have to live through whatever was coming. And while he'd encouraged her to take the risk, because he knew she would regret it if she didn't, part of him wanted to turn around and take her back to Whisper Lake, keep her safe with the status quo, protect her from further pain.

She turned her head to meet his gaze and gave him a tentative, shaky smile.

"Second thoughts?" he asked.

"Second, third, fourth, fifth…" She gave a helpless shrug. "Am I making the right decision, Zach? Am I going to hurt people because I'm curious? And I'm including myself in that."

"It's not just curiosity, Gianna."

"What do you think it is?"

"It's not for me to say."

"What? Now you don't have an opinion? You always have an opinion, Zach."

"This is your journey. I don't need to put my thoughts on it."

She frowned at his comment. "I would really like to know what you think."

"Okay, but don't shoot the messenger."

"What does that mean?"

He thought about not answering her, because he didn't think she'd like what he had to say, but the stubborn gleam in her eyes told her she was ready to fight someone, and right now it was him.

"Here it is," he said finally. "You've always said that you just want to know your heritage, your medical history, whether you look like your parents. But I think it's more than that. You hurt down deep inside from what you perceive as your mother's rejection. She gave you away, and you can't understand it. You can't accept it. No matter how much your adoptive parents love you, there's still this raw wound that you can't seem to heal." He glanced over at her, seeing thoughtfulness in her gaze, but not anger. He was relieved that she hadn't immediately gotten defensive.

"That's very insightful," she said slowly. "Do you think all adopted kids feel that way?"

"I don't know. I just know you."

"I'm sure that Jill gave me up because she was sixteen and too young to have a kid. She probably wanted me to have a good life and thought she was being generous in allowing me to be raised by two people who desperately wanted children. It's hard to blame her for that. I have had a wonderful life, an amazing family. Maybe Jill made the right decision."

"But it's more complicated than that."

"Yes. I do feel that burn of rejection, even when it makes complete sense that she gave me away. I don't know that meeting her will change that. But whatever happens today, at least one thing will change—I won't have to keep wondering who she is and why she did what she did."

"That alone could be life-changing."

She drew in a breath as she met his gaze. "I hope I'm ready."

"You are."

"Thanks. And by the way, Zach, I'm glad you're here."

"I wouldn't want to be anywhere else."

They walked into the bakery café together, but while Zach got in line to get himself coffee, Gianna headed for the middle-aged blonde woman sitting alone at a table. The woman hadn't seen her; she was checking her phone. Gianna slowed her steps, taking a minute just to look at Jill. She was much older, but she was definitely the girl in the photo.

As she took another step forward, the woman raised her head, her brown eyes meeting hers, and in that moment, Gianna knew the complete and utter truth. She didn't need an introduction, a confirmation, a blood test—this woman was her mother. It was like she was looking into a mirror, seeing a future reflection of herself.

It gave her some joy that Jill was attractive. Her blonde hair was shoulder length, her face was thin, and she was dressed in skinny jeans and a sleeveless top that made her look younger than her forty-five years.

Jill stood up as she arrived at the table, giving her an awkward, hesitant smile. "It's you," she said. "I think I would have known you anywhere."

"I feel the same way. I'm Gianna."

"And I'm—Jill."

She wondered if Jill had started to say she was her mother, then thought better of it.

"Gianna is a pretty name," Jill continued. "I was going to call you Allison."

"Really?" It was strange to hear even that tiny, unexpected detail.

"Yes. I don't know why; I just liked the name. But you're definitely a Gianna." Jill licked her lips. "Do you want coffee or something else?"

"No, I'm fine."

"We should sit."

"Yes."

They sat down across from each other, and neither one could seem to find a single word to say. They were an island of silence in a bakery filled with conversation, background music, and the sounds of the espresso machine and coffee grinder.

Finally, she cleared her throat. "Thanks for meeting me."

"When Tammy called me and said she had met my daughter, I almost fell out of my chair. I never ever thought I would see you again. I wasn't even sure I could believe it. But she was quite convinced."

"When Tammy said she knew you, I couldn't quite believe it, either."

"How—how are you, Gianna?" Jill asked tentatively.

"I'm good. I'm healthy and happy."

"And the people who adopted you? I prayed they were good to you."

She very much appreciated the heartfelt sincerity in Jill's eyes. "They were great parents. They still are. They love me a lot, and I love them."

Jill blinked away tears. "It's both good to hear and a little hard."

"Why did you give me away?" It was the question she'd wanted to ask since she'd first learned she was adopted, and she knew she couldn't leave this meeting without asking it.

"We're getting right to it," Jill said, with a shaky breath.

"Sorry if that was blunt, but I would like an answer."

"I was really young—sixteen. My mother was a single mom. When she found out I was pregnant, she insisted I give the baby up for adoption. She said she knew how hard it was to raise a kid alone, and she'd been almost thirty when she had to do it. She wanted me to finish high school and go to college and not get derailed by a child."

"I guess that's understandable."

"I didn't want to do it, but I didn't have a choice, Gianna. I know you must think I did. But I had no money, and my mom wouldn't help me. She wouldn't let me live at home if I kept you. I was going to have to do it all alone, and maybe I should have been stronger, tougher, but I couldn't fight her. She has a really strong personality."

"I know that. I saw her the other night. She actually told me you were never pregnant and never had a baby."

"I'm not surprised. It has always been a secret shame for her. She sent me away to live with her sister the last three months of my pregnancy, which happened to be over the summer. I was so young and thin that I was barely showing at six months. No one in town ever knew I was pregnant. By the time school started again, I was no longer a mother. It was a terrible time for me. I felt tremendous guilt. And I missed you."

Now, it was Gianna's eyes that were blurring with moisture. "You thought about me?"

"All the time. I couldn't stop thinking about you. I drove my mother so crazy she sent me to college out of state, so she wouldn't have to see me moping around."

"I didn't think you were from Whisper Lake. The adoption agency told my parents you were not local."

"I don't know anything about that. My mom handled everything. She said it was better for me not to know where you were. She thought it would be easier, but there was nothing easy about it. I only got to hold you for a minute before they took you away. I gave you the only thing I had with me at the hospital, my locket."

"It led me back to you," she said softly. "I wore it until I was fifteen years old, and then I lost it at Echo Falls Camp. I think now your mom took it. She must have seen me wearing it and realized who I was. She didn't want to take the chance that someone might remember her daughter wearing a similar locket. I don't know if that's true, but it makes sense to me."

"I wouldn't put it past her," Jill said. "She's not a horrible person. She just loves in her own way."

"And she couldn't love me."

"She couldn't see past my mistakes. It wasn't you she was angry with; it was me. But you paid the price." Jill let out a sigh. "I have so many regrets, Gianna, but I never regretted having you."

"I'm glad. Tammy said that you're married, that you have other children."

"I married a wonderful man sixteen years ago. I have two daughters, Grace and Lily. They're fifteen and thirteen." She paused. "They don't know about you, but my husband does. I told him before we got married. I had kept the secret for more than a decade, but I didn't want to marry him without him knowing that I'd given up a baby. Fortunately, he was able to understand and accept my choice."

"Does he know that you're meeting me today?"

Jill shook her head. "No. I had to be sure it was really you. What about your parents?"

"I didn't tell them. I felt the same way. I didn't want to upset anyone unnecessarily until I knew the truth."

"Your parents didn't want you to look for me?" Jill asked.

"They were all right with it, but I wouldn't say they were super happy. I think they had mixed feelings."

"I can't blame them for that. They raised you."

"And I love them very much," she reiterated. "I've just always wanted to know where I came from, who my parents are. What about my biological father?"

Jill's eyes filled with guilt. "I wish I could say we were in love and that it was a long relationship, but the truth is that I went to a party and I drank too much, and I had sex with a guy in my class who I had a crush on, but I barely knew."

"Not the greatest love story of all time," she murmured.

"I really wasn't that slutty. I was just careless and stupid. It was actually my first time. I didn't have sex again for about six years after that."

"Did he know about me?"

"I never told him. That's the part my husband got really angry about. He thought the guy had had a right to know. He probably did, but I can't imagine he was in a position to take care of you, either. He was sixteen—same as me."

"You don't want to tell me his name, do you?"

Jill hesitated. "If you really want it, I will tell you. It's your turn to call the shots."

"I'll think about it."

"All right. So, what do you like? What do you do? Are you married?"

"I'm an artist, and I'm not married."

"An artist? Oh, my God, I love art," Jill said with an amazed look filling her eyes. "I was an art history major. I worked at the Met in New York the year after I graduated from college."

"I can't believe it," she said, both surprised and excited that they shared a common interest. "I guess art was in my genes."

"I'd love to see some of your work."

"Does that mean you'd like to do this again sometime?"

"I would. But it's up to you. If it's just answers you want, I'll try to provide them. But if you're interested in more…

"I'm interested," she said, meeting Jill's gaze. "I'd like to know you."

"I feel the same way. I don't have the right, but I do have the desire."

There was love in her mother's eyes, and she wanted to cry, but somehow, she managed to hold it together, because she didn't want to ruin the moment—the moment she'd dreamed about forever.

"I have to go out of town this weekend," Jill continued. "I'll be gone a week. We're going to see my husband's side of the family for the Fourth of July. But maybe after that, we could meet again. I want to tell the girls about you."

"I'd love to meet them, but only when you think it's the right time."

"They're going to be thrilled. Is there more I can tell you now?"

"I don't know. I have a lot of questions, but they all seem to be out of my head at the moment. I also have to get back to Whisper Lake before one."

"I can't believe you live in Whisper Lake. I thought you were a million miles away."

"I've actually been living in LA for the last several years. I came home to help my aunt in her antiques store. She broke her leg and has to be off her feet. Do you live here in Paxmore?"

"Yes. We moved there three years ago. My girls love to ride, and I missed the mountains." Jill took a breath. "This has been amazing."

"It really has."

"I hate to leave, but I know we're both short on time today. Do you want to walk out together?"

"Actually, I have a friend over there who's going to give me a ride." She tipped her head toward Zach, who sent back a smile.

"No wonder he was watching us so closely. He's very handsome. Is he your boyfriend?" Jill asked curiously.

"I honestly don't know what he is, but he's a good guy."

"That's the important thing." Jill stood up, and she did the same. "Would it be awkward to give you a hug?"

"Probably, but let's risk it," she said, exchanging a brief embrace that felt weird but also right.

"I'll text you when we get back to town," Jill promised.

"I'll be looking forward to it."

As Jill left the café, she walked over to Zach's table and sat down, expelling a long, pent-up breath.

"That looked like it went well."

"It was great. So much better than I imagined it could. She was an art history major, Zach. She worked at the Metropolitan Museum of Art in New York City. Can you believe it?"

"That's crazy."

"Her husband knows about me; her teen girls do not, but she wants to tell them. She wants us all to meet, to have a relationship."

"Is that what you want?"

"It is. She seems like a nice person, and I want to get to know her. I just have to figure out a way to tell my parents that without hurting them."

"When they see how happy you are, they'll be supportive; I'm sure of it."

"I don't know about that. They did all the hard work. They raised me. Now I want to hang out with my real mom? I see a lot of potential pain."

"You know what I see?" he asked.

"I hope it's something good."

"I see you having enough love and time to give both of your moms and your dad, too. Hey, what about the bio father?"

"He never knew about me. They weren't in a relationship. It was a party mistake."

"At sixteen, that can happen."

"Jill said she would give me his name if I wanted it, but right now, I think I'll stick with her."

"Do you want some coffee or a pastry?"

"No. We should go back. Thanks again for driving me, for encouraging me, for being your usual pushy self."

"Any time."

"I still feel like I'm in a dream, and I'm going to wake up and none of it will be real."

"It's all real, Gianna. All of it. And I'm not just talking about you and your mom."

"You're talking about us," she finished, meeting his gaze.

"Yes. We're good for each other. You have my back; I have yours. When we're together, we're unstoppable. We're amazing."

She smiled at his words. "You're making us sound pretty awesome."

"We are."

"But there's so much uncertainty in both our lives, Zach. You have Hailey, and I don't even know if I'll stay in Whisper Lake."

"You'd be closer to your biological mother."

"But further away from my career," she countered. "We might

find ourselves miles apart again, just like before. Thinking about a future together seems unwise. It's too complicated."

"The best things in life are complicated," he argued. "When we were teenagers, we didn't have a choice where we had to go. We do now. If we find ourselves anywhere—chances are that's exactly where we want to be. You just have to decide where that is."

"So do you."

"I already know."

"How can you?"

"Because I do," he said simply.

Her heart skipped a beat at his words, at the look in his eyes, at the promise in his smile. "You are making this hard, Zach."

"Good. It should be hard. But you don't have to decide anything now. Come on. I'll take you home."

CHAPTER TWENTY-FOUR

GIANNA THOUGHT about Zach's words on the way back to the lake, but when she arrived at the store, the place was packed, and she was kept busy and distracted the rest of the afternoon. Then it was time to fill in her parents on her meeting with Jill.

It went better than she'd expected. It started out with tension and awkwardness and then eventually evolved into understanding and relief. She'd assured her parents that they were still the most important people in her life, that meeting Jill didn't change that. And by the end of their long conversation as well as dinner and ice cream sundaes, they'd all gotten to a good place.

Saturday morning, she woke up fresh and eager to take on the day. There were so many new possibilities in her life, and she was excited by all of them. She was also wary, too. Zach had told her that she'd end up wherever she wanted to end up. He was definitely a believer in choice. He would never act like a victim. He would own his decisions, good or bad.

She was trying to own hers, too.

But owning the past was a lot different than deciding the future. There was still risk there, still the potential of heartbreak. Of course, there was also the potential of real happiness. There wasn't just killer chemistry between her and Zach—there was an honesty that had been missing in her previous relationships. There was also a genuine friendship. She would miss him if she left—if he left.

Sighing at that thought, she put Zach out of her head and focused on the task at hand. She wanted to get some pieces from the storeroom moved into the front room. Kellan would be coming in later, so she could use him for some of the heavier furniture, but as she dug through a box of smaller items, including scarves, mittens and beanies, she found herself staring at a bright-red notebook with the words *My Diary* scrawled across it.

The diary had probably been dumped out of a drawer along with the other items, and the owner hadn't realized it.

The owner...

Was this box from the Carvers? Was this what Helen had been looking for?

She pulled out the diary and opened the first page, her heart stopping when she saw the words: *This diary belongs to Rebecca Carver.*

The date was seventeen years ago. Rebecca would have been twelve when she started writing in the journal.

Gianna turned the page and read through the first entry. It was all about getting the diary and how she was going to write down all her thoughts, all the things she wanted to say but couldn't.

The next page was filled with school ramblings: getting Mr. Collins for seventh-grade math, wondering if she could change her seat so she could sit next to Michael Gregory, who was so cute.

Gianna took the diary over to the couch and sat down, skimming through the next several entries. She felt a little guilty reading through Rebecca's thoughts, but Zach was so certain that Rebecca had a secret, and this might be the only way to find out if that was true.

As she read through the journal, huge chunks of time were skipped. They went straight from the seventh-grade winter carnival to the first day of eighth grade, to Rebecca's thirteenth birthday, and then to middle school graduation, to the start of high school.

When she turned the next page, the writing was somewhat streaked, as if water or tears had smudged the ink.

Her stomach tightened as she read a more disturbing entry...

He's at the house again. He keeps watching me. I know it's wrong. I told Mom I wanted to sleep at Dana's house, but she wouldn't let me go. I shouldn't be scared of him, but I am. I'm just being silly, aren't I?

She turned the page.

The next entry was four days later.

I want to die. I found Mom's anxiety pills. I was too scared to take them all, so I just took a couple. I felt better for a little while. But then I remembered what happened. Mom says I dreamt it, or that I'm making it up to cause trouble. But I'm not. She's just trying to cover for him. I told her that, but she won't back down. She loves him too much. She loves him more than me. That's why she's protecting him instead of her daughter. I want to leave. I want to run away, but I can't. I feel trapped.

Gianna drew in a deep breath, more than a little bothered by Rebecca's last entry. Someone had hurt her. A man who had been at the house. It didn't sound like Ron, but it was someone her mother loved.

God, she hoped it wasn't Mitch. But that wouldn't make sense. Mitch was four years younger than Rebecca. He would have been ten at the time of this entry. It had to be someone else. She was almost afraid to find out.

Her phone buzzed, and Zach's name flashed across the screen. "Hello?"

"How are you?" he asked. "I missed you last night."

"I missed you, too. Zach...but something has happened."

"What?" he asked warily. "You're not going to tell me that you want to take another break, are you?"

"Not at the moment, but..."

"But what? Did things go badly with your parents last night? Your text sounded like it went well."

"It did. I sound funny because I just found Rebecca's diary."

"Are you serious?" he asked in shock.

"It was in a box filled with winter gear. I don't think anyone knew it was in there."

"Have you read it?"

"I'm reading it now. Someone hurt her, Zach. I haven't gotten to who yet. But I think you should read it."

"I'll be there in ten minutes. I'm leaving the inn now."

"I'm in the storeroom. We don't open for another half hour, so come in the back door." She paused. "Do you want me to stop reading?"

"No, keep going. Then you can tell me what I need to know."

"Okay. I'll see you soon." As she set down her phone and picked up the diary again, she wondered if it would be difficult for Zach to read Rebecca's thoughts. For him, it would be a much more personal experience. Maybe it was better if she continued on. She would be able to prep him before he had to actually hear Rebecca's voice in his head.

The next entry was two weeks later...

I didn't sleep at all last night. Every time the floor creaks, I imagine it's him again. So, I stay awake. I keep Mitch's baseball bat by my side. I have to be ready. Because she'll let him back in the house. I know she will. She's weak. I used to think she was the strongest person I knew, but she's not. She's afraid of what people will think. She's afraid of everything. I want to tell Dad, but how can I? He'll look at me differently. He'll think it's my fault, too. He always thinks it's my fault.

Gianna's heart went out to Rebecca, to the fear she'd been living in. She'd been fourteen, whenever this horrible thing had happened. Gianna had known Rebecca when she was that age, and she'd had no idea. Rebecca had never shown her turmoil on the outside. She'd been popular, the life of the party...but she'd had a terrible secret.

She flipped through the next few entries, which turned away from the darkness. It seemed like Rebecca was making an effort to be normal, writing about school again. And then there was another jump in time. It was two years later.

He came back tonight. He looked at me like nothing had ever happened. He wanted to joke, to laugh. He wanted me to care about him. And she wanted the same thing. She wanted me to pretend. God, I hate her. Fortunately, I was able to climb out the window and go to Maggie's house. I won't go back until he's gone.

Gianna frowned, wishing Rebecca had written down a name. But maybe she just couldn't bring herself to do that.

The next entry was a year later.

I am going to college today. Thank God I can finally leave this house. I'll never live here again. Hopefully I'll be able to sleep at college. I feel like this is my fresh start. I can be someone else. I don't know who that is. Maybe if I can sleep, I'll be able to figure it out. I'm leaving you behind, diary. I'm leaving everything behind. I'm sure my mom will read these pages and I don't care. I want her to know what she did to me, how badly she hurt me. It was worse than what he did. I'll never ever let any child of mine go through what I went through.

Gianna looked through the rest of the diary, but Rebecca had kept her promise not to write again. As she fingered through the somewhat yellowed pages, she knew that Helen had read the diary, probably many times, and her heart had torn a little more each time.

The door opened, and Zach strode into the room, purpose and fire in his eyes. "Well, what did you find out?"

She stood up. "Rebecca was abused in some way. She doesn't go into detail. She doesn't name names, but she states that her mother protected this person, this man—that it was someone Helen loved."

"Ron?"

"No, it wasn't her father. She says once that she wants to tell him, but she's afraid. She thinks he'll blame her."

"You're saying that someone molested her in her house?"

"Yes. And she told her mom. But her mom said it wasn't a big deal and that it would never happen again."

"Wasn't a big deal? What does that mean?" He ran a hand through his hair, his eyes troubled.

"I don't know. I feel like it was a relative or a friend of Helen's.

The first entry was when she was about fourteen. But he was there again two years later. She said she climbed out the window to sleep at her friend's house. She only posted one more time when she was leaving for college. She said she hoped she could finally sleep again. I guess because she couldn't rely on her mother to protect her, she had trouble closing her eyes. She used to sleep with Mitch's baseball bat."

Bleakness filled his gaze. "I told you before she had trouble sleeping when she was with me. And she had to have two exits, a front door, and a fire escape. I asked her more than once if something had happened to her, but she always said no. Why did she lie?"

"I think there was shame. She blamed herself in some way. But not as much as she blamed her mother for forcing her to keep the secret, for protecting the person who hurt her." She paused. "What are you going to do about it?"

"I'm going to confront Helen and Ron. It's time to put all the cards on the table."

"I agree. In Rebecca's last note, she says she'd never let anything happen to any child she had. That she would protect them. If there's someone in Helen's life that could possibly still be around..."

Anger flared in Zach's eyes. "Then Hailey could be in danger. Hell, something could have already happened, and I wouldn't even know."

"You should read the diary. You might understand more than I did."

"I'll do that right now."

"Why don't you take it upstairs? Nora will be here any second, and she's a lovely person but a big gossip. My apartment door is unlocked."

"Okay. Thanks."

"I'll be up soon." She wanted to sit next to him as he read the diary, but she had to get the store open. And maybe it was better if he had a few moments to himself.

Rebecca's voice, her pain, haunted him. Zach leaned his head back against Gianna's couch and thought about what he'd read. He'd never imagined a secret this big. *But why hadn't he? Why hadn't he pushed her to open up to him, to tell him why she couldn't sleep, why she felt she had to drink and do drugs? Could he have gotten her to talk if he'd tried harder? Could he have changed what happened? Could he have saved her life?*

The questions ran around in his head. He'd felt guilty before, but now it was so much worse, because he knew the truth, or at least part of it. Helen would have to fill in the rest.

She'd resist. She'd call him a liar. She'd try to get Ron to kick him out of the house, but he had the diary, and he was no longer willing to sit back and be patient, to try to find a compromise. He needed to protect Hailey now. He needed to do that not just for Hailey but also for Rebecca.

Picking up his phone, he called Mitch.

"Hey, what's up?" Mitch asked.

"I found Rebecca's diary. I'm going to take it over to your parents' house today. You might want to be there."

"Why? What's in it?" Mitch asked warily.

"You don't know? You never looked in your big sister's diary?"

"No way. She kept that hidden. Where was it?"

"In some box that your dad gave to the antiques store when he went on his cleaning binge."

"Let me read it before you talk to my parents."

"No," he said flatly. "I'm sorry, Mitch. I have to confront your parents. If you want to be there, you can all hear it at the same time."

"I don't know if they're home."

"Then I'll sit on their porch until they return."

There was a long pause on the other end of the phone.

"It's that bad?" Mitch asked, a heavy note in his voice.

"Yes. I now know why Rebecca couldn't sleep, why she had a falling out with your mother."

Mitch drew in a hard breath. "You're sure you want to do this?"

"I'm sure I have to do this. Hailey is living in that house."

"I grew up there, too. I was fine."

"You're not a girl."

"Oh, God," Mitch muttered. "It's not my dad. Tell me it's not my dad."

"No, but that's all I'm saying. I'll see you at the house." As he ended the call, Gianna came into the apartment, her brown eyes shadowed with concern.

She took a seat next to him, putting her hand on his leg. "Are you all right, Zach?"

"I'm not the one who was hurt."

"I know. Rebecca was hurt. I feel bad that I thought she was just a mean girl, a party girl. I had no idea what secrets she was keeping. And I'm sure it's even worse for you."

"I keep asking myself why she didn't tell me or why I didn't figure it out, because it seems really clear now."

"She didn't want you to know, Zach. And I'm sure she never imagined she would die so young, that her daughter would end up back in the house she'd run away from."

"I'm actually not sure about that. I think sometimes she was almost trying to die. That's why she should have told me, so I could have protected Hailey from the beginning."

"What are you going to do?"

"I'm going over to the Carvers' house."

"They'll say you're lying. They might even call the police."

"I know, and I can't be forced out of there before I get the truth." He paused. "I need your help, Gianna. I need you to go with me. You're an objective third party. You found the diary. You know that Helen broke into your shop. If the police show up and try to run me off, maybe you can back me up."

"Of course," she said, not hesitating for a second. "I want Helen to come clean on what she did. And I want to protect that little girl you love so much."

"I don't want Hailey to hear any of this. I asked Mitch to come, too. Maybe he can keep Hailey in the other room."

"Or I can. I'm pretty good with little kids."

"Thanks. I know this isn't your fight, Gianna."

"Maybe not as much as it's yours, but you had my back yesterday; now I have yours."

CHAPTER TWENTY-FIVE

"Are you nervous?" Gianna asked as Zach parked in front of the Carvers' home.

He glanced over at her. "No. I'm resolved."

"You do have a determined look in your eyes."

"I'm getting to the bottom of this once and for all."

"I hope there's a way to resolve this peacefully—for Hailey's sake. They are her grandparents."

"I'm very aware of that. But the time for patience is over. Hailey could be in danger."

He got out of the truck and strode quickly up to the front door, pushing the bell several times.

Ron opened the door, his eyes angry. "What the hell is going on?"

He held up Rebecca's red diary. "This."

"Mitch said you found Rebecca's diary in something I dropped at the antiques store." Ron's eyes darted to Gianna. "Why did you give it to him?"

"Because he was there," she said.

"You had no right," Ron said loudly. "I will put your aunt's store out of business for this." ·

"Don't threaten her," Zach said, stepping between Ron and

Gianna. He could see Mitch and his mother hovering in the hall-way. Mitch had his arm around his mother. Helen looked as pale as a ghost. "We're coming in." He pushed past Ron, feeling like he'd just gotten over one hurdle.

"I'll call the police," Ron said, closing the door behind them.

"Where's Hailey?" he demanded.

"She's in her room, and you are not seeing her," Ron said.

"Don't do this, Zach," Helen pleaded. "You don't understand. You don't know the whole story."

"I know enough. I know something terrible happened to Rebecca, and you covered it up."

"Oh, God," Helen said, now covering her face with her hands.

"What are you talking about?" Ron asked. "What is he talking about, Helen?"

Helen's shoulders were shaking but she refused to look at anyone.

"I'm going to make sure Hailey stays in her room," Mitch said.

"You should stay for this, Mitch," he said. "If it's all right, Gianna will keep Hailey company."

Mitch hesitated, then gave a nod. "I'll take you to her room, Gianna, and introduce you. And then I'll come back."

He waited until Mitch and Gianna had gone up the stairs, then turned back to the Carvers. Ron was still pissed, but he also had a worried, questioning expression on his face.

"Helen," Ron said. "What is Zach talking about? What's in the diary?"

She shook her head, still not removing her hands from her eyes.

Ron turned back to him. "Well?"

"Someone abused Rebecca. It happened here—in this house. She was fourteen years old. She told her mother, but Helen insisted that she must have dreamt it, that it hadn't happened, and that if she told anyone, they'd all think she was a liar."

"What? That's ridiculous. You're the one who's lying. I'm calling the cops." Ron pulled out his phone.

"You should call them. This should go to the police."

"Don't," Helen said suddenly, finally dropping her hands and looking at them through tear-filled eyes. "Don't, Ron. Don't call anyone." She walked out of the entry and into the living room.

He and Ron followed.

Helen picked up a photo of Rebecca from the mantel above the fireplace and stared down at it.

"She was such a sweet girl," Helen said, more tears streaming down her face. "I didn't want to believe her when she told me. It was unimaginable, unthinkable."

"What happened?" Ron demanded, angry pain in his voice. "What are you talking about?"

Helen looked at her husband. "It was Will."

"Your brother?" Ron asked in shock.

She nodded tightly. "He stayed with me for a few days when you were on a business trip. He was going through his divorce. He was really depressed, and I said he could stay on the couch."

"What did he do to Rebecca? My God, what did he do? Did he...did he...I can't even say it."

"Will told me that she'd had a nightmare and he was trying to comfort her. But she said he kissed her and touched her under her nightgown. She woke up and started screaming. I heard her yelling and went into the room. I didn't see anything. I didn't think he could be lying. It took me awhile to calm her down and I really wasn't sure who was telling the truth."

"How could you not be sure?" Zach cut in, furious at how she was trying to spin the story even now.

"Rebecca made up stories all the time, and I had grown up with Will; he was my little brother. I couldn't believe he would hurt my daughter."

Ron shook his head, looking at Helen like she was a stranger. "Why didn't you tell me?"

"Because it was too horrible. I thought Rebecca could get over it. It wasn't like he did—you know—everything. And I never let Will stay here again."

"That's not true," Zach said. "Rebecca wrote in her diary that he was there when she was sixteen, and she climbed out the window and went to a friend's house."

"Well, that was the only other time. He was distraught that night. His marriage was ending. I thought he was suicidal. He had mental issues."

"It wasn't the only other time he was in this house," Ron said. "He was here for holidays, for birthdays."

"But not overnight."

"That doesn't matter."

"She wasn't hurt, Ron. She was just scared."

"She wasn't just scared; she was molested," Zach said forcefully. "And it haunted her for the rest of her life." His words brought pain to Helen's face, but he didn't care. "She could never sleep without a light on. She had to have an escape route out of the apartment. She said the drugs and alcohol helped her forget the monsters. I thought they were in her head, but they weren't all in her mind. One was real."

"I didn't know she kept thinking about it."

"Because you wouldn't let her talk about it. It's in her diary— how you insisted that she not tell Ron. You made her think that everyone would believe she was a liar."

Ron sank down on a nearby chair, looking completely defeated.

"I can't believe this," Mitch said, walking into the room.

"You heard?" Zach asked.

"I heard enough," Mitch said tersely. "Uncle Will molested Rebecca, and you protected him, Mom. Everything makes so much more sense now, why you and Becca suddenly hated each other."

"And why Becca left home and would never come back," Ron muttered. "And she barely let us visit her until two years ago— when Will died."

Zach was surprised to hear that piece of information and was relieved that Will was no longer a problem. At least Hailey hadn't been put in that predator's path.

"I'm sorry," Helen said. "I really wanted to hold the family together. I knew you'd be angry, Ron. You'd want me to cut ties to

Will, and he was such a tortured soul; I couldn't turn my back on him."

"You turned your back on our daughter, and you kept me in the dark about something horrific that happened to her," Ron said. "I can't even look at you right now. I have to go. I have to get out of here." He jumped to his feet, anger and disgust bringing him new energy.

"Before you leave," Zach said, stepping in front of him. "This changes everything when it comes to Hailey. I want to raise her. I won't keep you out of her life. You can see her whenever you want, but she needs to be with me. She needs to be with someone who will always protect her."

Ron didn't say a word, just pushed past him, slamming the front door behind him.

Helen sat down on the couch, still clutching Rebecca's photo to her heart. "I loved her. I really thought she was okay, that she'd moved on."

"That's just what you told yourself, Mom," Mitch said harshly.

"And now you hate me, too?" she asked her son.

"I don't know how I feel. But I do know that Zach is right. He needs to take Hailey out of here. She needs to be away from this mess."

"I love Hailey. I would never let her be hurt."

"That's hard to believe after what happened to my sister. Why did you keep the diary, Mom? You must have known what was in it, how it could hurt you if anyone else read it."

"Because it was hers, and I missed her. After Will died, I thought we could start again, and it seemed like she was interested. But she was too…"

"Broken," Zach suggested. "Because she was broken."

"I didn't think it was enough to break her."

He couldn't begin to understand Helen's thought process, but he really didn't care. "I'm going to get Hailey. When I come back, I want you to wipe your tears and put a smile on your face and tell her that she's going to get to spend time with me, but that you'll see her soon."

"Will I see her soon?"

"Yes, because you're her grandmother. And she's already lost her mother. But I'll petition the court for custody, and you'll support me in every possible way."

"I don't know why you think you're better for her than we are. We're a family."

"I'm her family, too. I gave you the chance to make this work for all of us. Now, it's my turn. Your actions in the past do not give me confidence in your ability to take care of her."

"And you're going to take her to a hotel? Take her away from her grandparents, her uncle, her room? Hasn't she had enough trauma?"

"I'll find a rental as fast as I can."

"Here in Whisper Lake?"

"For now."

"Zach, I want to talk to you for a minute," Mitch said, tipping his head to the hall.

"All right." He hoped Mitch wasn't going to try to talk him out of taking Hailey, but he'd hear him out.

———

"That is so pretty," Gianna said, as she and Hailey painted on a pad she'd found on Hailey's desk.

"It's not as good as yours," Hailey said, pointing to her brightly colored butterfly. "How did you do that?"

"I've had a lot of practice. I started painting when I was your age."

"Grandma doesn't like me to paint in here. She thinks I'll make a mess."

Gianna felt a little guilty about suggesting they paint, but she'd wanted to distract Hailey after Mitch left.

"Where's Zach?" Hailey asked. "He's taking a long time to talk to Grandma and Grandpa."

"He'll be here soon. Did you know I taught Zach how to paint a butterfly when we were kids?"

"You knew each other when you were kids?"

"Yes. We were teenagers. We met at summer camp. He was actually really good at drawing. I didn't know then he was going to grow up to draw houses for people."

"He said one day he'd draw a house for us." Her face fell. "But Mommy went to heaven."

"I'm sorry about that."

"She can't come back. But Zach says she's watching over me. Do you think she likes my picture?"

"I'm sure she does." She felt a little out of her depth, but thankfully Hailey was already turning her attention back to her painting.

"I want to paint some flowers now," Hailey said. "Can you draw them, and I'll paint them?"

"Absolutely." She sketched out some flowers for Hailey to color.

As the little girl focused on her picture, she thought about what might be going on in the living room. It was taking a long time. She hoped that was a good sign, that they were really hashing things out. She had to believe after everything they'd learned today that Zach had a much better chance of getting Hailey back into his life. But he still wasn't blood, and who knew how much that would factor into any legal opinion.

The bedroom door finally opened, and Zach walked in. There was a new light in his eyes and a smile on his lips.

"Zach," Hailey said with delight, running over to him.

He swept her up in his arms and gave her a tight hug.

Hailey put her hands on his face. "What took you so long?"

"Sorry. Your grandparents and I had a lot to talk about."

"Am I going to come and live with you?"

"Well, we still have to make some plans, but soon."

She was a little surprised that he wasn't taking Hailey out of the house immediately. She didn't think he'd be comfortable leaving her with the Carvers after what he'd learned, but maybe there was more to the situation than she knew.

"Tomorrow?" Hailey asked, pressing him for an answer.

"We'll see. What have you and Gianna been doing?"

"Painting. She draws good."

"I know she does." He gave her a grateful smile, then set Hailey back down. "I need to talk to Gianna for a minute. Can you finish your picture?"

"Okay. But come back faster."

"I will," he promised.

She followed Zach into the hall. She could hear voices downstairs as they paused on the landing.

"What's going on?" she asked.

"It was Helen's brother who molested Rebecca. She woke up and screamed. When Helen went into the room, her brother said he was comforting Rebecca after a nightmare."

"And Helen didn't know he was lying?"

"She didn't want to believe it."

"That's disgusting and unforgivable."

"I agree. Ron knew nothing. He was horrified. So was Mitch. Ron took off a while ago. I'm not sure how he's going to get past Helen's lie, the terrible secret she kept from him."

"What about you and Hailey?"

"I wanted to take her now, but Mitch said that I really need to find an apartment or a house with two bedrooms, and he's right. I can't take Hailey to the inn."

"Can you risk leaving her here?"

"Helen's brother died two years ago, so he's not a threat. Mitch is willing to watch over Hailey for a few days, so I'll leave her where she is. I know he loves Hailey, and she loves him. I don't want to rip her out of this house and scare her."

"That makes sense."

"I also have to be smart about all this. I need to show I can provide a good home for Hailey."

"Do you think the Carvers will stand in your way?"

"No. If they try to keep me out of Hailey's life, they'll have to talk about what happened in the past." He held up the diary still in his hand. "I'm going to hang on to this. I'm so glad you found it. If you hadn't, we might never have discovered the truth."

"I got lucky. If you need to find a place to live, you should talk to Keira. Her real estate company handles rentals, too. I'll text you her number."

"Good idea. I'm going to hang out here today. Do you want to take my truck back to the shop?"

"No, I'll call for a ride."

"Are you sure? Maybe I should drop you off and come back."

"Don't be silly. I'll be fine. Hailey needs you. She has been talking about you the whole time. I actually learned a lot about you —your fascination with the *Little Mermaid*, your love of singing 'Baby Shark', and the way you mix three cereals to make one great one."

He smiled. "Hailey can be chatty."

She smiled back at him. "Yes, and we're going to need to talk about the mermaid thing at some point."

"Jealous?"

"No," she said. "And I'm not just talking about the mermaid."

He knew exactly what she meant. "I'm glad. But you are also very important to me, Gianna."

"The only person you need to worry about right now is Hailey." She gave him a quick kiss, then walked down the stairs and out the front door, not wanting to interrupt the tense conversation she could hear Mitch having with his mother.

There was a good chance Helen was going to lose everyone she loved. Maybe that's what she deserved.

CHAPTER TWENTY-SIX

GIANNA DESERVED MORE *than he was giving her,* Zach thought, as he left the Fourth of July barbecue and headed toward her apartment on Wednesday night. It had been four days since he'd seen her walk out of the Carvers' house. They'd called and texted, but they hadn't found a minute to get together. He'd thought she'd be at the town party. She'd said she was going, but he hadn't seen her. Neither had any of her friends, who had all said that not only was Gianna supposed to be at the barbecue, but that she was also supposed to be going out on Adam's boat in a half hour to watch the nine o'clock fireworks show from the water.

He didn't know what was going on with her, but he was pretty sure he was responsible for her absence. He'd felt her starting to pull away from him, finding ways to get off the phone, being vague about her plans. He didn't like the feeling he was getting.

It probably wasn't fair to ask her to take on the situation he was creating, but he wanted her in his life. He'd told her she was important to him, but he hadn't backed that up with action. He had been too busy locating a rental house, getting it set up for Hailey, and trying to find a compromise with the Carvers that would allow them all to have Hailey in their lives but still be the best situation for Hailey. They hadn't gotten to an answer, but at least they were talking.

Actually, he was talking...

Ron was giving Helen the cold shoulder, refusing to speak to her directly. The only good thing about that was that Ron was now willing to talk to him. He had stopped being the villain in Ron's eyes. That was Helen's role now.

He actually felt a little sorry for Rebecca's mother. Not that he also didn't feel tremendous anger for the way she'd dismissed what had happened to her daughter, how she'd protected her brother over her child, but he could also see that she was suffering. In her own selfish way, she had loved Rebecca, and she had lost her, and now she was losing Hailey, too.

He actually wanted Hailey to have all of her family. She'd already lost too much. But getting them to a place where they could peacefully coexist and raise Hailey together was going to take time and effort and focus.

Which brought him back to Gianna.

She was backing off because she knew as well as he did that his priorities were shifting. But he didn't want to lose Gianna in the process of getting Hailey back. He wanted them both.

He probably wanted too much...

He parked on the street in front of the store and rang the doorbell for the apartment. There was a light on upstairs, and since she wasn't at the lake with everyone else in town, hopefully she was home.

A moment later, her voice came over the buzzer.

"It's me," he said. "Can I come up?"

"All right."

It wasn't the most welcome tone he'd ever heard, but she did buzz him in.

He jogged up the stairs, eager to see her again. Everything would be better once they were talking in person.

She met him at the door, a hesitant look in her eyes.

"First things first," he said, pulling her into his arms and kissing her sweet, sexy mouth.

Her initial stiffness dissipated with their kiss, and she kissed him back with a somewhat desperate fervor, as if she were trying to savor one last minute together, but he didn't want it to be their last.

When they finally came up for air, she gave him a breathless look and said, "That wasn't fair."

"I wanted to get that in before we talk, before you push me away."

"Why aren't you at the barbecue or on Adam's boat? The fireworks will be starting soon."

"I was at the barbecue, but you weren't there, and your friends didn't seem to know where you were. I told them I would find you."

"I got caught up in my painting, and I'm not that big on fireworks."

He moved into the apartment, a little surprised at the sight of a new painting on the easel as well as two other canvases standing up against the wall, each one in a different degree of completion. "You really are painting."

"Did you think I was lying?"

"More like avoiding me. But I can see you've been busy."

"I've gone a little mad," she admitted. "I couldn't figure out what I wanted to do, so I set them up next to each other, hoping it would give me clarity."

"I like them all. Although, the first one, the teens at the lake, is still my favorite." The other two were darker images. One was a fiery dragon looming over a baby. The third was a house by a lake, smoke swirling from the chimney, a swing in the yard, an empty deck, and an open front door.

"You like the first one because you're in it," Gianna pointed out.

"So are you." He pointed his hand to the second canvas. "The dragon lady is Theresa and the baby is you. It's a rather frightening image."

"That one came out of a dream I had last night. I got up at two to paint it."

"And the last one?"

"I'm not sure."

He looked at the house. "It's not happy, but it's not sad, either. It's...waiting."

"That's an interesting way to put it."

He turned back to her. "Is that how you feel, Gianna, like you're waiting?"

"Not everything I paint is me."

"And yet it is," he said with a small smile. "At least these three pictures."

"I was thinking about you and Hailey, the house you got. Keira told me it was by the lake. That it had a swing set."

"But there are no people in this picture."

"No. I didn't have a vision of that."

"I've been neglecting you."

"You haven't," she said quickly. "You've been doing what you need to do. You don't have to worry about me, Zach. I'm an adult. Hailey is your priority. Where is she tonight?"

"She's with her best friend Maddie's family for a sleepover. She was invited a few days ago, and we all thought it was good for her to do something normal."

"How is she? Does she understand what's going on?"

"She's good, but she is confused. She's not sure where she's going to be spending her time. I showed her the house yesterday. She liked it. She wants to live there with me. But she also loves her grandparents and her uncle. So, she keeps asking if she can live in both places."

"Can you all share her?"

"We're working on the details of that. There are a lot of hoops to jump through because I'm not biologically connected to Hailey, nor was I married to her mother. The only reason anything can happen is because the Carvers are willing to make it happen. Mitch has also stepped up. He was trying to help me before, but he was always reluctant to go against his parents. Now that he knows what happened to his sister, he is taking charge."

"It's a difficult, complicated situation."

"But worth it." He put his hands on her shoulders. "You're worth it, too, Gianna. I haven't forgotten about you."

"Hey, we were just having fun," she said lightly. "You don't owe me anything."

Despite her words, he saw a sadness in her eyes. "Don't down-play our relationship into mindless fun."

"And you shouldn't try to make it more than it is."

"We don't know what it is yet. Would you consider staying in Whisper Lake past the summer?"

She stared back at him. "I don't know, Zach."

He frowned at her answer. "I need to be here for a while."

"Yes, you do."

"I know I'm asking a lot. You have your career in LA. You have a life there. But you could have a life here, too."

"You and Hailey need to be together. I would mess that up. She would be even more confused, wondering why you were bringing some other woman around."

"She'd understand why over time."

"It's too much, Zach. I had trouble committing in my past rela-tionships, and they were a lot simpler than this."

"I don't give a damn about your past relationships. This is you and me. We're different."

"Are we?"

"Yes," he said forcefully, gripping her shoulders. "I'm in love with you, Gianna. I've been in love with you since I was sixteen years old."

"You've loved other people, Zach."

"So have you, but that doesn't change the fact that our connec-tion was made a long time ago. And maybe we both ended up here and now, because this is our time."

"Or we say good-bye and we move on. We accept that our rela-tionship was always meant to be short."

"You're killing me," he said, feeling both anger and disappoint-ment at her words. "What we feel—we both know it doesn't come around very often. Are you really going to walk away from it?"

"I'm good at walking away," she said with a touch of self-recrimination. "Just ask anyone."

"I don't care what anyone else thinks. And I don't believe you'll walk away from real love. Those other guys weren't right. I am."

"But you have become a package deal."

"That's true. I know you'd be sacrificing a lot, Gianna. It's not the ideal love story, but it is a love story, and it could be a good one."

Her eyes blurred with tears. "I do care about you, Zach. But it's too fast."

"Then we'll slow things down. We'll table this until the end of summer. But until then we stay together."

"I don't think so. It wouldn't be good for Hailey if we start something we can't finish. It wouldn't be good for us, either."

"I'm not willing to walk away. I fight. I want you to fight, too," he said, feeling a bit desperate to convince her.

A buzzing phone drew her attention away from him. "Let me check that."

"Can it wait?" he asked in frustration.

"I—I don't know." She slipped away from him to pick up the phone. "Hello? Chloe?" She paused. "What? Oh, my God! I'm on my way. I'll be there in five minutes."

"What happened?" he asked, seeing the fear on Gianna's face.

"Chloe got a call. Kevin is missing in action. I have to get over there. She can't get a hold of anyone else. They're all on the boat. She's alone."

"I'll drive you."

"Okay," she said, grabbing her bag, then leading him down the stairs.

"Kevin has to be okay," she said, as she got into his truck and fastened her seat belt. "Chloe is having his baby in less than two weeks. She can't lose him now."

He wanted to be positive, but all he felt was a terrible fear. His mother had never gotten a call that his father was missing. She'd just learned that he was dead. Hopefully, the outcome for Chloe's husband would be different. He'd be found. He'd come back. He'd be able to be a father and a husband.

But deep down inside, he wasn't sure he could believe that, and he had a feeling Chloe couldn't believe it, either.

———

Gianna's heart was pounding as she ran up to Chloe's door, with Zach following close behind. She hit the bell and then tried the knob. It turned. She walked into Chloe's house and saw her sitting on the couch, her phone in her hand, tears streaming down her face.

She sat down on the couch next to Chloe. "I'm here."

Chloe stared back at her with wild, dazed eyes. "They don't know where Kevin is. He got separated from the team two days ago. *Two days ago!* They waited this long to tell me that no one knows what happened to him."

"What about the other men? The other wives?"

"The wives are only now finding out. The whole team was out of communication for over a week on some super-secret mission that they still can't tell me about. I don't even know what continent he's on, Gianna."

She licked her lips, not knowing what to say. "Did they tell you anything else?"

"That they're doing everything that they can, and that they'll be in touch. I didn't even know the guy who called. Couldn't one of his friends have spoken to me?"

"They probably didn't want to put one of his friends in the position of having to lie to you," Zach interjected, sitting down on the other side of Chloe.

"You think they know where he is?" Chloe asked, turning to him.

"I think they know more than they're saying," he replied. "But missing is better than the alternative."

"That could be coming. They could be calling me next to tell me he's dead. I can't believe this is happening."

Chloe's face twisted with pain, her breathing shifting, as she gasped her way through a few more breaths.

With her hand rubbing her belly, Gianna suddenly had a new, terrified thought. "Chloe, are you having contractions?"

"They're probably false. I had some yesterday. I went to the clinic. They said it wasn't real. They sent me home and told me it could be a few more days."

She didn't like the sound of that, especially as Chloe started panting once more. "Is that another one?"

"I'm just upset about Kevin. It's not labor. The baby can't come until Kevin is back."

She exchanged a quick look with Zach and saw the concern on his face. "We need to get you to the clinic."

"They're going to call me back about Kevin. I can't leave."

"You can take the phone with you."

"When we get to the hospital, they won't let me use it. And the longer I stay here, the longer it will be before I have the baby." Chloe gasped as another contraction hit her.

"We're taking you to the medical center right now." She and Zach helped Chloe to her feet, but then Chloe cried out, doubling over in pain as her water broke.

"Whoa," Zach said in alarm.

"It's okay. We just need to get her into the truck," she said.

"There are only two seats in the truck," Zach reminded her.

"Right. Where are your car keys, Chloe?"

"I don't want to go to the hospital. I want to wait here until Kevin comes home," Chloe said stubbornly, dazed by the pain and the trauma of the last hour.

"Honey, you have to go to the hospital. You have to take care of your baby."

"I'm going to call 911," Zach said. "We'll get her an ambulance."

"Oh, God!" Chloe cried, screaming with pain. "I think the baby is coming now."

"Now? It can't come now," she said.

"I can feel it," Chloe said, giving her a panicked look. "What am I going to do?"

"Let's get you back on the couch," she said, helping Chloe stretch out against the pillows as Zach got on the phone with the 911 operator. She could hear him demanding an ambulance, but there seemed to be some sort of argument going on.

"It hurts," Chloe told her, panting once more. "I can feel its head, Gianna. I need to push."

"No, don't do that. Just breathe."

Chloe tried to breathe, but then said, "It's not working. Can you look?"

Gianna drew in her own shaky breath. "Okay." She pushed up Chloe's sundress and pulled down her panties, seeing the tip of her baby's head. She was shocked and terrified, feeling completely out of her depth. "The baby is coming." She looked up at Zach, who had paled in the last minute, getting his own glimpse of the problem. "Is the ambulance on its way?"

"There's a multi-vehicle accident on the west shore. Both of the city ambulances are there. It's going to be awhile. They're patching us through to the medical center for advice."

"Advice?" she echoed. "We don't need advice. We need a doctor."

Chloe screamed again, then yelled, "Help me."

Gianna pulled herself together. There was no one coming, so they had to take care of Chloe. "Hand me the phone."

Zach did as she asked, then said, "I'll get some towels."

"Hello?" she asked. "Yes, we need help." She put the phone down on the coffee table, leaving the speaker on so she could hear the instructions and help Chloe at the same time.

Giving her friend the bravest smile she could, she said, "Okay, Chloe, we're going to do this together."

Chloe gave her a terrified look. "I can't lose the baby, too, Gianna."

"You're not going to lose this baby." She desperately hoped that was the truth.

Zach came back with towels and she slid them under Chloe

while helping her off with her underwear. For the next ten minutes, she followed the nurse's instructions while Zach stayed by Chloe's side, talking her through the contractions and letting her grip the hell out of his hand.

It was scary and amazing and messy all at the same time. But when the baby was finally born, he let out a howl, and they all laughed with relief.

She wrapped the baby in a blanket and placed him on Chloe's chest.

More tears streamed down Chloe's face as she looked at her son. "He's—beautiful," she gulped.

"Perfect," she said, feeling like crying herself. "You have a son."

"He needs a name," Chloe said. "We were going to wait until Kevin came home to decide. He wanted to see him. See what name fit him best. But now..."

Her heart broke at the thought that Kevin might never see his son. He and Chloe had been together forever. He'd been one of her best friends, too, and he would be an amazing father. "You'll come up with the right name," she said. "And by the way, he has a good pair of lungs."

"He does," Chloe said. "And he was determined to come out. Do you think he knew I needed him?"

A tear fell out of her eye at that poignant comment. "Maybe," she said. "You're not going to be alone, no matter what happens with Kevin."

Chloe stroked her son's head, quietly soothing him until he fell silent and just stared at his mother with big, dark eyes. "I'm going to make sure he has a happy life," Chloe promised. "If I have to do this alone, I'll do it alone. An hour ago, I didn't think I could. But now I feel certain that I can and that I will be able to do whatever I have to do. Because this is my life. This is my child. And he needs me to be strong."

At the sound of a siren, Zach got to his feet. "That's the ambulance. I'll let them in."

"Zach is a good man in a crisis," Chloe said. "You both helped me bring my baby into the world. I'll never forget it."

"I don't think I'll forget it, either. I saw it all happening, and I still don't know how you did it."

"We do what we have to do for love."

"Yes," she murmured, getting to her feet as the paramedics came through the door. They put mom and baby on a stretcher and took them out to the ambulance. Before they left, Gianna told Chloe she'd let her friends and family know what had happened and then they'd check in on her in the morning.

As the ambulance drove away, Zach put his arms around her. "Wow," he said. "You delivered a baby tonight."

"I have no idea how I held it together. But I really didn't do much. That kid was coming out, no matter what. Thank you for helping to keep Chloe calm."

"No problem." He flexed his hand. "I think she broke a few fingers, but otherwise no big deal."

She smiled up at him. "It's hard work bringing a kid into the world."

"It's one of the most amazing things I've ever seen."

"Me, too. I just hope Kevin makes it back. I don't want Chloe to have to raise her son on her own."

"I don't, either." He paused as a loud blast rocked the air.

She looked up as fireworks lit up the sky. "Well, this is appropriate," she said with a laugh. "Tonight is definitely a night for celebration. But you might have enjoyed this more from the water."

"Are you kidding? This is absolutely perfect." He put his arms around her as they watched the show.

It was beautiful and spectacular and wrapped up in Zach's embrace, she felt like there was no place she'd rather be.

When the show ended, she let out a little sigh. "I guess that's it."

"We could go back to your place, start up our own fireworks."

She smiled at him. "I want to clean things up here before we leave. And then I have a lot of calls to make."

"That's fine. I'll help."

"You've done enough, Zach. You should go back to the inn or go down to the water. The party will still be going on for a while."

"No. I'll see this through with you."

He would see it through. He wasn't the kind of man who would ever walk away, ever quit, ever shirk his responsibility. *Was she really going to be able to walk away from him?*

They got back to Gianna's apartment at one in the morning. Gianna had called all of Chloe's friends and family, leaving messages or sending texts to let them know about the birth and also about Kevin's worrisome status. Chloe would have a stream of visitors in the morning. She would definitely not be alone.

"Tired?" Zach asked as she flopped down on the couch.

"I am, but I also feel strangely invigorated. I wonder if doctors feel this way after delivering a baby."

He sat down next to her, putting his hand on her thigh, as he gave her a smile. "You did good."

"So did you. You were able to keep Chloe calm and focused."

"I was trying not to look at what was happening on your end," he said dryly.

"It freaked me out a little, too. I saw it, and I still don't know how she managed to deliver that baby."

"I prefer not to think about it."

She laughed. "Well, we can chalk that up to one of our craziest experiences."

"I'll say. It happened so fast. I thought women went through hours of labor."

"I think Chloe was in labor for a while, but she was so distraught over Kevin, so determined not to have the baby without him that she tried to pretend it wasn't happening." She paused, thinking how Chloe's whole attitude had changed after the baby had arrived. "But becoming a mother made her fierce. That little baby turned Chloe into a fighter, even with all the fear running through her. I'm in complete awe of her. She made me feel like a wimp."

"You're not a wimp. Look what you did tonight. You delivered a kid."

"Because I had to."

"That's usually when courage comes out."

"But I'm scared of too much," she said, shifting to face him. "I was trying to break up with you earlier."

"I know. My life is complicated. You'd be taking on a seven-year-old. You'd have to deal with the Carvers and figure out what kind of career you could have here, at least for the foreseeable future. It's not fair of me to ask you to make all those sacrifices, but I love you too much to be fair. I wanted to be with you. That's the bottom line."

She sucked in a quick breath at his intense words. "I love you, too, Zach. I've just made so many mistakes when it comes to men. I don't want to make another one. I don't want to get hurt, and I don't want to hurt you."

"There are no guarantees in life. You have to trust yourself. And if it helps, you should know that I trust you completely."

"Unless I decide to break up with you. Then you'll think I'm an idiot."

"No. I'll just think I need to work harder to get you back."

"You have so much else to work on."

"I can't imagine a future that doesn't include you, Gianna. I've never been able to talk to anyone the way I talk to you. I've never felt so connected, so crazy in love, and I do mean *never*. I have cared about other people, but the way I feel about you is different. We came together a long time ago. And I don't think we ever really let each other go. This is our time."

His impassioned speech made her heart swell with love and hope. "I want it to be our time."

He grabbed her hand and squeezed her fingers. "Then give us a chance. You don't have to make final decisions right now. I'm not proposing, Gianna."

"Thank goodness," she said with a little laugh.

He gave her a happy grin. "Let's see what happens. Let's make as much time for each other as we can. I want you to get to know Hailey, and for her to get to know you. I can see our life together, but you need to see it, too. You need to feel what I feel." He took her hand and put it on his heart, and she could feel it pounding against his chest. "Finding you again—it put my heart back together."

She blinked back a tear. "That's a beautiful thing to say."

"It's the truth. I know you, and you know me."

"Better than anyone," she whispered. "Better than I know myself. I never thought I'd find love back here in Whisper Lake, but I did."

"I did, too." He leaned forward and gave her a tender kiss.

"Let's go to bed. I don't want to just tell you how I feel; I want to show you."

His eyes lit up. "I thought you'd never ask. And I promise to let you get some sleep…at some point."

She laughed as she got to her feet and pulled him up. "I can't promise that at all."

CHAPTER TWENTY-SEVEN

Zach stifled a yawn as he and Gianna walked into the medical center at eleven the next morning. Gianna had made good on her promise not to let him get much sleep, but it had been totally worth it.

Having laid their hearts bare, they'd made love with even more intense emotion than they ever had before. This was the woman for him. He didn't imagine he could ever love anyone else. But he'd promised to go slow. As long as she didn't push him away, he'd move at whatever pace she wanted.

When they got to Chloe's hospital room, they found her holding her son and surrounded by some of her friends: Hannah, Keira, Lizzie and Adam.

Chloe looked better this morning—her eyes brighter, her skin not as pale, and at some point, she'd brushed her hair and pulled it back in a ponytail. Zach was happy to see the smile on her face. She'd been through a lot in the past twenty-four hours.

"Here they are, my delivery team," Chloe said, waving them over to the bed.

Gianna gave Chloe a hug and took a peek at her sleeping son. "He's still perfect," she said.

"Thanks to you," Chloe said. "Should I call you Dr. Gianna now?"

"Not for a second. I have even more appreciation for real doctors now and for women giving birth. I don't think I'll be doing that any time soon."

"I would have liked to see you delivering Chloe's baby," Keira said with a laugh. "As I recall, you almost fainted once when you had to give blood."

"Trust me, I had to fight that feeling," Gianna said with a laugh. "It was a crazy time. But Zach helped, too."

"I just held Chloe's hand," he said, as the group focused on him. He saw varying degrees of emotion in their individual gazes, some of which were suspicious, some of which were approving. Gianna's friends were protective of her, and he could appreciate that. He didn't want anyone to hurt her, either.

"Sorry if I squeezed your hand too hard, Zach," Chloe said.

He gave her a smile. "Whatever pain I was going through was nothing compared to what you were going through. I don't know how women do what they do."

"We are the stronger sex," Hannah said with a grin.

"I can't argue with that."

"I'm just sorry we were all out on the boat when you went into labor, Chloe," Lizzie put in. "We didn't have reception, so we didn't get Gianna's calls and texts until after it was all over."

"I know you all would have helped if you could," Chloe said, her gaze sweeping the group. "But I am glad that Gianna was home. I was very upset, hysterical, in fact. I don't really remember a lot of what I said. Everything was happening at once. It was quite an extreme range of emotions." Her eyes dimmed as she stroked her baby's head. "I think this little guy knew he needed to make his appearance early."

"Has there been any more information about your husband?" he asked.

Chloe shook her head. "I spoke to the leader of Kevin's unit this morning. They're very hopeful that they'll be able to bring

Kevin home, but he couldn't tell me anything else. I could feel his optimism, so I'm trying to stay positive."

"You should."

"We're here for you," Adam said, putting a comforting hand on Chloe's shoulder. "Whatever you need, whenever you need it. I hope you know that."

Chloe gave Adam a sweet smile. "Thank you. You're all spoiling me."

"You deserve it," Lizzie said. "And Chelsea sends her congratulations. She'll be in to see you later."

"I'm sure you're going to have a steady stream of visitors today," Gianna said. "I know Kevin's parents are trying to get here as soon as they can."

"It will be nice to see them," Chloe said. "I did speak to them a little while ago. They're very concerned about Kevin, so I think seeing the baby will be a good distraction."

Despite Chloe's outward smiles, he could see the struggle in her eyes to contain her fear. But at least she wasn't alone. She had her friends, and she had her son. He moved to the side as a nurse brushed past him.

"Okay, this is a little too much excitement for our new mom," the nurse said. "She needs to rest. Out you go."

They said their goodbyes and then filed out of the room.

Adam waylaid him on his way down the hall.

"I spoke to Ron Carver yesterday," Adam said. "He told me you've worked out your differences and that they're going to relinquish custody of their granddaughter to you. I felt like I was talking to an entirely different man."

"Ron had a change of heart," he said, not going into detail. One part of his agreement with the Carvers was that Helen's secrets would stay secrets. He didn't think Ron even knew that Helen had broken into the antiques store. But he was dealing with enough heartache and betrayal, so there was no need to bring that up.

"I'll say he did," Adam said, giving him a speculative look. "But Ron was very tired, very pale. He seemed defeated. I'd like to know what happened."

"I think he and Helen are having some problems, but I'm sure they'll work it out," he said carefully.

"And you're not going to tell me."

He shrugged. "If you have more questions about the Carvers, you should ask them."

"Well, I'm glad the custody situation is being resolved. I hate to see a kid caught in the middle of that."

"Thankfully, that battle appears to be over."

"And you'll be staying in Whisper Lake?"

"Yes. I'm going to run my business from here."

"That will be good for Hunter."

"And for me. I'd like to see the camp all the way through the remodel."

"The camp is another reason I'm glad you and the Carvers have made peace. I was afraid Hunter's dream was going to take a beating in the planning commission."

"Hopefully, that won't happen." They walked down the hall to where Gianna and Lizzie were waiting by the elevator. The others had already left.

"Everything okay?" Gianna asked, giving him a concerned look.

"It's good," he assured her. "Adam was just telling me how happy he is that I'm working things out with the Carvers. Now he won't have to arrest me."

"That wasn't exactly what I said, but the sentiment is correct," Adam said dryly. He turned to his sister. "Where is Chelsea? She skipped the boat ride last night and I called her this morning, but there was no answer."

Lizzie shrugged. "Who knows? She sent me a quick text to say congrats to Chloe, but that was it. She hasn't been talking to me much."

"I remember when we couldn't get her to shut up," Adam said. "She used to talk all the time."

"And sing," Lizzie said. "It's sad that she doesn't do that anymore. It was so much a part of her."

"I hope she's all right," Gianna put in. "Maybe I should reach out. I know what it's like to not be doing what you were born to do. I was in an artistic slump until Zach helped me get out of it."

"How did he do that?" Lizzie asked with a curious smile.

Gianna flushed, and he laughed. "Are you going to tell her?" he asked.

"No," Gianna said pointedly.

"That sounds like a good story," Lizzie said.

"Let's just say Zach reminded me that art is a part of me and it's the way I express myself. Anyway, I'll give Chelsea a call."

"It can't hurt," Lizzie said, stepping into the elevator as the doors opened.

They rode down to the lobby and then parted ways with the Cole siblings in the parking lot.

"What do you want to do now?" He took Gianna's hand as they walked back to his truck. "Do you have to work?"

"Nora said she could cover the store today. I told her what happened with Chloe and she said I should get some rest."

"So, we can go back to bed—I like it."

She laughed. "You always like it."

"I do. I like you."

"You don't have to get Hailey?"

"No. Mitch will pick her up from her friend's house this afternoon and take her to the movies. I'm free to hang with you for a few hours."

"You might regret that," she said with a small laugh.

"Why is that?"

"Because I promised to meet my parents for lunch. How do you feel about seeing my dad again?"

"I'm fine with it. I'd like to get to know your parents better."

"And I want them to get to know you. But let's not tell them we're in love. I don't want to freak my father out."

"I won't tell them, but I have a feeling they might guess—like the rest of your friends have."

"Probably. But as long as you don't give me a ring any time soon, we can hopefully keep their concerns at bay. My father wants me to think before I jump."

"Too late. We've already jumped."

"Let's keep that as our little secret."

He put a hand on her arm as she was about to open her door. She gave him a questioning look.

"What?" she asked.

"I am going to propose to you one of these days, Gianna. I want you to know that."

"You wouldn't be scared I'd say yes and then bail on the wedding?"

There was real concern in her voice. "Not even for a second. When we decide to get married, there won't be any doubt."

"No, there won't," she agreed. "I didn't know who I was before, but I do now."

"Speaking of which—any more word from your bio mom?"

"She sent me a happy Fourth of July text and said her daughters are looking forward to meeting me when they get back from their trip."

He was happy that her search for her mom had turned out so well.

"Oh, and Jill asked her mom about my necklace, and Theresa admitted to taking it. She said she saw me pulling the locket back and forth on its chain every time I came to the dining room, and she knew instantly that I was Jill's daughter. She was afraid someone else might connect the locket with Jill, so she took it. She apparently still has it, so I may actually get it back."

"Do you think you'll speak to Theresa again?"

"I don't know. I'm not that interested in a relationship with her. Lying at the time of my birth was one thing but lying to my face a few days ago was ridiculous. I don't need to spend time with someone who is that uninterested in knowing me."

"Her loss," he said, putting his hands on her waist.

"What are you doing?" she asked with a laugh.

"I need a kiss before we get in the truck."

"You can't wait?" she teased.

"It's been hours, and I've been waiting for this—for us—since I was sixteen."

"I'm glad we got a second chance, Zach. Let's not blow it."

"We won't," he promised.

She put a hand against his chest before he could take the kiss he wanted. "I've already made one decision, Zach. I'm going to stay in Whisper Lake. It's my home, and the friends I have here are important to me. But they're not the reason I'm staying; you are. I love you. When I said I know who I am now, it's not because I found my birth mother—it's because I found you again, because you made me remember the girl I used to be, and you gave me the courage to push past my fears and my insecurities. I owe you a lot."

The love in her eyes almost undid him. "I owe you more, Gianna. You've had my back in my fight for Hailey. You've been there when I needed you. And I'm not just talking about now. You brought me back to life a long time ago. I always thought the lake healed me, but it was you."

"I always want to be there for you, Zach. You said you could see our future, but I needed to see it, too. Well, I can see it, and it's going to be amazing. And one day, if you ask me, I will walk down the aisle, and I will not run away."

"Whenever you're ready," he promised. "I know you're making sacrifices for our relationship, Gianna. You're not just taking me on but also Hailey. But I am going to do everything I can to make you happy."

"I know you will. But I'm not really sacrificing anything. I can paint here. I can make my career work. And hopefully, I'll be good for Hailey, too. What's most important is that we're together. We have our second chance. I don't want to waste it."

"We won't. Can I kiss you now? Because it has been way too long."

She lifted her sweet lips to his, and he couldn't help thinking that if this kiss went on forever, it wouldn't be nearly long enough.

THE END

I hope you enjoyed Gianna and Zach's love story. There is a lot more to come in the WHISPER LAKE SERIES. You'll want to keep reading to find out what happens with Chloe's missing husband, learn more about the Coles, and watch Gianna, Zach and Hailey become a family. You'll also meet interesting new characters, who will bring you romance, drama and adventure in every story.

Don't miss the next book in the series, MY WILDEST DREAM, where Chelsea Cole's dark past threatens the new life she is building for herself.

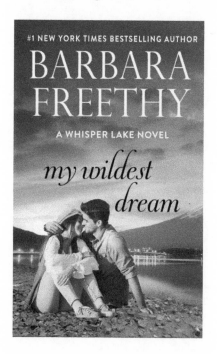

ABOUT THE AUTHOR

Barbara Freethy is a #1 New York Times Bestselling Author of 68 novels ranging from contemporary romance to romantic suspense and women's fiction. With over 12 million copies sold, twenty-three of Barbara's books have appeared on the New York Times and USA Today Bestseller Lists, including SUMMER SECRETS which hit #1 on the New York Times!

Known for her emotional and compelling stories of love, family, mystery and romance, Barbara enjoys writing about ordinary people caught up in extraordinary adventures. Library Journal says, "Freethy has a gift for creating unforgettable characters."

For additional information, please visit Barbara's website at www.barbarafreethy.com.